KT-449-609

# BLOOD BROTHER

Jack Kerley worked in advertising and teaching before becoming a full-time novelist. He lives in Newport, Kentucky, but also spends a good deal of time in Southern Alabama, the setting for his Carson Ryder novels. His love of the suspense genre was sparked at age thirteen, when his father gave him a collection of Saint stories by Leslie Charteris. When not writing, Jack likes to relax in the mountains with his fishing rod.

Visit www.AuthorTracker.co.uk for exclusive information on Jack Kerley.

Also by Jack Kerley

# JACK KERLEY

## *Blood Brother*

HARPER

Harper
An imprint of HarperCollins*Publishers*
77–85 Fulham Palace Road, London W6 8JB

www.harpercollins.co.uk

A Paperback Original 2008

1

A catalogue record for this book
is available from the British Library

ISBN- 978-0-00-726907-5

Set in Sabon by Palimpsest Book Production Limited,
Grangemouth, Stirlingshire

Printed in Great Britain by
Clays Limited, St Ives plc

# ACKNOWLEDGMENTS

Thanks as always to my wife, Elaine, for putting up with my frequent spur-of-the-moment trips from Kentucky to coastal Alabama where, ostensibly there to write and research, I am often found fishing.

Special thanks to Mike Ward, Supervisor, Kentucky Medical Examiner's Toxicology Laboratory, for superb ideas and input regarding various nasty substances. I employed his ideas at my whim, and any errancies are mine alone.

Thanks also to Julia Wisdom and Anne O'Brien of HarperCollins UK for excellent input and editing.

And finally, thanks to all the folks at the Aaron M. Priest Literary Agency.

*For April and Mark, my brother and sister . . .*
*Siblings without rival.*

# PROLOGUE

*Rural Southern Alabama, mid 1980s*

The boy is in his teens, slender and blond, kicking a pine cone down the red-dirt country road, dense woods to his left, cotton field to his right. Though the Alabama sun lays hard across the boy's bare arms and legs, his skin is pale, like light bounces off, never sinks inside.

A sound at his back turns the boy's head to a bright truck grille a hundred yards behind. He steps to the road's edge to let the truck pass. But it glides slower and closer until his nose fills with the oily stink of the engine. The truck pulls even.

"Hey, I saw you in the newspaper," the driver calls through the open passenger window, a man

1

in his early thirties with tight-cropped hair, angular face, eyes behind wraparound mirror sunglasses. His face is built around a smile, his voice is pure country twang. "You're that kid who got a perfect score on the STA, right?"

The boy's water-blue, almost feminine eyes drop with embarrassment. He mumbles, "SAT, Scholastic Aptitude Test."

"And now you got free college and all that. You do us proud. Wanna ride?"

"I'm fine walking. But thanks."

The driver grins with bright, even teeth. "It's gotta be ninety-five degrees. We can't have our local genius getting heat stroke. Where you need to go?"

"Town, then. The library."

The driver nods, pleased. The boy climbs in the truck. Hard muscles on the driver's arm dance as he shifts. He drives for a quarter mile before swerving on to a dirt lane scarcely wider than the truck. Branches squeal against the vehicle's sides.

"Hey," the boy yips. "You said we were going to town."

The truck bounces to a small clearing and jolts to a halt. The boy's eyes dart from side to side. Insects buzz from the trees.

"You recognize this place, son?" the driver says. "You been here before, right?"

Something in the man's voice has gotten harder. The twang has disappeared.

"Lissen, mister. I uh, I need to get back to –"

"It was last year, son. A dead man was found tied to that big pine tree yonder. Someone took a long time to kill him. A real long time."

The boy's hand sneaks to the door handle. He pulls the latch and dives against the door. The door doesn't give. The boy's terrified face turns to the driver.

"Locked," the man says, his voice calm. "Under my control. It's all under my control. Look here . . ."

The driver lifts his blue work shirt to reveal a pistol in his belt. Pictures and voices from the past align in the boy's mind. He recalls who the man is, when they met, what was said.

The boy closes his eyes, thinks, *It's over.*

The driver looks into the shadowed woods. "There was blood everywhere the day that man got torn apart. Someone said he didn't know people had that much blood in them."

"You're wrong, mister," the boy protests, his voice high and tremulous. "I didn't do anything. I never been here before. I swear I ain't never –"

3

"SHUT THE FUCK UP, KID!"

The insects are silent. Birds freeze in the trees. It's as if time has stopped. When the man's voice starts again, so does everything else.

"I've studied on that day a lot, son. More than you can believe. You know what I came up with in my thinking?"

"What?" the boy whispers.

"I've never heard of so much anger busting free. So much . . . letting out. You know what I mean by letting out?"

A long pause. "No. Not really."

"Letting out is like floodwater piling up behind a dam. You can picture water rising behind a dam, right?"

The slightest motion as the boy nods. The driver continues speaking.

"The dam holds back the water – keeps it inside, under control. But a dam can't stop the rain. So let's say it keeps raining, day and night. The water rises and that held-back lake gets longer and wider and deeper. You know how that goes, don't you? Maybe from experience?"

"Yes." The boy's whisper is almost lost in the sound of the insects.

"The dam's a strong one and wants to hold. But that rain whips down day and night. Water

4

keeps backing up, pushing harder. What do you think happens next?"

The boy's face quivers and his eyes shimmer with liquid. A crystal tear traces down his cheek.

"It keeps raining. And the dam breaks."

The man reaches over and erases the boy's tear with his thumb.

"No, son. The dam opens just in time. And that's how it saves itself."

# ONE

It was a morning for firsts.

My first landing at LaGuardia Airport, my first escort from a 737 while the other passengers were ordered to remain seated, my first hustling through a terminal by security police, my first ride in a siren-screaming police cruiser through gray Manhattan rain.

And I, Detective Carson Ryder of the Mobile, Alabama, Police Department, had accomplished them all in the past twenty-three minutes.

"No one's gonna tell me what this is about?" I asked my driver, a Sergeant Koslowski by the nameplate. We skidded sideways through an intersection. Koslowski spun the wheel, goosed the gas, and we straightened out two inches from tagging a taxi. The hack driver gave us a bored glance and I wondered what it took to scare a New York cabbie.

"No one told me nothin'," Koslowski growled. "So how can I tell you somethin'?" The growl fit; he looked like a bulldog in a blue uniform.

"What were you told, exactly?" I asked.

"Pick up your ass at the airport and deliver it to an address in the Village. There, now you know as much as me."

Two hours ago I had been at my desk in Mobile, drinking coffee and waiting for my detective partner, Harry Nautilus, to arrive. My supervisor, Lieutenant Tom Mason, had called me into his office and closed the door. His phone was beside the cradle, thrown down instead of hung up.

*"You're on a new case, Carson. You got to be on a plane to New York City in twenty minutes. Your ticket's waiting. The plane too, probably."*

*"What the hell? I can't just up and –"*

*"There's a cruiser waiting outside. Move it."*

Koslowski did the sideways skid again, setting us on to a slender street. He jammed the brakes in front of a three-story brick warehouse. We threaded past four radio cars with light bars flashing, a Forensics van and what I took to be

8

a command van. There was also an SUV from the Medical Examiner's office. Whatever had gone down, the full cast and crew was present and accounted for.

I saw a portly man shambling our way, his black hat tucked low and his gray raincoat rippling in the wind. Mr Raincoat opened my door and I stepped out.

The guy looked in his late fifties, with a round face as morose as a bloodhound. His nose was large and beaklike. His eyes sagged above, bagged below, and probably looked sad even when a woman said *Yes*. Unlike everyone else, he seemed in no hurry. He offered his hand. "My name is Sheldon Waltz, NYPD. Friendlier folks call me Shelly, which I invite you to do. How was your flight?"

The warmth and sincerity in his voice made me drop pleasantries in favor of the truth. "I hate jets, Shelly. I'd have preferred being shot here by cannon." I paused. "You gonna tell me what's going on?"

He sighed and patted my back. Even his pats seemed doleful. "Actually, I was hoping you might tell me."

The warehouse reeked of stale water and fresh rat droppings. We walked a plank floor toward a service elevator. A print tech dusted the paint-peeling wall for latents. I thought the tech was shooting me curious side-eyed glances, but realized he was studying Waltz. Also eyeing Waltz was a young guy in a Technical Services jacket who sat cross-legged on the floor with a small video monitor in his lap. He looked ready to spring into action, just as soon as someone told him what the action was.

To the right the corridor opened into a side room, the light coming from a bank of ancient fluorescents, bulbs sizzling and giving a jittery quality to the scene. I saw three detectives inside, the Alpha dick spotlighted by a sharp bark as the others bobbed their heads. Alpha was a woman, early thirties, with an ovoid face, slender lips, dark hair pulled straight back and held with a rubber band. Efficient and aerodynamic. Her rust-colored, no-frills business suit had a gold badge hanging from the jacket pocket. Her eyes flashed with intelligence and she looked as hard and fit as a dancer.

The woman's eyes found me and glared, like I'd spit in her soup and run away laughing. I flicked a genial wave. Alpha showed me her back and her puppets followed suit. I heard one of the men's voices mutter the word *yokel*.

"Who's that woman, Shelly?" I asked as we stepped into the elevator, a cage with a floor. Waltz thumbed the button and we jolted upward.

"It doesn't matter right now."

The elevator clattered to a stop and we stepped into a maze of semi-finished sheetrock walls dividing a large room. Waltz said, "The building's being turned into lofts. The construction foreman stopped in at six a.m. to leave instructions for the workers, found the victim. The foreman's an older guy with angina. The sight had him grabbing at his chest. The med types didn't want him to add to the body count, so they sent him to a nearby ER." Waltz nodded to a second doorway. "The victim's back here."

I followed Waltz to a framed-in space I suspected would be a complete unit when finished, fifty feet long, twenty wide. At the end of the space a pair of sawbucks carried a sheet of plywood. Atop the wood was a blanketed shape I knew was a human body. I shivered, then realized the air conditioning was cranked to meat-locker level.

"The cold's helping stabilize the body," Waltz said, seeing my puzzlement.

"Until what?"

"Until you got here."

11

There was a plastic runner on the floor, a path to walk without disturbing evidence. I saw a snip of hair beside the runner, a slender brown comma. Beside it was a tuft of white. I crouched, pursing my lips and puffing at the debris. The result floated in the air. "Several colors of hair," I said. "Strange."

Waltz turned. "Come on, Detective. We don't have much time. Forensics will deal with the minutiae."

The runner was slick and we walked with the care of men on ice. When we reached the form Waltz grabbed an edge of the white blanket. I took a deep breath and nodded, *Go.* Waltz pulled back the cover. I saw a woman's body, headless. *No,* my mind suddenly screamed, *the head was there.* It had been jammed into a slashing cut made in the abdomen. The head, its eyes wide, stared at me from the belly. The scene was horrific and utterly incongruous.

Then I realized: I knew the face in the belly.

I gasped. My knees buckled and the room veered sideways. Waltz grabbed beneath my arm. I closed my eyes. Long seconds passed before they opened again.

"You know her, right?" Waltz looked at my face. "Take your time."

I waited until the room stopped spinning. Found the breath to rasp out words. "Her name is Dr Evangeline Prowse. She's the director of the Alabama Institute of Aberrational Behavior. It's where some of the country's strangest killers are kept, walking nightmares."

"I know of the Institute. You're sure it's her?"

I nodded and strode to an open window to suck in air, hoping to stop the spinning in my head. Waltz appeared with a paper cup of water. He steered me to a chair.

"Better?" he asked as I gulped water.

"Getting there," I lied.

"How well did you know her?"

"She consulted on several cases for the Mobile police. We enjoyed one another's company. I guess you could say we were the kind of friends who always promise to see one another more, but can't find the time."

We'd never find the time. I'd never speak to Vangie again, an incredible loss.

"When did you last see Dr Prowse?" Waltz asked.

"Two months ago. I was in the Montgomery area and stopped by. We shared a sandwich in her office, spent a half hour talking. That was all."

There was more to it than that. Much more. But only five people in the world knew that particular secret. Evangeline Prowse had been one of them.

"Did she mention anything about coming to New York?"

"Vangie grew up in Queens, lived in the city until her early thirties. Coming here was a regular event, no big deal."

"How about a professional angle? You and Dr Prowse weren't working together? A case?"

"Not for a couple years."

"You're sure? Nothing?"

"Shelly, why the hell am I here? Why not a co-worker or a –"

He blew out an exasperated breath. "There's a bit of a mystery going on. Follow me."

I accompanied Waltz back down the elevator to where the other detectives were waiting. The sleek Alpha lady was leaning against the wall with studied nonchalance, legs crossed at the ankles, cellphone nudging a high cheekbone. "I dunno what the Southern guy's supposed to do. I'm waiting for him to pull the magnifying glass from his pocket, ask if there's any footprints he can follow . . ."

She hung up and tapped her watch with a

crisp pink talon. "I've got places to be, Waltz. And given that goddamn convention, I expect you do, too. Let's open and close this little play right now."

Waltz pursed his lips and whistled. The young guy in the Technical Services jacket appeared, cradling the battery-driven video playback unit as if it was an infant. His nameplate read J. Cargyle. The kid held the unit at chest level. Waltz tapped Play. Everyone gathered close.

A shiver of electrons and my heart climbed to my throat: Vangie's face in close-up, a white wall at her back. The camera's tiny microphone distorted background sounds into a rumbling sludge. She was holding the camera close and her hands were shaking, her face moving within the frame. Vangie looked worn, her brown eyes circled with shadow.

*"If you have found this recording, I ask that you contact Carson Ryder of the Mobile Police Department."*

I startled at my name, but kept my eyes on the screen.

*"I have worked with dozens of specialists in the profiling and apprehension of the homicidally deranged. Detective Ryder is the best I know at understanding these people, a dark gift, but a*

15

*gift nonetheless. I am currently doing things that make little sense. But I needed a serious –"*

A sudden thump, a noise like a growl. Vangie's eyes widened and the camera spun. I saw the edge of a mirror, a seam of wall and ceiling. The thump and growl repeated. The screen showed a flash of palm and fingers, then went dark.

"It's almost over," Waltz said. "She put the camera in something. Her purse, probably."

"What does it mean? Where was it –"

"Wait." Waltz pointed back at the screen. As if adding a post script, Vangie lifted the still-recording camera from her purse and aimed it at her face. Tears were streaming down her cheeks.

She said, *"Carson, I'm so sorry."*

# TWO

"Do you know what she's talking about, Detective?" Alpha Lady said, arms crossed high on her chest. "Outside of you being hotsie-totsie with the loonies?"

"No."

"You have no idea what she's doing that makes little sense?"

"No idea, Lieutenant."

"Ms Prowse says, 'I needed a serious . . .' Something interrupts. Serious what?"

"How would I know that? Where was the recording found?"

Waltz said, "The memory card was in an envelope that read *Open in Event of Emergency*. It stood out, given the circumstances. I immediately had Tech Services play the video. One thing led to another and . . ."

"And now we've got an investigation on hold for hours and an outsider tromping through the scene," the Lieutenant finished, shaking her head.

Waltz sighed and turned to the woman. "I've never heard of a case where the expertise of another detective was referenced by the victim. I thought it best to retain the death tableau and bring that detective here for a look. The ME's people did their part, and forensic processing slowed but never stopped. If you have a problem with my decision, Lieutenant, I suggest you convey your displeasure to the powers that be."

Waltz pulled a cellphone from his pocket, dialed a number. He held the phone up for the Lieutenant to take. The room was dead silent. I heard ringing from the phone, then a pickup.

*"This is the office of the Chief of Police . . ."*

The Lieutenant turned white.

*"Hello? Is anyone there?"*

She snatched the phone from Waltz's outstretched palm, snapped it closed, thrust it back at him: A surrender. She turned her anger from Waltz to me, her voice angry and demanding, pushing her frustration my way.

"What was left of her clothes looked like a

runner's garb. Like she went running, got grabbed off the street, brought here. Did she like to run?"

I said, "She ran marathons, even at sixty-three. She was a fitness junkie."

"She ever run late at night?"

"She ran whenever she found the time, or was stressed. Were there any defensive wounds?"

"How about you shut up and let the Lieutenant ask the questions?" snapped a detective a few years past my age of thirty-four, a hulking monster with a Greco-Roman wrestler's neck and shoulders. His face was pale and acne-scarred, making his small eyes look like green buttons floating in a bowl of cream of wheat. His hair was neither brown nor blond, but some shade in between, brond, perhaps. I'd heard someone call him Bullard.

Waltz said, "Her forearms are bruised, probably defensive. No tissue is visible beneath her nails. They're cut close, unfortunately. The Forensics crew will vacuum the floor when we leave, maybe find something important."

Another interruption from Alpha Lady. "Why did the victim give the big-ass sales job on your behalf? She was sorry about what?"

"I just got here. How would I fucking know?"

"Hey," snapped Bullard. "Watch your goddamn

19

mouth." He stood to show me he was taller than me. Wider, too.

Alpha said, "Stay calm, Bubba. I'm trying to get a handle on things. Waltz told me about the box of crazies where she worked, this Institute. Is it possible a former patient might have held a grudge?"

I shook my head. "Couldn't happen."

"You psychic as part of your talents?"

"The only way out of the Institute is to stop breathing. They don't rehabilitate, they analyze."

Waltz nodded. "He's right. I know of the Institute."

I said, "Have you checked Dr Prowse's whereabouts since she arrived, Lieutenant? Maybe she was targeted by the perp earlier. Maybe as early as at the airport. You might want to –"

She held up her hand. Shot me a fake and indulgent smile. "I'm sure you do fine on your home turf, Detective. But the NYPD actually looks into such things. We've done it a few times before." She turned the fake smile to Waltz. "Take him to lunch, Detective. Show him the Statue of Liberty. Let him buy some postcards. But then it's time for Mississippi to get its missing policeman back."

Before I could correct her, she showed me her back and strode away with the sycophants in tow. The little turf war now over, Waltz seemed unperturbed.

"Somewhere in the good Lieutenant's soliloquy I heard the word lunch. There's a decent deli a couple blocks away. Give it a shot, Detective Ryder?"

The deli was little more than a long, narrow counter, and a few tables against a wall decorated with faded posters of Sardinia. I was without hunger and fiddled with a salad. Waltz seemed light on appetite as well and nibbled at a chicken sandwich.

I couldn't quite figure out Waltz's position in the hierarchy. His rank was detective, the Alpha Lady – named Alice Folger, I'd discovered – was a lieutenant. She was brusque to Waltz, but was obviously afraid to push him too far. Another big question: What gave Waltz the power to slow an investigation for several hours so I could be flown here? That would have taken sledgehammer clout.

I was about to ask when Waltz slid a mostly uneaten sandwich to the side of the table. "Let's say Dr Prowse felt she was in danger. Why didn't she ask the NYPD for protection?" He paused.

21

"Unless, of course, she wasn't in danger. That fits with her taking a midnight run through the neighborhood."

"What about the recording?"

"We have no idea when it was made. Or why. Are you sure you have no idea why she'd record a testament to your abilities vis-à-vis psychopaths?"

Waltz was conversational, but I knew I was being interrogated. I looked down, realized it was a tell for a person about to lie. I scratched my ankle to give my down-glance a purpose.

"I'm as much in the dark as you, Shelly."

"You have no idea what she was sorry for? Or anything about the serious whatever she was seeking?"

This time I could look him in the eyes. "I'm utterly dumbfounded."

"What's your background, Detective Ryder – if I may ask?"

"Eight years on the force, five in Homicide. I studied at the FBI Behavioral Division for all of a month. I also work in a special unit called the PSIT: the Psychopathological and Sociopathological Investigative Team."

"Impressive."

"In name only. The whole unit, which everyone calls Piss-it, is me and my partner

Harry Nautilus. We're activated maybe five times a year, usually a false alarm. Though we do have a decent solve rate when the action is bona fide."

"Which is?"

"A hundred per cent. Still, like the unhappy lady lieutenant said, this is New York. Y'all deal with more crazies in a day than Mobile does in a year."

Waltz spun his glass of iced tea. "Dr Prowse said you had a special gift for investigating psychos. She called it a dark gift. What's that mean, if I may ask?"

I repeatedly punctured a piece of romaine. I didn't want to lie, but couldn't tell the truth. Not fully.

"I was a Psych major in college, Shelly. I did prison interviews with psychos and socios. Dr Prowse thought I had a rapport with them, made them drop their guard. That's probably the gift she was talking about."

I sensed Waltz didn't believe I was telling the full story. But he shifted the conversation. "I'm not ready to close this box yet. I've convinced those in command to give you a few days here in case we need your input."

I raised an eyebrow at Waltz's ability to

sidestep immediate authority. "Sounds like you went above Lieutenant Folger."

"A step or two. That's not a comment on her, either personally or professionally. She seems unhappy with some aspect of her life, and it makes her brittle, but the Lieutenant is blessed with a highly analytical mind. She's destined ever upward, as the sages say."

"She seems young for all the authority."

"She's thirty-two, but has been climbing the ladder three steps at a time. After a degree in criminal justice – top of her class, highest honors – she started in uniform in Brooklyn, grabbed attention by using her head, analyzing crime patterns, offering realistic solutions. She worked undercover for a while, setting up sting operations, pitting dope dealers against one another, busting a fencing operation that reached from Florida to Canada . . ."

"Not your ordinary street cop." I felt a sudden kinship with Alice Folger. My departmental rise began by solving a major crime while still in uniform.

Waltz nodded. "She seemed almost driven to prove herself as a cop. It got her noticed by a few people with clout. They touted Ms Folger to the big brass at One Police Plaza – HQ. Her supporters suggested the brass jump her in rank and send her here to be tested. We're a big precinct and our homicide teams handle everything from street craze-os to murderous stockbrokers. It's a plum placement for a detective displaying more tricks than usual."

*Perhaps like you, Shelly*, I thought.

"I'm a fellow officer. Why does Folger think I'm useless?"

"Johnny Folger, her late father, was NYPD. All three of Johnny's brothers were on the force, one died on 9/11. An aunt works in the impound. That's just this generation. Before that . . ."

I held up my hand. "I get your point, Shelly. Folger has cop in her DNA."

"Or overcompensating to create the genes."

"What?"

He waved it away. "Nothing. I always found families more custom and tradition than blood, but that's my take. What it boils down to is that Folger's a partisan. She sees you as a –, as um . . ." Waltz fumbled for the word.

"As a rube," I finished. "Someone to stumble over while the pros handle the heavy lifting."

Waltz sighed an affirmation. I slid my unfinished salad over to join his sandwich and leaned forward, arms crossed on the table.

25

"How did I get here, Shelly? You know what I mean. How does a detective push the pause button on a homicide investigation, and get the NYPD to pull me from Mobile to New York in a heartbeat?"

Waltz looked uncomfortable. His fingers traced the rim of his glass. "Five years ago a councilman's daughter ran off with a cult leader, a psychopath. I tracked him down in Alaska and personally brought her back. She had a successful deprogramming and the whole nasty incident stayed under wraps."

I pursed my lips, blew silently. "There's a grateful councilman on your shoulder? No wonder you could call the Chief direct."

He shrugged. "That and a few other successes have given me a reputation for dealing with cases like your PSIT handles, the psychological stuff. I'm allowed latitude others don't have. An input role."

A thought about Shelly's clout hit me. "Were you one of the supporters responsible for Alice Folger's jump to the major leagues?"

He waved it away like it was no big deal. "I saw talent, I passed her name upstairs."

I figured Waltz had seen a bright spark in Alice Folger and decided to drop it into an oxygen-laden environment to see if it would blaze or burn out. Judging by the veiled admiration in his voice, Folger had blazed bright.

I said, "Where do I go from here?"

"I've arranged you a hotel room nearby. Check in, get whatever you need and you'll be reimbursed. You can come in to the department, or I'll send reports to your hotel. I simply want you to see if you can add anything."

"That's all?"

"It's what the lady wanted, it's what the lady gets."

*Lady wanted*, I thought, not *victim wanted*. Good for Waltz.

Waltz offered to drive me to the hotel, but needing to clear my head I started walking. I ducked into the continuing mist, my mind swirling into the events that had slammed my life into Dr Evangeline Prowse, with repercussions that would forever echo in my soul. Events I had not, could not, tell Sheldon Waltz.

The Alabama Institute of Aberrational Behavior housed an average of fifty criminally insane men and women. It had become one of the more enlightened such institutions under the stewardship of Dr Prowse, who had made a career-long study of psychopathy and sociopathy. It was claimed no doctoral candidate in abnormal psychology could write more than five pages without citing Vangie.

In one of her cases, a sixteen-year-old boy had murdered an abusive father, disemboweling him with a knife, a slow and hideous death by vivisection. The homicide was so savage that the local police did not suspect the boy, an intelligent and gentle soul, barely questioning him.

Starting two years later, five women were murdered in a grim, violent and symbolic manner. After the third mutilated victim appeared, the FBI gave the case material to Vangie. She studied the bizarre and ceremonial crime scenes, detecting signs of a tormented child. The police finally turned their eyes toward a twenty-six-year-old man whose father had died in the woods years before. He confessed, was ultimately pronounced insane, and Dr Prowse petitioned for him to be brought to the Alabama Institute of Aberrational Behavior.

I was in college at the time of the killer's capture. Dr Prowse and I had met through that case, and had been bound by it for years.

The father was my father. The killer was my brother, Jeremy.

*"Get back here, Jeremy, you little coward . . . stop that squealing . . . I'll give you something to squeal about . . ."*

*"Don't, Daddy, please don't, Daddy . . ."*

Though my father, Earl Eugene Ridgecliff, functioned as a respected civil engineer, he was diseased with anger. As children, my brother and I lived with the fear that anything – a word, a glance, a misperceived gesture – could explode into horror. My brother, older than me by six years, became the focus of our father's physical rage, and I still awoke in cold sweats with my brother's screams razoring through my home.

*"Help me, Mama, help me, Mama . . . Daddy's trying to kill me . . ."*

I had never used the word murder for my brother's actions against our father, preferring "attempted salvation". Had Jeremy been caught and tried he might be free today, a jury figuring anyone suffering such agony had little recourse but to kill his tormentor.

But years of abuse had planted a seed of madness inside my gentle brother. Even as we built our neighboring forts in the oaks, signaling to one another with torn sheets like ship's flags, fished for catfish in the slow Southern creeks, or lay in the summer grass and stared at clouds, the seed grew into vines that wrapped and strangled his soul.

My mother was a beautiful and emotionally fragile woman twenty years of age when my father, eighteen years her senior, passed through her small country town on an engineering project. Married within two months, my mother expected a storybook life. Instead, she found herself embroiled in a hellish drama so far beyond comprehension her only recourse was retreating to her room to practice her sole skill: the sewing of wedding dresses, white and flowing waves of satin and tulle.

The mutant seed within my brother caused him to believe our mother could have intervened in the nights of terror at the hands of our father. She could have more easily stopped the tides with her fingertips.

*"The Alabama State Police today announced a suspect in the bizarre and brutal killings of at least five women . . ."*

So deep was my brother's belief in our mother's complicity in his suffering that a few years after killing our father, Jeremy began

30

killing our mother. I speak metaphorically: To actually kill *her* would have consigned me to a foster home – and he would not have done that – so surrogates fed his unfathomable need. Shamed by my brother's actions, I changed my name, hid my private history behind veils of obfuscation, and refused to visit him.

It was Vangie – with input from Jeremy – who tracked me down and convinced me to re-establish a relationship with my brother. Jeremy and I had even collaborated – if that's the word – on several cases where his unique insights helped me understand the crimes. He was so finely calibrated for madness he once boasted he could walk through a mall and point out a half-dozen people "either convinced Martians are reading their minds, or thinking things so dark they'd make Torquemada retch".

My brother was not only insane himself, he was a Geiger counter for insanity in others.

# THREE

The desk staff at the mid-town hotel were expecting my arrival and treated me with deference though I was in sodden clothes and my shoes squeaked footprints across the marble floor. They directed me to a nearby shop where I secured denim jeans, three cotton dress shirts, a white linen sport coat, a pair of upscale walking shoes plus underwear and socks.

Finally in my hotel room, a third-floor double dressed in somber monochrome – black, gray, gray-white – I showered, then snapped on a muted CNN to add color and distraction to my world. I unwrapped my new dress shirts and rinsed them in the sink to remove the creases and factory starch, squeezing them as dry as possible. In the cool and arid air conditioning they'd be set to iron in the morning. I did the same to the tees.

The phone rang, the desk advising me a package had just been delivered. A small Hispanic gentleman brought an envelope to my room, NYPD stamped on top left corner, the information Waltz had promised. As he had noted, it was spare, the investigation barely off the launching pad.

The prelims from the forensic teams in Vangie's room featured all the No's: No signs of struggle, No blood or body fluids visible, No seeming thefts, No signs of a search. I noted the mention of a closet with casual-type wear that seemed good for a week's stay. It appeared she had packed for a normal visit to NYC.

Yet before this particular visit, Vangie Prowse turned on a video camera, noted my experience with serial killers, then proclaimed she'd made a strange decision, and was *"doing things that make little sense. But I needed a serious –"*

She'd had to hang up before finishing the sentence. Needed a serious what? Doing what things that made little sense? As if that wasn't cryptic enough, she'd looked into the camera and apologized.

*"Carson, I'm so sorry."*

What the hell had Vangie done?

I lay on the bed and studied the ceiling and ran that question in front of my eyes a hundred times until I drifted into a sweaty, twitchy sleep.

A ringing phone at the bedside awakened me. I dropped it, picked it up by the cord and bobbled it to my ear.

"Hmmp?"

Waltz. "We've got a dead woman, Detective Ryder. It's a bad one."

"Do I know her?" I mumbled from between two worlds.

"Jesus, wake up, Detective. You don't know her. God, I hope not. I'm on scene and sending you a car. Be out front."

"Waltz, um, wait. Let me get myself toget—"

The phone clicked dead. The clock said it was 8.10 p.m. I'd slept for two hours. My washed shirts were soggy. All I had was the one I'd worn through the day, reeking of sweat and despair. Holding my breath, I pulled it on and headed outside.

Day was failing fast, oblique light soaking the sky with an amber hue. City noise echoed down the man-made canyons, giving the sounds a reverberant depth. A police cruiser waited on the sidewalk, almost to the hotel steps. I was barely inside before the cruiser roared into traffic. I looked at the driver: Koslowski. He wrinkled his nose at my used clothes, shot me a glance, and rolled his window down.

"Where's the scene?" I yelled over the siren. The traffic was mainly taxis. Koslowski kept his foot deep in the pedal, expecting cabs to open a path by the time he got there, and somehow they did.

"SoHo. If I don't get you there in five minutes, Waltz is going to chew my ass."

"I can't imagine Waltz chewing ass."

"He does it without words. It's worse that way."

"He's an interesting guy," I said, fishing for more info about the sad-eyed detective. "What's your take on him?"

Instead of answering, Koslowski pulled to a brick Italianate duplex, a FOR SALE sign in the tiny front yard. I saw one cruiser by the curb, and a battered SUV with NYPD TECHNICAL DIVISION stenciled on the door. Beside it was a van from the Medical Examiner's office. A blue-and-white was sideways across two lanes to keep gawkers distant, its light bar painting the street in shaking, multihued bursts. I jumped out and hustled toward the house.

"Hey, Dixie," Koslowski called.

I spun. "What?"

"You asked me what I thought about Shelly Waltz." He jammed the cruiser in gear. "When it's nighttime for the whole world, and everyone is asleep, Shelly Waltz flies through the sky on a silver unicorn."

"*What*?"

But Koslowski's taillights were already flowing away. Shaking my head, I entered the house. A man and woman from the Medical Examiner's office stood inside the door, opening a case of equipment. They looked shaken, ashen. They directed me down a hall to a bedroom. I smelled blood and my stomach shifted sideways.

I entered the room. Like the front rooms, it was devoid of furniture. Shelly was alone, standing above a draped figure in the center of the floor. The white cover was turning red as I watched. Waltz was rubbing his eyes with his palms.

"What is it, Shelly?"

He shook his head, lifted the cover. A woman's nude body. Her eyes stared wide from the center of her own belly. Blood and fascia and yellow fatty tissue surrounded the head, having squirted out when the head was jammed into the wound. I let it all register for a five count, then closed my eyes.

"We've got a bad problem," Waltz said.

"Bad as it gets," I affirmed.

Waltz let the cover fall back over the corpse. When it fell it puffed out air, swirling hairs on the floor, the same amalgam I'd seen at Vangie's crime scene: hairs of various colors and textures. Looking closer, I saw them scattered everywhere. On the tile floor, laying atop congealing pools of blood, on the window sill.

We turned to a thunder of footsteps approaching down the hall followed by Folger's bray.

"Waltz? Are you back there?"

The footsteps turned into three agitated faces, Lieutenant Folger and Tweedledum and -dee from this morning – the hulking Bullard and Abel Cluff, a smaller and older guy with bulging eyes and the forward-pointing facial structure of a stoat. Cluff was wheezing, like he'd run a dozen flights instead of walking up a five-step stoop out front. Both men were in dark suits and white shirts, Bullard's plank-thick wrists hanging two inches from his sleeves, like he'd grown since he'd bought the suit.

The trio moved past, stepping around the blood pools and smears. Cluff bent and lifted the cover from the corpse. His eyes showed neither surprise nor emotion and I figured being an older detective with the NYPD, he'd seen every possible permutation of horror.

"Oh Christ," Folger moaned when she saw the body. "Tell me I'm dreaming, we don't have a mad butcher out there."

"Removing the head could be an attempt at depersonalization," I ventured, trying to be helpful. "But inserting it in the abdomen could be a show of control: Behold my power. Or it might –"

Folger snapped her face to me. "What the hell are you doing here?" She sniffed, wafting her hand past her nose at my scent. "Jesus, they don't have soap or deodorant where you're from?"

Waltz said, "I invited Detective Ryder, Lieutenant. Given his experience with disturbed minds, I thought he might –"

"He's not needed," she said. "Stick him on a bus and aim it south."

Bullard pinched his nose and gurgled a laugh. "You may want to spray him with something first."

"Have you seen all you need, Detective?" Waltz asked. He shot me a look that said he knew I hadn't, but it was time to let the Lieutenant win one. I nodded yes for the sake of harmony, and we retreated outside. There were now three cruisers on scene, one ambulance, an ME vehicle, a forensic vehicle, a large command vehicle and Waltz's dinged-up blue Chevy Impala. The area was cordoned with yellow CRIME SCENE tape. The kid from Tech Services, Cargyle, jogged by, phone to his face and a heavy case slung over his shoulder.

I said, "Looks like you people are about to ramp into full investigative mode, Shelly. I'll catch a cab."

"One question, Detective. The eyes of the two victims. What do you make of the eyes?"

"That they're open?" I said. "Not closed or covered or mutilated?"

"Yes."

"He feels no shame at his actions, Shelly. There's a good chance he feels pride his victims get to watch him at work."

Waltz nodded sadly and turned as white as a man struck by lightning. Photoflash. I spun and saw a photographer a dozen feet distant.

*Flash*.

"Hey, Detective Waltz, s'up in there? Who's dead?"

*Flash Flash.*

I saw blue squares floating in the air. Waltz gestured for a uniform to move the guy away. The photog retreated on wide and flat feet, grinning like a donkey, holding his hands up in the *I surrender* pose. He was a short guy, round, round, and round – face, belly, and butt, respectively.

I looked at Waltz. "One of the local media elite?"

"That piece of waddling excrement is the infamous Benny Mac. The prize scribbler-slash-camera jockey from the *New York Watcher*. It's the newspaper for citizens who don't like to read. We'll be in it tomorrow, unless something important takes the space, like a celebrity getting a DUI or a cat that uses a toilet."

I watched the guy pad across the street, shooting an arm into the air like an imperious wave. An engine roared to life down the block and a double-parked white Hummer sailed to Benny Mac's side. He climbed inside, barked some command to the driver, and was whisked away, smirking through the window as he went.

# FOUR

*"Meester Ryder? Room service. I brought breakfas'."*

The Spanish-accented voice and knocking seemed too close. I felt something hard against my nose, something gritty pressing my cheek.

*"Meester Ryder?"*

My eyes popped open. I was on the floor by the door, nose against the wood, cheek on the carpet. I'd been dreaming.

"Just a minute," I mumbled, staggering upright. "Be right there."

I saw covers, sheet and pillows trailing from the bed to the door. Having dreams so disturbing I'd try to crawl away from them happened several times a year. The imagery was consistent: moaning shadows, faces comprised solely of teeth, a house

41

where all windows faced inward . . . dreams generated during childhood.

I scooped the bedclothes up, threw the pillows and covers on the bed, wrapped the sheet around my naked body to answer the door. If the room service lady thought it unusual to find guests in ad hoc togas, her face didn't let on. In fact, she beamed with recognition, and grabbed a newspaper from her cart. The woman waved the paper in my face, said, "Ees chew."

"No thanks." I thought she was offering me the paper. "Ees chew," she repeated, snapping the paper open and pushing it to my face again. "Chew ees famous."

I pushed it aside to look at her. "Pardon?"

"*Aqui*," she said, tapping the third page with her finger. I saw a photo of Waltz and me. Beside the photo was a brief article.

### Savagery in SoHo

New York's Finest are close-lipped about a woman found with her abdomen sliced open in a vacant SoHo property. Perhaps the gruesome crime scene explains the look on the face of renowned Detective Sheldon Waltz, here conferring with an unnamed colleague . . .

At the housekeeper's request – "Chew so famous!" – I autographed the article and took my breakfast tray inside. Naked on the bed with plate in one hand, fork in the other, I displaced the bad-dream bilge in my stomach with over-cooked eggs and undercooked bacon and yearned for cheese grits with andouille. I show-ered for fifteen minutes, wishing I were at home on Dauphin Island, a hundred yards from the Gulf of Mexico, cool at this time of year, invig-orating.

I dressed and walked to the cop shop, finding it kin to every station house in the civilized world: agitated bodies and loud voices, the smell of burnt coffee and all-nighter sweat, phones ringing, jammed-together desks piled with files. Waltz was in a glass-windowed office along the far wall. When I entered his office, he held up a copy of the *New York Watcher* turned to our photo.

"Must not have been any celebrity malfunc-tions overnight. You take a better picture than me. Have a seat."

I sat. Waltz fixed me with a despondent gaze. "The techs are at their wits' end, Detective. The hair you noticed on the floor at the scenes? It's from hundreds of people. Men's hair, women's, different races. Plus dozens of fiber types, all mixed together."

"*What?*"

"They did some tests, figure the killer collected hair from barber shops and beauty salons, fibers from anything. It's an evidentiary nightmare."

"Jeez, Shelly, even if you found something in the room that ID'd the guy . . ."

"The evidence would be polluted," Waltz finished. "No sane DA would bring it to trial. It's brilliant. How many madmen could figure out a ploy like this?"

*I know one who could*, I thought. But to everyone's good fortune, my brother was in the fortress called the Alabama Institute for Aberrational Behavior, locked up tight and forever.

Waltz pushed aside files on his desk to make a place for his elbows and flicked a paper at me, *Office of the Medical Examiner* on the letterhead.

"The prelims on the autopsies. Both were done last night and side-by-side. Folger and I pushed it through."

I grimaced at the bullet-pointed information. "The womb was taken?"

"Basically, the victims received amateur hysterectomies. I attended the post mortem. The pathologist told me it was like an angry monkey hacking away with a knife. When all that was over, the head was pushed into the wound."

The picture that came to my mind was so ugly I shut it off.

"Jesus. Forensics find anything useful?"

"We're screwed by the hairs and fibers on the scene. But we did ID the victim. Dora Anderson, thirty-six years of age. She works for the realtor. She went there to meet a prospective buyer."

"Alone? At night?"

"It's a fairly upscale neighborhood. The guy must have presented himself benignly on the phone. She felt safe in his presence, obviously."

A man who could tear another person apart and still present a perfectly normal appearance and demeanor was a total psychopath, a human chameleon. I shivered involuntarily and tossed the prelim on Shelly's desk. It felt greasy in my hands, like the vileness of the murder had tainted the paper.

"You realize our perp hates women, right? More than anything?"

He nodded. "By removing the womb, he castrated her. I've seen my share of gender kills, though nothing quite that extreme."

"Shelly, you've got a real nightmare brewing out there."

Waltz's phone rang. He grabbed it up. I turned my eyes away and pretended not to listen but, like everyone in the world, cops especially, kept an ear tuned to his voice.

"I'm in the middle of a . . . *She's* in town? The Chief wants me specifically? No, I can do it. I've got to do it, right? Listen, we have a guy here, a specialist in, uh, people with bad intentions. OK to bring him along? Good. We're heading there now."

He hung up. "I know you heard that, Detective. I'd be disappointed if you hadn't."

"I take it we're going somewhere?"

"There's a political convention in a week or so, women from around the country, leadership types. I'm supposed to vet the threats, determine which are hot air, which are truly dangerous."

"Threats?"

"The keynote speaker is Cynthia Pelham."

"Holy shit," I whispered. Cynthia Pelham had been on the American political scene for over twenty-five years. Her saga started at age twenty-three, when the county sweet-potato queen with two years of junior college married a fifty-eight-year-old senator from Georgia.

By thirty, she was making statements contrary to the senator's positions regarding women's right to equal pay and maternity leave. She had three-fourths of a law degree, obtained at night, since she'd had to spend her days on the senator's arm and smiling the sweet-potato smile at cameras.

By thirty-five, she had the degree, but not the senator. Following a high-profile divorce, the senator's allies, of whom there were many, spread rumors that Cynthia Pelham was – depending on the day and rumormonger – a lesbian, a woman who bedded every man she saw, frigid, a drug addict, a drunkard and, according to the *New York Watcher*, maybe even an extraterrestrial. Ms Pelham's friends, of whom there were few at that time, simply said, "She grew up."

By forty, Pelham was representing a mainly poor congressional district with such concern and passion she was uncontested in the next election. Since she was unmarried, held centrist feminist ideals, and kept her personal life personal, rumors of lesbianism persisted, her denials met with scorn. Websites and blogs sprang up calling for either her vilification or beatification.

By fifty-two, her present age, she had been convinced by grass-roots support and a generous helping of ambition – never denied – to run for President of the United States. Though bitterly divisive among partisans and ideologues, she wielded enough centrist appeal that odds were even money she'd win.

A few nights back I'd seen news from a typical Pelham event in Miami. Three-quarters of the crowd were supporters, the others ranting, waving fists, and carrying signs and posters. One showed a mangy female dog with bloated teats, Pelham's face in place of the dog head. The caption said, "Time to Put the Bitch to Sleep."

I said, "How long will Pelham be here, Shelly?"

"She's coming to coordinate the eastern seaboard campaigns. The lady will be in and out of town all the next week."

"What about the Secret Service?"

"They'll accompany Pelham while we vet everything else."

"'We' meaning you?"

"Basic security isn't my problem, a special team handles the bodyguard routine, checking traffic routes and so forth." He sighed. "The Chief wants me to explain to Ms Pelham's handlers how the NYPD will keep snakes from wriggling under her door."

I nodded my sympathy. Given Pelham's flashpoint index it would take someone with experience to determine which threats were hot air and which were dangerous. It was nasty work, like dredging sewage with your fingers.

Waltz stood and grabbed his hat. "Like you heard, I bartered you into the mix. Straighten your tie and let's get running."

The powwow was at Ms Pelham's NYC head-quarters, a storefront near Cooper Union. There were the usual banners and posters and photos of the candidate. The desks were staffed by earnest-looking folks with phones in one hand, pencils in the other.

We met in a back room with Ronald Banks, a square, bespectacled African-American Secret Service agent in charge of the operation. I took the room to be a place for strategizing, a large map of NYC on the wall, broken down into precincts, voting registrations or projections sticky-taped to the map. There was a round table, a few chairs. Boxes of campaign flyers on the floor.

"She getting many threats?" Waltz asked Banks.

"People love her or hate her. The ones who hate her all seem to have rabies. Good luck, Detective Waltz."

Our heads turned to a commotion in the work area: Cheers, applause, whistles. Either someone was dispensing free money, or the candidate was visiting. Three minutes later, Cynthia Pelham entered our room, two aides de camp in her slipstream. Somewhere along the road the sweet-potato queen had been replaced by a whirlwind in a pantsuit and sensible shoes. She ran to a corner, cellphone to one ear, finger in the other, talking as loud as if she were alone for miles around.

*"Dammit, I don't care how much money he has, the sonuvabitch is trailing garbage. The day after we take his donation the bastard will be indicted for screwing a goat or something. See if you can piss him off and maybe he'll give the money to the other side . . ."*

The second she snapped the phone closed it rang again. She listened for a ten-count. "The answers are, respectively, Yes, Yes, No, Hell yes, and the lobster bisque." She switched the phone off and tossed it to a woman beside her, a petite blonde with quiet eyes and a square jaw who tucked the phone in a fat briefcase I figured doubled as the candidate's purse.

The sweet-potato queen had turned from a pretty girl into a handsome woman, auburn hair now mixed with gray, her form shaded to the heavier side, skin lined with experience. The eyes that looked piercing on television seemed more curious in real life. She aimed the eyes at Waltz and me, moved to us as if pulled by gravity.

"You gentlemen look official. Am I triple-parked again?"

Waltz did his best to make his sad face smile. It looked like he was fighting a sneeze. "We're here because a lot of folks don't like you, Congresswoman. Men especially. At least that's what I hear on the news."

Pelham laughed, hearty and deep and bordering on bawdy. Unlike many candidates, she wasn't afraid laughter would mark her as more human than machine, therefore unfit for high office.

"A lot of ladies don't like me either. Hell, a lot of people's pets don't like me, if I'm to believe my mail."

"You do seem to seriously set some folks off," I said.

She raised an eyebrow at my voice, then the eyes went serious. "A lot of politicians get hate mail from people who live under rocks, but mine seems to come from the people beneath the people under the rocks. I showed a few letters to Rich Stanzaro when we were primary opponents. He said, 'I see some strange shit, Cyn, but no one ever wants to cut my tits off.'"

"Rabies, like I said," Banks noted to Waltz.

Pelham turned the curious eyes to me. "You're the first NYPD cop I've ever met with a Southern accent." She raised an eyebrow and grinned. "South Bronx, maybe?"

"I'm with the police department in Mobile, ma'am. I'm consulting on another case and Detective Waltz thought I might have a useful insight or two."

"Because you've done something like this before? Helped guard against the angry people?"

"In a way. Back in Mobile I'm part of a unit that deals with mentally unstable criminals."

"How unstable?"

"They'd not only cut your tits off, ma'am, they'd bread 'em and fry 'em up for supper."

Eyes widened around us. Even Waltz raised

52

an eyebrow. There was a moment of silence before the congresswoman barked the laugh, slapped my shoulder.

"I'm glad they sent out for Southern cooking, hon. You got some pepper in your gravy."

Pelham shot us either a peace or victory sign and scurried off to pump up the cheerleader section out front. I stayed quiet as Waltz explained to aides and senior staff how he'd be checking the hate mail and unsavory phone calls, cautioning everyone to stay alert for strange people, incidents, and items in the mail.

The whole trip to and from Pelham's HQ took under an hour. Cargyle, the young guy from Technical Services, ran across the floor as we returned to the detectives' room, excitement in his voice and a tape cassette in his hand.

"Dr Prowse's arrival was caught on security cameras at LaGuardia. I found two sections when she's on camera. The first is by the baggage carousel, the second is going out the door. She seems normal, picking up her bag, heading out to grab a cab. She talks to a man beside her for a second. Probably small talk with another passenger."

"Folger and her crew in?" Waltz asked.

"Due back shortly, but I don't know exactly when."

"Let's get a preview."

Cargyle wheeled a playback system into a conference room. He had a bag of tools and tape and electronic doohickeys slung over his skinny shoulder. His wristwatch had more buttons than my truck's dashboard. He had not one but two skinny telephones. If Cargyle was like our Tech Services crew in Mobile, he read schematics instead of books.

"You just now find the footage?" I asked him.

"I've been at LaGuardia all night. Found one image at three, the other a half hour ago."

"There all night, here all day? You ever sleep, buddy?"

Waltz said, "Cargyle's assigned to the precinct, his training phase. I'm making sure he gets the full learning experience."

"Full and more," Cargyle grinned. The tape stuttered into action. The quality was better than your standard convenience-store cameras and I figured Homeland Security had a bigger budget than the Gas'n'Gulp.

"Here's the first segment," Cargyle announced. "By the baggage carousel."

I held my breath as Vangie stepped into the frame, flight bag over her shoulder. She ran to the carousel and snatched her suitcase. She paused, then spoke to a white-shirted man beside her, slender, facing away. The scene lasted all of five seconds.

"That's snippet number one," Cargyle said. "The second is a couple seconds longer, but not much."

The edited video jumped to the next scene. The camera was positioned above the door, the crowd herding tight for the exit like cattle down a chute.

"Here she comes," Waltz whispered, picking Vangie from the on-rushing mob while she was still a blur. I leaned close to the screen. It took a second to discern the familiar features, the large eyes, dark and compact hair, rosebud lips. The eyes looked wary and tight with tension as Vangie exited the terminal with the slender man by her side, his head again canted away. At the last moment, he snapped his face toward the camera. His grin was ecstatic, his joy dominating the screen.

My spine turned to ice. I couldn't choke back a gasp.

"What?" Waltz said. "You know him?"

"I've seen him before," I whispered. "He's a patient at the Institute. Brilliant and murderous and unpredictable."

I didn't add that he was my brother.

# FIVE

"The crazy's name is what?" Folger asked.

"Jeremy Ridgecliff," Waltz said. "He killed his father when he was sixteen, then brutally murdered five women. Ridgecliff has been in the Alabama Institute for Aberrational Behavior for over a dozen years."

Folger turned to me. "Didn't you say they never got out of that place?"

I barely heard her and made no response. I sat in the corner, stunned. Somehow, Jeremy had escaped and forced Vangie to New York. Vangie was dead, mercilessly and bizarrely mutilated by my brother.

*Tell them,* my mind said. *Tell them he's your brother. You've got to tell them now.*

I opened my mouth to speak as Waltz waved

57

everyone silent, holding up pages fresh from the fax machine. "Our first look at Ridgecliff. He likes knives, mutilation and symbolism. And he's had years of incarceration to dream up new stuff. That's the good news."

A detective in the back of the room, Perlstein, looked up from his note-taking. "If that's good, Shelly, what's bad?"

"He has a higher IQ than anyone in this room, I'd wager. I'm talking maybe thirty points higher."

Low whistles, groans. A killer with creative intelligence could be as elusive as a black shark in a midnight ocean.

*Stand up and tell them,* my mind repeated. *They're cops. You're a cop.*

Folger's heels ticked on the floor as she paced. "Ridgecliff somehow coerced the Prowse woman into bringing him here, then killed her, no longer needed. What he did to her got him so juiced he had to do it again. Like Waltz said, this monster's had years to let his fantasies cook. His feet barely hit pavement and we've got two women torn to bits."

What would happen when I told them? I'd become their information machine, held distant from the investigation, used but not completely trusted. It was the smart thing to do. It's what I would do in the same situation.

Waltz's voice broke into my thoughts. "It was Detective Ryder who ID'd Ridgecliff, saving hundreds of man-hours. We all owe him a debt of gratitude."

My face burned as the other faces in the room turned to me. Cop faces, my brethren, nodding thanks at me. I heard scattered handclaps. Folger walked over.

*Tell her.*

"Job well done, Detective. Waltz is right. We all owe you one."

"Listen, Lieutenant, uh, I'd like to tell you about Ridgecliff. He's —"

Folger's hand, firm and cool, found its way into mine. "Sorry we got off on the wrong foot. You know how protective departments are about turf, right? You can head home and we'll have Ridgecliff nailed in a day or two. Drop him back in the box. Or even better, lay him in the ground."

"Bang," Bullard said. "Problem solved."

"Uh, listen, Lieutenant . . ."

*But what if . . . What would change if . . . I said nothing. What was affected as long as I stayed near the investigation? Vangie could have*

59

*mentioned Jeremy was my brother. Why didn't she?*

"Yes?" Folger said, a dark eyebrow raised.

"About Jeremy Ridgecliff . . . I'm part of a special unit that handles the edgy stuff, psychotics, sociopaths. I can help you more than you think."

"We have homicidal crazies in New York, Ryder. I think the NYPD can handle –"

Waltz interrupted. "You recognized Ridgecliff right off the bat, Detective Ryder. Am I to assume you studied the suspect?"

I kept my face neutral and my voice even. "I have had conversations with Mr Ridgecliff. Quite a few, actually."

Waltz turned to Folger. "Not only does Detective Ryder know a bit about Ridgecliff, it might speed up communication with Southern law enforcement if we had a liaison. And a local professional to interview the staff at the Institute." Waltz looked to me. "You can handle the Southern pipeline on both counts, Detective Ryder?"

Though my heart was pounding like a hammer, I kept my voice nonchalant. "I have excellent contacts in the Alabama State Police and can have my partner handle interviews at

60

the Institute. He's experienced in psychological crimes."

Folger said, "I don't think we need –"

Waltz clapped his hands once, not applause, but finality. "That should settle things and sit well with the brass. Detective Ryder will be with us a few days longer. A consultant, if you will."

*Don't go down this road. Tell them now. It's your last chance.*

I studied my shoes. My mouth stayed closed. *What am I doing?*

Folger departed briskly, Bullard and Cluff on her heels. Waltz headed to a meeting with the DA on another case. I stood on unsteady legs and checked my watch: Ten thirty a.m. It was an hour earlier in Mobile. I blotted sweat from my forehead with my sleeve, took a deep breath and dialed my cellphone. Twelve hundred miles away in Mobile, my partner, Harry Nautilus, picked up.

"Cars? Jeez, what the hell's going on? Are you still in NYC?"

I pictured Harry frowning into the phone, a six-four black man in a forty-eight long jacket, probably yellow or neon green. The pants might be plum, or mauve. Harry loved color and no one dared tell him it sometimes didn't love him back.

"I'll be here for a few days, Harry."

"Why? I mean, one minute you're here, the next you're –"

"Jeremy escaped," I said. "He's in New York."

"*What*?"

"He somehow coerced Vangie Prowse into bringing him here. Vangie's dead, Harry. Jeremy killed her and another woman. He did terrible things to the bodies. He's exploding."

"Lord Jesus," Harry whispered. "How in the hell did he get out?"

"I don't know. Some kind of ruse. Maybe he got hold of a weapon, or found some security failing. It should have been impossible, but he did it. Listen, Harry, I know the State Police will be handling it, but could you take a look at the Institute, find out how –"

"Did you tell them, Cars? Did you tell them he's your brother?"

I couldn't find my breath. The day seemed to come crashing in and my eyes filled with tears. I gasped, wiped my face on my shoulder. Waited for Harry to tear into me, to tell me I was an idiot. Or worse.

Instead, Harry said, "Tell me what you need me to do, bro."

We talked for a few minutes. After hanging up, I slunk toward the exit carrying a paper bag bulging with copies of the files faxed to Waltz by the Alabama State Police. On the way out I saw Alice Folger in a shadowy meeting room by herself, watching a television like something major depended on the outcome. I couldn't see the screen or hear the audio, and wondered if it was a news program with NYPD featured in some way, or perhaps a verdict on a case she'd worked.

I crept by to the other side of the hall, shot a glance at the TV screen. I saw a suited man pointing at colored lines bisecting the nation's midsection.

Alice Folger was hypnotized by the Weather Channel?

# SIX

I returned to the hotel and set the files on the table, pushing them to the far side. Guilt at my inability to tell the cops the truth pooled in my guts like cold oil. There was more to feel guilty about: Even though a specialist in psychological crimes, I had never read the details of my brother's murders. I had always feared that, in reading the cold facts of Jeremy's cases, I might see a monster, and not the tormented child who killed his father after years of unspeakable misery . . .

*I am just past my tenth birthday. Jeremy is sixteen. One day, playing alone in one of the forts Jeremy and I built in the woods behind our house, I walk from the trees to find the county police at our house. There is a policeman on the*

64

dirt drive of our house, another at the wheel of the car. The cop in the drive is looking at my mother, three steps up on the porch. Jeremy is on the porch as well, sitting a dozen feet away in the glider. He looks between the policeman in the car and the one in the drive, his eyes pensive.

The policeman's hat is off and he is holding it over his privates. He is tremendously old, fifty maybe. He removes his mirrored sunglasses, his face creased with sorrow. I hear his words in soft groupings.

"I'm so sorry, ma'am . . .

"The coroner's there now, no need for you to see such a . . .

"We'll find this madman, ma'am, this person . . ."

I look to the police car and see the second policeman through the open car door. Younger. He's reloading one of those cameras where the film turns into pictures as you watch. He sets the camera aside and his eyes study me. Strangely ashamed, I look at the ground. When I look up again, he is studying Jeremy. Then the moment passes and the cops turn to dust in the hot air. My mother stands in the yard like a statue. Jeremy rocks the glider to and fro, a faraway smile on his face.

I had never asked Jeremy about the day our father died. I had hated the man. When he left for work in the morning, I watched the truck disappear down the road and prayed for his death. A retaining wall cave-in, crushed under a bulldozer, falling from a bridge. I had a dozen hopeful scenarios.

*Please God, make him die today in a gasoline explosion . . .*

Instead, it was my big brother who finally exploded. Only later, after interviewing a hundred fiercely dysfunctional minds, did I realize Jeremy's explosion had saved me from an escalating madness destined to end in a house full of dead bodies with the standard news bites from the neighbors.

*"We never knew the Ridgecliffs real good, but they seemed decent enough . . . Earl didn't seem the kind of man to do that to his family and hisself . . . it's a tragedy, is what it is . . ."*

Jeremy knew how it would end, and took the only course he could take. I am alive because my father never got the chance to kill me.

Every breath I take is a gift from Jeremy.

I arrayed Jeremy's files before me in chronological order, starting with paperwork generated

66

the day my father died. One of the first officers at the scene was Jim Day of the county police. Though higher-ranking officers had been in early attendance – Sergeant Willis Farnsworth, Lieutenant Merle Baines, Captain Hollis Reamy – it was Day who wrote up the report. It may have been that Farnsworth, Baines and Reamy wanted to avoid paperwork, not unusual for guys with the rank to lay the work on others; but it could also have been Day's eye for minutiae and vocabulary for description.

*Victim's intestine*, Day wrote, *appeared to have been severed at lower end and pulled like rope from the slit in victim's abdomen. This "rope" extended across the ground for a dozen feet.* And later in the report: *A kidney appears to have been thrown with great force into a tree, bursting like a water balloon. Fragments were on the ground at the tree's base.*

And near the conclusion of the report, Day noted that, *"the scene seemed one of total anger. The feeling was of a threshold crossed, some form of decision acted on."*

It took an hour to read Jim Day's details and descriptions. When finished, I was soaked in sweat and my hands shook, forced to experience the crime as it unfolded. I'd heard the screams for mercy, smelled the cut-copper reek of flowing blood. My mind's-eye watched my brother cut my father apart with a knife I'd used to slice bologna.

I blotted sweat from my brow and pushed aside the six-inch-tall stack of copies generated by Jeremy's remaining murders of the five innocent women. I'd get to them later.

Tomorrow for sure.

Twilight painted the air a clean and fragile blue as Jeremy Ridgecliff rode a subway car downtown. He was feigning sleep while shooting sidelong glances at his quarry, a pasty little man, fortyish and balding. He was dressed in khakis and a gray wool cardigan, and had wary, flickering eyes that often shot to the tattered briefcase locked beneath his arm.

Jeremy had spent the afternoon wandering in the library, never going too far from the Political Science stacks and the Archived Newspapers: Cheese for a very special kind of mouse.

Had he found one?

Jeremy had watched the man working in a carrel, muttering to himself and making notes. After an hour, the man exited the library cautiously, clutching the briefcase to his chest and jitter-stepping to the street, shooting glances over his shoulders.

Jeremy had followed, his antennae quivering.

The man had stopped at a cart for a sandwich. He opened the bread like it was booby-trapped, and inspected the interior. After wolfing the sandwich down, he'd skittered to the subway entrance. Jeremy slipped his Metro Pass from his pocket, followed the man into the ground.

*Next stop Chambers Street . . .*

The train slowed. Jeremy saw his quarry's hands tighten on the bar, ready to exit, but not wanting anyone to know. The wheels squealed to a halt. Doors snapped open. People entered and exited. At the last possible moment, the man jumped from his seat and slipped through the closing doors.

Jeremy was already outside, waiting in the shadows. The man walked east for a dozen blocks, entering a neighborhood of expensive high-rise apartments and condos.

Jeremy slipped ahead with the stealth of a cat, appearing at the man's side.

"Keep walking," Jeremy growled. "Walk or die. Don't make a sound."

The man moaned. Jeremy steered him to a paved area outside an empty dog run. A dirty streetlamp turned the twilight into yellow haze. Jeremy's finger jabbed the man toward a bench.

"Sit," he demanded.

The man sat and held up the briefcase like a shield. "I-I have c- copies. If anything h-happens to me, copies g-go to the *New York Times*, the *Wuh-Washington Post*, the *Chicago T-Tribune* and the *R-Rocky Mountain News*."

"Shut up or I'll slice your throat. Show me what you have."

The man fumbled at the locks with trembling fingers. The open case revealed hundreds of tattered pages. He selected what seemed an important page, names and dates linked by colored arrows. He pushed the page at Jeremy.

"You c-can't hurt me. It's all backed up. I have c-copies."

Jeremy moved beneath the streetlamp. He studied arrows and lines snaking from *Trilateral Commission* to *Ronald Reagan* to *the House of Saud* to *GW Bush*. The Bay of Pigs was represented, as were the Kennedys. Each name was followed by a half-dozen exclamation points.

Jeremy stepped to the man's side. Shook the page in front of the man's eyes. "How long have you known about this?"

"T-Twenty-two years."

Jeremy replaced the anger in his face with calm. He surprised the man by gently squeezing his shoulder.

"It's terrible, isn't it? They used hidden speakers to fill my house with noises at night. They were always sneaking up on me, dressed as repairmen. They put things in my food to make me sick."

The man's eyes widened. "You're . . . one of us?"

Jeremy looked from side to side, whispered, "They were after me for a decade, but I managed to get free."

"HOW?"

Jeremy put a finger to his lips and pointed to an approaching jogger, a man in white sweats, MP3 player wire running to his ears. The jogger shot an uninterested glance as he padded past.

"He saw us," the man gasped. "Do you think he's one of Them?"

"He'd been wired for sound," Jeremy said. "Did you notice one wire was black, the other one white?"

The man's hand swept to his mouth. "Oh Jesus . . ."

Jeremy crouched to look the man in the eyes. "Things are falling apart in Washington. They might be willing to forget you. I made them forget me."

"TELL ME HOW! I'll do anything!"

"Shhhhh. I bribed them. And I was free."

"The NSA takes bribes? The CIA?"

Jeremy rubbed his fingers in the money-whisk motion. "It's Washington, everything slides on the green grease."

"What do they want?"

"What can you give them?"

The man's brow wrinkled in furious thought as his fingertips drummed his briefcase. "Paper money's going to be worthless soon. I can get my hands on Krugerrands, gold coins. Most gold is radioactive, but the South Africans make Krugerrands immune to the rays. I can't get many – seventy or eighty thousand dollars worth or so." He shook his head. "It's nothing to Them."

"They'll soon be the only currency left. Give them half. It's what I did."

The man's wary eyes returned. He pulled the briefcase to his chest, pages spilling across the pavement. "You could be one of Them. You'll steal from me and still follow me."

Jeremy patted the man's forearm, one friend to another. "If I was after your money, wouldn't I ask for all of it?"

The man absorbed the information, sighed with relief. "I don't want to meet them. Can you take the gold for me?"

Jeremy straightened, put his hands in his pockets, shot furtive looks from side to side.

"I'll have to catch the red-eye to DC tomorrow. Can you get the gold tonight? And maybe some cash to tide them over?"

# SEVEN

The next morning I entered the detectives' room to a heavy smell of sweat and adrenalin. Bodies were moving fast, papers shuffling, phones ringing. Cluff was on the phone and staring down at his fax machine. I watched a heavyset detective cross the room with a cup of coffee, enter a cubicle a dozen feet away, start talking with a colleague.

"Too freakin' much," the chunky guy said, laughing.

"What?"

"Len and me just got back from a condo in Tribeca. Ritzy place, owned by a husband and wife, the guy manages an investment firm. Good people, they keep a room for the wife's brother, Gerald. Gerald's forty-two, got a few head problems, mainly he's paranoid-schizo. Gerald does

74

OK until he skips his meds, then he weirds out, hides from the Feds, that sort of thing. The boys in blue track him down a couple times a year, bring him home."

"Conspiracy type?"

"In spades. Seems Gerald came home last night, snuck in the husband's office safe and grabbed forty-seven grand worth of Krugerrands the investment guy had stashed."

"Uh-oh."

"Yep. By the time Mr Investment finds the shiny coins missing this morning, Gerald's given them away, plus twenty-six thou in cash. Said he was buying his freedom from the CIA."

A laugh. "Who'd Gerald give the stuff to? He say?"

"Won't say anything, except he's finally free and they're all safe. He's a happy camper. Showed us some backward scribbles on a piece of cardboard, claimed it was his receipt from the CIA . . ."

I shook my head and walked away, seeing Waltz arriving, opening the door of his office, tossing his hat to the corner of his desk. I crossed the floor, making my face benign, guileless. I had chosen duplicity over truth and there was no turning back.

My fear of discovery wasn't overwhelming. I'd gone to a fair amount of trouble to wall myself off from my past. Except for paying a computer-savvy friend to delete items from a college database, it was mostly legal, changing my name and spreading carefully chosen rumors. Unless the few who knew of my connection to Jeremy Ridgecliff pointed my way, anyone looking for the missing brother of a blighted family might think the guy boarded a steamer and fell beneath the horizon, never seen again.

"What's up, Shelly?" I asked, poking my head through his door.

"Cluff dug up tax records from Ms Dora Anderson. She wasn't born a realtor, it was a career change."

"From what?"

"A social worker in Newark. It was years ago, but . . ."

We were in Newark a half-hour later, in the city's social services department. It resembled the detectives' room at the precinct – a large space jammed with cubicles and filing cabinets and lined by small offices and conference rooms. Unlike the detectives' room, the workers were predominantly women, the scent tending to perfume and hand lotions and other womanly nostrums. There were more pictures of families on the desks, fewer guys grinning beside large fish.

We had been directed to Jonnie Peal, a fortyish woman who held her head sideways as she talked, looking away every few seconds, like someone was whispering in her ear a half-dozen words at a time.

"Dora worked in the office all day. A mid-level administrator. Assignments, mainly, coordinating the schedules of our contact staff. I recall her having her realtor's license back then. A part-time thing, weekends. One day she went for it full time. Guess she got tired of scheduling. Pay was better. Couldn't be worse."

"No contact with clients?" I asked.

Ms Peal nodded to a row of wide cubicles separated by tall gray dividers. "She worked in cubicle fourteen. Sat there all day long."

I looked at Waltz. Desk-bound workers rarely made enemies that mutilated your body. It was the caseworkers, the folks on the street who were avoided, jeered, cursed, spat on, and sometimes harmed as they thrust themselves into situations where they were neither understood nor wanted. Cohabitational situations were bad, toss in kids and things got worse. Though parents might allow an infant to wallow in filth for days, let a social worker suggest inadequate care and things could explode into violence. But Ms Anderson had been insulated from those situations.

"That's wrong," said a voice. "Dora wasn't always at that desk."

We turned to see a petite, sharp-dressed Hispanic woman a dozen feet away. She stood up from a desk where she'd been on the telephone. Her phone rang. I figured it rang all day.

"Excuse me?" I said.

She punched a button on the phone and walked over. "I'm Celia Ramirez. Been here twenty years. Dora started in Social Services as a caseworker when she was fresh from college. It didn't work out, I guess. She was put in filing, worked her way to scheduling."

"She worked out of here? This office?"

Ms Ramirez pointed to an adjoining annex. "Back then she worked in Children's Services. You know what kind of nastiness they see over there?"

"Yes," I told her. "Unfortunately, I do."

We followed Ms Ramirez's directions to the Child Welfare section of the department. It mirrored government offices everywhere: cubes, chairs, desks with piled-high in-baskets, cabinets. But I knew horrors lurked in the cabinets and case files, the seeds of serial murderers. Psychopathic killers are created in childhood. They come from backgrounds of physical and psychological abuse on a scale almost inconceivable to the normal American mind.

No matter how childhood is stripped away, by sex or pain or perverse and relentlessly inventive combinations of the two, it leaves, or never begins. Many children endure these cauldrons of despair to create what we call productive lives. But endurance is a skill, not a foundation. Many are wounded in some way, unable to form normal relationships, or know anything akin to inner peace. Others have all vestiges of personality destroyed, as if an angry fire had seared away their soul. Nothing remains to hold evil at bay, and everything becomes a possibility.

Waltz noted my silence, said, "Are you all right, Detective Ryder?"

"I've been in too many of these places, Shelly."

"Don't I know it. Listen, two of us might seem heavy handed. Want to keep it one-on-one again, you being the one?"

I nodded. "Sounds right."

He squeezed my shoulder, then stood on tip-toe and scanned the floor. "I've got to find a restroom. I drank two cans of diet fudge goo this morning."

I wandered until I found the director, Eugenie Brickle, a slender and handsome black woman in her fifties with searching eyes. They searched me from toes to hat before deciding I was on the side of the angels.

"How long was she a caseworker?" I asked as we strolled the sidewalk in front of the building so Ms Brickle could have a cigarette. She didn't really smoke, just sort of touched the cigarette to her lips and inhaled as she pulled it away, puffing out nothing. I figured her for a long-time smoker who'd found a way to get the motion without the potion.

"Dora worked with us for two years. Then she was moved to clerical. It was that or be let go."

I paused, waited for a loud bus to pass. "Dora wasn't good at her job?"

"Maybe too good, too sensitive. She didn't know how to compartmentalize. Every child was Dora's child, every situation could have a happy ending. If it didn't, the failure was Dora's. It was tearing her up. It wasn't doing the staff a lot of good either, finding her weeping in the washroom three times a week."

"It seems strange she left the field completely."

We came to the end of the block, turned around. Ms Brickle had not-smoked the cigarette almost to the filter.

"Her mother lived with Dora and had been ill for several years. It's why Dora did real estate on weekends, to help with the bills. Her mom took a turn for the worse and the bills piled higher . . ."

"Dora jumped for the added pay."

"I imagine she was a super realtor, working to give every buyer a happy ending, find the dream home. Maybe that's what she threw herself into. But she never let go of her social-work days completely."

"Why do you say that?"

We stopped at the door. Ms Brickle pressed the cigarette into the sand of a receptacle, tapping it deep, so all that remained was a tan circle the circumference of a .32 shell.

"I was over in the city, saw her about a month back. She was clicking down the street in high heels and print dress flapping in the breeze, looking bright and happy and about to jump straight up into the blue sky. I asked if she'd just sold Donald Trump a building. She laughed and said she'd crossed paths with a client from her Child Welfare days, and he had made it through hell; not just survived, but was building a good life for himself."

"She say who it was?"

She shrugged. "We see so many kids I probably wouldn't have recalled the name. Just someone she'd seen in the course of her job."

"A success story."

"Even Dora had figured him for a lost child, too broken to ever be made right. But there he was, a responsible adult, working a good job and making a difference in the world. That day it wasn't the real estate work lighting her face up, Detective. It was a case from years and years ago. Dora got her a happy ending."

# EIGHT

"Could you please stop pacing, Doc?" Harry Nautilus said. "It's driving me nuts."

Nautilus rolled a chair behind Dr Alan Traynor, bumping the back of Traynor's knees. The psychiatrist half sat, half fell, into the chair.

"I'm trying to stay calm," the acting head of the Alabama Institute for Aberrational Behavior mumbled. He ran pink fingers through thinning white hair, tiny blue eyes twitching behind wire-framed bifocals. "It's all so mystifying. What would make Dr Prowse do such a thing?"

Nautilus sat another chair in the book-filled office that had belonged to Dr Evangeline Prowse. He rolled toward Traynor until their knees touched, hoping to lock the nervous shrink in place.

"I need to understand Dr Prowse's last few weeks."

Nautilus had left Mobile at six a.m.. He'd spent most of the drive on the phone with the State Police, making sure they were working together, not at odds. For now, the death of Dr Prowse was being disseminated as inconclusive. That a patient was missing was being played close to the vest. Had Jeremy Ridgecliff been prowling the Alabama countryside, there would have been a full shrieking alert. Roadblocks. Helicopters. Bloodhounds.

"Dr Traynor?" Nautilus prompted. "Did you notice anything strange?"

"Like I told the State Police, I wasn't here. She sent me and the three other senior staffers to a conference in Austin. It was last minute and strange."

"Strange how?"

"The conference had little bearing on what we do at the Institute. It was on interpersonal dynamics, personality assessments, psychometrics . . ." Traynor's hand rose to cover his mouth. "Oh Lord. Do you think Dr Prowse sent us to Austin to keep us away while all . . . the bad stuff was going on?"

"I don't know enough to answer that. Was anything unusual?"

Nautilus watched Traynor's face contort through memories. "She'd been nervous the past three or so weeks. But there wasn't any major incident. One thing stood out, though it wasn't recent. About six weeks back I was working second shift. Near midnight, I saw the Doctor in her office. I poked my head in, asked if I could help with anything. She said she was perplexed by a case."

"I'd figure perplexing cases were pretty standard here."

"She was more than perplexed, she was upset, though trying to hide it. I asked if I could help with anything. She said there might be confidentiality issues involved."

"Confidentiality holds in here?" Nautilus frowned down the long white hall toward the patient section of the Institute, separated by shining steel doors. Every fifty feet of wall held a button labeled *Emergency*. It wasn't referring to fires.

"Not at the Institute," Traynor said. "But doctor-patient privileges could have been involved if she was talking about a private client."

Nautilus raised an eyebrow. "Why would a

world-renowned specialist like Dr Prowse want to see folks with sibling rivalries, panic attacks . . ."

"The standard afflictions? She wouldn't. For Dr Prowse to accept an individual patient, he or she would be very compelling in some way. Of interest."

"I'd imagine she sees all kinds of 'interesting' in here," Nautilus said. "Jeremy Ridgecliff, for example."

Traynor nodded. "Patricide following years of childhood abuse, mental and physical. That wasn't overly unusual, a child reaching the breaking point, taking revenge. What was unusual was the shifting of anger to a disconnected mother, or rather, surrogates. And the startling amount of physical violence inflicted on his victims. Unfortunately . . ." Traynor shrugged, shook his head.

"Unfortunately what, Doctor?"

"Dr Prowse never fully opened Ridgecliff up. She figured ways to keep him calm and fairly reality based – that in itself was a monumental success – but she never reached the primal judgment."

"Primal judgment?"

"Sorry . . . a term the Doctor and I used for

the underlying motivator in killings. Another staffer calls it 'The Fire that lights all fires'."

"I thought abuse was the underlying factor."

"That's the fact of the case. The primal judgment is how the patient transforms that fact into his own beliefs. How the fact is perceived, interpreted and, in Jeremy Ridgecliff's case, turned into a murderous impulse against women." Traynor raised a wispy eyebrow, a note of condescension in his voice. "The concept is perhaps a bit difficult for the layman. A drunken and abusive man beats three sons. One son reads it as a form of contact, a misshapen display of love, and manages to love his father back. The second interprets it as hatred, responds in kind. The third son . . ." Traynor paused, tapped his fingers to his chin, trying to come up with an example.

"The third son," Nautilus said, "might do something wholly different, such as judging the pain to be a message from God or Allah or the Universal Oneness – a sign that he's been chosen for something, and the suffering is necessary."

Traynor stared at Nautilus as if seeing him for the first time.

"Exactly, Detective. But Dr Prowse never

found Jeremy Ridgecliff's primal judgment, probably because he knew she was looking for it. They danced around the subject, almost playfully at times."

"Playfully?"

"Both knew it was serious business, but Jeremy Ridgecliff had his whole life to play the game, his form of hide-and-seek. He held tight to his secrets."

"So the two, uh, toyed with one another. Is that the right word?"

"Ridgecliff could actually be puckish. And wholly charming, when he wished. Lovable, almost. If you didn't know his history."

*Lovable.* Nautilus tumbled the word in his mind. Dr Evangeline Prowse was a friend of his partner. If Carson had a blind spot, it was overlooking imperfections in those close to him. Nautilus narrowed an eye at the nervous Traynor and decided to push him a bit.

"Tell me about the phenomenon known as transference, Doctor."

Traynor frowned. "There's no way Dr Prowse would allow transference to occur."

"Transference of romantic feelings from patient to therapist . . . all kinds of patients fall for their therapists. Sometimes those vices get versa'd, right? The docs fall for the patients?"

The psychiatrist's forehead reddened with anger. "There's no way Dr Prowse would ever have a relationship with a patient."

"Then why did she go to such lengths to smuggle Ridgecliff out?"

"She didn't smuggle him out. He made her do it."

"It was Dr Prowse who changed guard schedules, falsified medical transfer papers, made up a half-dozen false scenarios over at least two weeks' time. You yourself suspect she diverted you to a conference to get you out of the way. Maybe it was all her idea."

"I just told you, that is impossible!"

"She did all this while he was locked up. No knife at her throat, gun at her back. It seems irrational. Which leaves emotion. Powerful emotion. What possible leverage could Ridgecliff hold over Dr Prowse except for an emotional one?"

Traynor stood abruptly, sending the chair toppling. "I don't know, goddammit! I DON'T FUCKING KNOW!"

Nautilus glanced at the toppled chair, raised an eyebrow at Traynor. "And when this transference happens under everyone's noses, there's surprise and anger. That's because of something called denial, right?"

The psychiatrist turned his head away. Said, "Yes."

# NINE

I grabbed a pastrami sandwich upon our return from Newark and brought it back to Waltz's office. I ate as Shelly nursed a can of something fished from his mini-fridge.

"Ms Anderson had a short tenure at Child Welfare," he said. "Ridgecliff's family never lived in Jersey, you're sure about that?"

*We never lived any further north than a brief stint in Knoxville when I was five. All I recall is my father ranting about mountains. He hated mountains, he hated plains, he hated whatever was in between.*

"It's in the records sent by the Alabama police, Shelly. The family never resided or even visited above the Mason-Dixon line."

"Anderson worked with dysfunctional families.

The Ridgecliffs were dysfunctional enough to register on the Richter scale. It's an interesting coincidence. I wish I could dig up the other kid. Charles Ridgecliff. Maybe he could make some sense of this."

I faked a yawn. "I doubt it, Shelly. He's long gone."

Waltz frowned. "You think Anderson was purely an opportunistic kill, right? Nothing in her background to tie her to Ridgecliff?"

"It's possible she'd been nice to him at some point in the last few days. It's one of his triggers."

Shelly shot me the sad eyes. "I forgot there's a switch in Ridgecliff's head that only flicks when a woman reminds him of his mother."

*My mother. My pathetic, terrified, mousy mother who scampered off to her goddamn sewing room every time my father's voice rose . . .*

I said, "It's key to Ridgecliff's delusion that his mother allowed the father's abuse to continue. That she was complicit in the horror."

"I saw in the records the mother's deceased."

I nodded. "Cancer took her."

*Took her with pain so hot it melted her hands into permanent fists. With screams that burned away her voice box until all she could do was*

92

*rasp. She never took any medication or allowed me to do anything for her. She thought dying in hell might somehow help her gain entrance to heaven.*

Waltz said, "Sorry. Off the track. You were talking about his target process?"

"Ms Anderson was medium build and blonde. At thirty-six she was squarely in an age range from early thirties to early forties. That describes every woman Ridgecliff has targeted because it basically describes his mother. He'd never kill a black or Oriental woman. Or an obese or very thin woman. They're outside his mother image."

"Dr Prowse didn't fit the image."

"He killed her to gain his freedom, Shelly. It also would have been personal."

Waltz closed his eyes. He made a curious squeak and turned away. Coughed. Pounded his chest so hard I winced.

"You OK, Shelly?"

"Dry throat." He took a pull from the can, followed it with a deep breath, regained his train of thought. "So Ridgecliff sees Anderson, his mind lights up with the word *Mommy*, and his juices start flowing. That how you think it went down?"

"Maybe they were on the street. He drops

something, she picks it up. The action and her looks flick his switch. He can't help following her. She walks to the realtor's office. He manages to find out her name. From there it's a simple deception to lure her to the property. He was probably laughing while he waited."

"Folger's got dicks and uniforms working for five blocks around, plus checking out Ms Anderson's and her office on 26th, and her neighborhood in Brooklyn. They're bracing people in the neighborhood, showing Ridgecliff's pic."

I thought for a moment. "Folger can pull the team from Brooklyn, Shelly. Ridgecliff's in Manhattan."

Waltz stared. "How the hell do you know that?"

"Uh, it's more a hunch than anything."

"I doubt Folger's gonna pull a team on your hunch." Waltz shook the can and glared like it was a personal irritant. I smelled chocolate and noticed a dark smudge over Waltz's upper lip, like he'd borrowed Little Richard's mustache.

"Are you drinking chocolate syrup?" I asked, happy to change the subject.

He held up the can. I saw the words *Slim-EEZ Chocolate Fudge*.

"It's a diet drink," he said, patting his gut. "The endless damn fight."

"Chocolate fudge is diet?"

He sighed. "It's one of those meal-in-a-can things. I remember when drinking your lunch meant three scotches. That was a lot more entertaining."

"How's the stuff taste?" I asked.

"Like pureed compost."

He lobbed the can into the wastebasket. The intercom on Waltz's phone buzzed, the desk sergeant. "Got a walk-in at the desk, Shelly. Guy wants to see the Southerner, Ryder."

Waltz shot me puzzlement. Maybe two dozen people knew I was here, all officials of some stripe.

"A walk-in for Ryder? Who is it, Moose?"

"Ray Charles died, right? We're sure about that?" The desk man chuckled and hung up. We hustled down the hall to the entrance. An older black guy sat on one of the benches, lanky as a pole vaulter, with ebony skin, tight pewter hair, wraparound shades. I put him in his mid-seventies, but he could have been a decade older. He wore a bright yellow blazer over a cream polo shirt. His pants were as white as the cane across his knees.

The desk sergeant saw us, grinned. "This is

Mr Zebulon Parks. He wants to tell Ryder something."

"Mr Ryder?" the blind man called out. "Mr Carson Ryder?"

"Right here, sir."

The dark glasses turned to me. "You got a place we can sit? By ourselves?"

"You can talk here, Mr Parks. It's fine."

"I'm s'posed to tell you what I got in private."

"There's a room we can use." I moved to him, held up my arm. "Would you care to hold on to my –"

"Just lead on," he said. "Walk."

I headed for a nearby conference room, Mr Parks's cane tapping at my heels. Waltz shot me a conspiratorial eye and nodded down the hall. I winked assent and he tiptoed ahead and slipped into the room.

I entered with Parks behind me and closed the door. Waltz sat motionless in a far corner. Parks reached forward, finger-tapped the table, set his hat on it. His hand found a chair and angled it toward him, sitting straight as a rail. I watched his nostrils study the air.

"Now, Mr Parks, you said you had something to –"

"We alone?" Parks interrupted.

"That's what you wanted," I finessed.

He flicked his head at Waltz. "Then who that fat guy sitting down there?"

I leaned forward, looked into Parks's obsidian-black lenses. I resisted the cliché of waving my hand before his eyes, but only barely.

"Can you see, Mr Parks?"

He nodded toward Waltz. "I heard his belly grumblin'."

Waltz looked at his gut, then at me; neither of us had heard a thing. Waltz sighed. "My name is Sheldon Waltz, Mr Parks. I'm a detective. Sitting in was my idea, and I apologize. But in law enforcement another pair of ears is often helpful."

"One pair works fine for me," Parks said. "They heard your sneakin' ass."

"For which I again apologize. Could you please explain how you knew I am, uh, a bit heavier than preferable."

"I smelled the air you walked through gettin' here. Stinks of that fat people's drink, Slim-Down or whatever. My sister drink a case of that stuff every week and the flo' boards still squeal when she walk crost 'em."

Waltz grimaced. "You have very good senses, Mr Parks."

"I hear birds light on branches, smell bacon cookin' a mile away. I remember the 'zact taste of ever' woman I been with."

Waltz raised his eyebrows, started to ask a question, thought better of it. I leaned toward Parks. "You mentioned to the desk man that you had something to tell me?"

Parks canted his head toward the door. "That coffee out there smells real fresh. Like it'd be good with two sugars but just a touch of cream."

"I'll be right back," Waltz said, returning seconds later with a Styrofoam cup of coffee. Parks sniffed from a foot away.

"Don't drink no fake sugar."

Waltz rolled his eyes, headed down the hall again. A minute later he set the coffee on the table. Parks sniffed the coffee and nodded approval.

"Well?" I asked.

"I was sittin' in Washington Square an hour back when footsteps come at my bench. A fellow axed me how my sense of humor was. I said funny's different to different folks. He said he was prankin' a friend and he'd give me fifty dollars to help. I poked my cane his way and said to git on wit' his sly bidness somewhere else."

"What happened next?"

"He sat down next to me. I grabbed tight to my money pocket. But he said, 'Do you hear inside the shadows, sir?' I said, 'What you talking about?' He said, 'Can you hear the music in the corner restaurant?' The joint was a block down and the jazz-band music was under the sounds of cars, trucks, people yellin' on the street, but sure, I could hear it. Next, he said, 'What you hear best?' I said it was the clar'net, but if I listened real hard I could separate out the bass notes on the piano."

"Most people wouldn't have heard anything but street sounds," I said, my heart beginning to pound.

"Yep, the music was deep under things. Then the man told what he was hearing, and damn if he wasn't hearing ever'thing I could. It come to me that maybe he was blind, too."

Cold prickles danced across my spine. "He wasn't blind, was he, Mr Parks?"

"Nope, though he was sure tuned up scary high for someone ain't never had to live in the dark."

"Did he frighten you?"

Mr Parks frowned, like doing a puzzle in his head. "He had a strange feeling pouring off him, like he had to do a job so important the need was pushing from his skin like heat. That's as close as I can get with words. Did I feel like he wanted to hurt me? No. But something underneath his voice said I wouldn't ever want him mad at me."

"What did you do?"

"Once I could feel he didn't mean no harm, I got interested in how high he was tuned. We started listening and smelling and talking about how much there was to hear and taste and smell, stuff most people never knew was going on, though it's right there in their ears and noses and mouths. After we talked a bit I decided to come here to pass on his words. I thought maybe they were important in a way I couldn't know."

"What exactly did the man say, Mr Parks?" I asked.

The frown again. Trying to get it just right, Parks spoke slowly. "'Tell Mr Ryder to consider George Bernard Shaw's thoughts on sanity in the US.'"

I closed my eyes, suspicions confirmed: I heard Jeremy's precise diction echoed in the old man's words. Waltz was staring at me. His silent lips formed the question, *Ridgecliff*?

I could do nothing but nod, *Yes*. Waltz jumped

toward the door. "Shaw, sanity, America. I'll Google it and see what hits."

I waved him back to the table. "Don't bother, Shelly. I know the quote."

"What is it?"

"An asylum for the sane would be empty in America."

Mr Parks chuckled and snatched his hat from the table. He set it on his head at a jaunty angle.

"I picked up that the man seemed interested in you, Mr Ryder. You close wit' him?"

"What made you think that?"

"He called you something nice, said you was —" Parks again paused to emulate my brother's crystalline diction — "'ever the hero on water or land'. Seems a nice thing to say, right?"

Waltz walked stiffly but quickly, his hand angling me into his office. Sweat sluiced from my armpits and I hoped it wasn't soaking through my sport coat. Jeremy had sent the message just to prove he could. At least he hadn't said anything to suggest our connection.

Waltz closed the door, shut the blinds. "We can send people to Washington Park. Maybe Ridgecliff's still in the area."

I waved the idea off. "He's not close to the

park any more, Shelly. Jeremy Ridgecliff doesn't take those chances. Trust me on that."

Waltz sat heavily, wiped his face with his hands. "Ridgecliff saw your picture in the *Watcher*, the only way he'd know you're in New York. Why would he send you a message?"

"We developed a strange sort of rapport. He sees me as friend and enemy."

"*Friend*?"

"Not in the usual sense. During our talks he was able to speak with me without being judged – that's how you get under the hood: Make no judgments and let them talk."

"And on the enemy side?"

"Part of him despises me for being able to open him up. He'd talk to me, then feel weak for opening up. These people hate being weak, Shelly. They need to feel strong and in total control."

It wasn't the whole truth, but close: My brother sought control in every direction, even over me. Being on the outside gave him more control than he'd had in fourteen years. It terrified me to consider how he would use that power.

Waltz said, "How long ago was it you interviewed him?"

"I talked to him a couple years back."

I'd also talked to him nine weeks ago, which I neglected to mention. After postponing a visit for several weeks, I'd run out of excuses. Though dreading the lost day, I'd taken a Saturday to make the run to the Institute, hoping to spend two or three mollifying hours with my brother, get back to my real life for another few months.

We'd been together in his room, the guard just outside the door. Jeremy had seemed in a regressive state, remote, bitter, bristling with tension.

*"Jeremy, what's bothering you?"*

*"You, Carson. You enter this stinking hell-hole whenever you want, leave whenever you want. I'm trapped in here."*

*I looked around his room: the special harmless furniture, the Mylar mirror that distorted reflections, the walls and floor constructed of the rubbery material used in children's playgrounds.*

*"Not the room, Carson!" he snapped. "I'M TRAPPED IN HERE!"*

*He slapped the side of his head. Then again, harder. He started punching his head and face as if they belonged to a hated rival, blood pouring from his ear and nose as I wrestled him* to the floor, Jeremy screaming about needing to be free, me yelling for the guards.

It had taken six of them to put my brother in restraints. As I wiped sweat from my face and retreated from the room, he'd called to me.

"CARSON!"

Jeremy was on the floor, bound tight as a chrysalis. An injected tranquilizer was kicking in as I stepped back inside the room, now reeking of anger and hatred and despair.

"What, Jeremy?"

His eyes began to glaze, his tongue to thicken. "The moment the old dog stopped breathing, someone became safe, right?"

No one but Vangie knew of my relationship to Jeremy. The guards heard only disassociated rambling. Jeremy was speaking of our father's death and how I had been kept safe, spared.

"Yes," I whispered.

A fierce grin blazed over Jeremy's face, the last sharp flare of light before a bulb dies. He shifted his voice to a perfect imitation of our father.

"I gave you life, Carson . . ." Jeremy hissed, leaving unspoken the words with which my father had always completed the phrase . . .

"And I can take it away."

Had Jeremy threatened me that day?

"Are you in there, Detective Ryder?" Waltz's voice pushed into my thoughts.

"Sorry, what?"

"I said I just called the Lieutenant. Get ready for a grilling."

Thoughts banging in my head like bumper cars, I slipped off to grab a bottle of water from the machine. Folger thundered in minutes later, Bullard and Cluff and several other dicks in tow. She paced the office, asking Waltz about the encounter, looking to me for the occasional confirming head bob. She was asking incisive questions; focused, like Waltz had said. She turned the focus to me.

"What Ridgecliff told you, Ryder – this Shaw quote – sounds like he was joking. You actually got along well enough with this crazy to joke?"

"Joking's part of the bonding process. Ridgecliff's big on quotes, since he spent most of his time reading."

"What was that bit about you being heroic on land or sea?"

"'Ever the hero on water or land' is the exact phrase," Waltz said, referring to his notes.

"Yeah, that."

I shrugged. "Land and sea may refer to my living a hundred feet from the Gulf. I may have mentioned one of my cases where I got rammed by a boat while in my kayak, but made it ashore alive and solved the case. I expect the hero reference is sarcastic."

"Ain't it cute," Bullard said. "Ryder tells police stories to his crazy buddies. Part of their beddy-bye reading, maybe."

Folger said, "You think he'll make contact again?"

I held up my hands, *No idea.*

"Then I want you people to start thinking about how to throw a net over this psycho. You got any ideas on how to do that, Ryder? This is your good buddy out there."

"I've been thinking about it."

"He's thinking?" Bullard mock-whispered. "We're fucked like five-buck whores."

One of the dicks in the rear of the room glanced up from his note-taking. "Instead of throwing a net over Ridgecliff, how about we do the world a favor and put this son of a bitch in the ground instead?"

Three detectives reached over and slapped the guy high fives. I understood how they felt, had thought the same about other killers on the loose. It troubled me. But not as much as my next thought:

*If Jeremy dies, I'm the one that's finally free.*

# TEN

Harry Nautilus pulled up the long gravel drive to Dr Evangeline Prowse's two-story frame house. It was tucked against a woods, a pair of ancient live oaks in the front yard, their branches like tentacles exploring the hot air. Nautilus stopped in the drive. He walked through dappled sunlight to the nearest oak, its trunk a good twenty feet in circumference, and laid his palm against the bark.

The tree had lived there since antebellum times and Nautilus always felt thrilled to touch a survivor. He patted the tree as if congratulating it on a good journey, then returned to his car and continued to the house. It was smaller than he had imagined, knowing Dr Prowse must have made a nice living from her books as well as a decent salary and a consultation fee now and then. He climbed the steps to the shaded gallery, waited.

Two minutes later a gray unmarked vehicle entered the drive, tires crunching over the gravel. A second man was in the passenger seat. The car stopped and a six-six black man in a blue suit stepped out, Sergeant Nathaniel Allen of the Alabama State Police, Western Montgomery post. Allen was two inches taller than Nautilus, but at a hundred-eighty pounds to Nautilus's two-fifty, he was a carrot beside a yam.

"Hey, Nate, s'up?"

"Hey, Harry. This is Bill Turnbow, best lock man in five counties."

Nautilus shook hands with the locksmith, sixtyish, who pulled a toolbox from the back seat, glanced at the lock on the door, shook his head, said, "Twenty seconds."

"So no one from your side's been in?" Nautilus asked Allen.

"The killing happened in New York. No need." Allen looked at the locksmith as he opened his case, and drew Nautilus a few feet down the porch, speaking softly. "A patient wandered?"

Nautilus nodded. "He's in New York."

"You're certain?"

"I'm positive. Carson's up there now, looking into it."

"We're keeping the lid on the box right now, don't want to freak out the entire county. But . . ." He raised an eyebrow at Nautilus.

"If he even looks south, Nate, we'll tell you." Nautilus shifted gears. "You said there'd been a police call here, right?"

"Three weeks back. I was working late, heading home, when the call came in."

"It's done," the locksmith said, pushing the door open with his pinky. "Eighteen seconds."

Nautilus and Allen walked back to the door. "You're good," Nautilus said to the locksmith.

"The lock's bad. Piece of crap. It cost a shit-load, so the homeowner thought it was good, but if the maker spent as much on the lock as on fancy sales brochures, it might even protect someone."

The cops went inside while the locksmith returned his tools to the car. The air conditioner had been left running and cool air poured through the portal. Nautilus breathed a sigh of relief, few things worse than searching through a furnace.

Nautilus was taken by the simplicity of the

décor, two massive couches and three matching chairs, the cushions of soft red leather. There was a bright Oriental carpet, abstract art on the walls reminiscent of Kandinsky. Nautilus shot a look through the window. The locksmith was leaning against the car and smoking a cigar. Judging by the length of the cigar, he'd be outside a while.

"Go on, Nate," Nautilus said to Allen. "The police call?"

"It looked like a standard B&E: Stuff scattered about, drawers open, the place tossed. Someone came through the front door, probably. Got past the lock."

"The upshot?"

Allen frowned. "To hear her tell it, nothing was missing."

"After all that work and scrabbling through the Doc's belongings?"

"She said nothing was missing. Not a penny. There was something going on, Harry. I could feel it."

"Tell me."

"She'd worked late – she leaves for the Institute at seven, never gets home before seven, twelve-hour days were short for her. She arrives at ten p.m., sees stuff scattered around, calls us.

111

She's waiting on the porch when I arrive. I ask her to check on missing items while I look around. She jumps for the chance to do something. And then a change of attitude."

"How so?"

"She checked in the bedroom, looking through the closet, a woman on a mission. The next time I see her she's got a smiley face on, saying, 'It looks like nothing's missing. No problem. Goodnight. Thanks for stopping by.' She did about everything but push me out the door. Something had her rattled, Harry."

"Something in the bedroom?"

"She went in loud and irritated, came out quiet. If I had to guess, Harry, I'd say she found something important had been taken. Something no one was supposed to know about, maybe."

Nautilus went upstairs to the master bedroom, Allen on his heels. He checked the walk-in closet. There were the ubiquitous dusty boxes on back shelves, the boxes heavy with yellowing photos and various keepsakes, typical. He saw a file cabinet in the back corner. He opened it and went through the sparse offerings.

"Looks like pieces of the past: financial stuff, mortgage records, old bank accounts, property

112

transfers, bills. All neatly catalogued, like I'd expect from the Doc. I've got every hang-file occupied except one, the description card on it saying nothing. It's simply blank."

"Probably wasn't anything there. But if there was, someone got it. Either the Doc or her visitor."

"Listen, Nate, I'm gonna look around a while. Thanks for your help."

Allen departed and Nautilus continued his search. The bathroom had the usual fixtures, the closets filled with bright towels and concoctions to scent, soothe, and soften. There was the hair-support system: blower, brushes, combs. The strongest chemical in the medicine chest was a bottle of ibuprofen. There were lotions and a bottle of perfume on a stand beside the sink.

Nautilus saved a small desk in an alcove off the kitchen for last; obviously the place Dr Prowse handled the domestic finances. He saw the standard stack of incoming bills for gas and electric, phone service, broadband, auto and so forth. There were credit-card statements. A bill from her wireless provider. Another bill for utility payments on an address in Gulf Shores, a resort-oriented seaside community on the eastern side of Mobile Bay.

The bills were a handful to plow through and he put the stack in a folder, tucked it into his briefcase for later. He'd been through the entire house. There was no office setting, or the kind of place he expected one saw patients. It seemed a bit off, given that several folks mentioned Prowse's occasional private patients.

He sighed. His next stop was Gulf Shores. It was an hour southeast of Mobile, the last place to check for evidence of a private patient. If he could dig some time free on his schedule, he'd go there tomorrow.

Senhor Cesar Caldiera stood before a set of mirrors in the tailor shop in Chelsea, a store selling custom-tailored and expensive off-the-rack suits. Caldiera spun one way, then the other, admiring the dark and silky garment as the mirrors presented it from all angles. He frowned, patted his belly.

"The pants feel a little snug in the waist. The tiniest bit."

Giuseppe Palmado, tailor, slipped a finger into the waistband of the trousers, wiggled the digit. "No problem, Signor Caldiera. Give me ten minutes with a needle, I'll give you ten years with a beautiful suit."

Caldiera beamed as he stepped into the changing booth, knowing he'd wear the gorgeous suit out the door, perhaps with the coral shirt. He was gaining quite a nice wardrobe.

Palmado took the pants to his work table, humming operatically.

Caldiera slipped back into his khakis and checked his watch as he walked to the storefront window. Yesterday she'd arrived about this time, left a half-hour later; back to work, probably. Was she a creature of habit?

Motion from across the street. Caldiera watched a dark-haired, oval-faced woman in her early thirties cross in his direction, wearing blue running garb and wearing a daypack that most likely held her work clothes. Caldiera glanced back at Palmado. The tailor was sewing at a distant table.

A rip appeared in Caldiera's face. Fingers pushed through the flesh and Jeremy Ridgecliff squirmed free of the false body. He took a deep breath and gazed upon the street, reveling in the clamor and motion of his new world. The length, width, depth and breadth of his new world. When he walked the streets he felt like raw wind charged with lighting, a force that was part physical, part pure magic. Women were

115

everywhere he looked. Sometimes it took all his strength to keep from screaming with joy.

Jeremy Ridgecliff watched Alice Folger pass a corner bistro – a hundred feet distant; he heard her footfalls over the traffic as she strode toward a tidy brick brownstone, bright flowers in boxes beneath its windows. Folger stopped at the door of the brownstone, slipped a key from her purse, went inside.

Ridgecliff heard floorboards squeak behind him and slipped back inside Cesar Caldiera. Giuseppe Palmado approached, holding up the slacks.

"They're ready, Signor Caldiera."

"As am I," Caldiera said. He stepped into the changing booth, slipped on the pants. He jumped back out a minute later, his smile a white crescent.

"*Perfeito*. Perfect."

Palmado studied his customer – black hair, dark eyes, olive skin. "Caldiera? Is that not Spanish, signor?"

"*Não. Meu nome é Portuguêse.*"

"My apologies. Portuguese, of course. I was wondering, is not Caldiera from the word for kettle, or cauldron? Like in the Italian, Calderone?"

Caldiera-Ridgecliff smiled into the mirror,

seeing the suit fitting like a second skin. Again, it took all his strength to keep from screaming with joy.

"*Sim*, Senhor Palmado, yes," Ridgecliff said. "I am most certainly a cauldron."

I'd banged around ideas with Waltz for a bit, went nowhere, my mind a lump of wet clay. Then he'd had to handle more dealings with the upcoming convention, so I'd returned to the hotel, taken an hour's nap, risen and showered. I was drying my hair when the phone rang, a grating sound that made my stomach sag. I believe in premonitions, the mind sensing threat through secondary channels and telegraphing warning via the body. I hesitated before lifting the receiver.

"Hello?"

Folger's voice. "I'm standing knee-deep in blood, Ryder. Guess what?"

"No," I whispered.

"Oh yes. It looks like your buddy struck again." Behind Folger's voice I heard male voices overstepping one another, feet on wooden steps, a wailing siren. "Get your ass to the station. We'll be back there in an hour or so. Be waiting."

"You're at the crime scene?" I asked.

117

"To repeat myself, Ryder, I want you to haul your countrified ass to the station. Take a shower, use soap, and get your butt to –"

Every time I interacted with Folger I felt like a puppet on steel wires. I was mentally worn, physically weary, tired of playing at the edge of the game. I hung the phone up.

It rang immediately. Folger said, "I hope we got cut off by accident."

"You want something from me, you stop treating me like mule dung. I'm included in all meetings, get copies of all reports. Not just Waltz, me."

"No way, Bubba. It's NYPD's show, not yours. That means I deci—"

I hung up and studied my watch. The phone rang fourteen seconds later. Folger affected a honey-drenched Southern accent, probably to keep from screaming.

"Howdy there, Swee'pea. Ah'm sending a radio cah. You prob'bly know Koslowski by now."

Not bad, I thought, grabbing my jacket from the closet.

I figured the doorman was getting tired of Koslowski parking half up on the sidewalk outside the front door, but there wasn't much he could do about it. I jumped in the cruiser, slammed the door. Koslowski checked the rear-view, stomped the gas, and we spun a perfect 180 into the street. He cranked on the music and light show and I watched our flashers bounce from glass-fronted buildings as the speedometer climbed. Koslowski cut between a bread truck and a cab. If there'd been another coat of paint on the cruiser, we wouldn't have made it.

Koslowski sniffed the air and seemed happier than last time. He raised an eyebrow. "Three times I pick you up. Three times a woman's dead. Anything you want to tell me, Dixie?"

"That's one unlucky woman."

He paused, caught it, laughed. It knocked a bit off the wall between us.

I said, "Listen, Koslowski, the other day when I wondered what you thought of Shelly Waltz, you told me –"

He cut the wheel and we swooped around a Con Ed truck, orange traffic cones racked on its bumper. "Yeah, yeah, about Shelly and flying and unicorns and whatnot. I was just kidding with you. Kind of."

"How so?"

He thought and dodged vehicles at the same time. I dared not look out the window.

"What I was trying to say is there's people that work stuck to the ground, which is about everybody, and a few people that don't. They're not as connected to the regular stuff."

"Folks like Shelly."

"Yeah. It's like he's so far up in his head, thinking, weighing things, that he's in a place gravity doesn't reach." He paused. "I'm not making sense. I ain't good with words."

"You're doing great, keep going."

"Because Shelly's alone up there with no distractions, he can look down and see how things really are. How they fit together. It makes him a real good detective, the best. But it also makes him alone. I guess that what I meant by Shelly flying through the sky."

"He flew at night, you said."

"Night's a more alone place to be." Koslowski braked, accelerated, braked again as if gathering momentum, then charged past a horse and carriage, getting wide-eyed looks from the passengers.

"What about the unicorn?" I asked. "What did that mean?"

He settled into the center lane, shot me a wink.

"Hell, Dixie, I just threw that in for a mythical reference."

We arrived minutes later. There was a cluster of onlookers outside the scene and Koslowski pulled to the curb. I nodded, started to open the door.

"Thanks for filling me in on things, Koslowski. When I get back South I'm gonna tell NASCAR about you."

He tapped my arm to stop me. "One more thing about Shelly. I think you'd like to know."

"What's that?"

"You know his face – sad, like he's always coming from a friend's funeral?"

"Hard to miss."

"I knew him thirty years back. He'd walk into the cop bar, O'Hearns, where it was dark as a friggin' tomb, and it was like someone let the sun in. Waltz was always smiling, laughing. He had a laugh so bright it was like dimes raining into a punchbowl."

"What changed?"

"No one knows. One day he showed up with the face he wears now, and it never went away."

The ageing apartment building had four doors facing the street, two ups, two downs. There was enough of a crowd that three uniforms had to keep people back while a third strung yellow scene tape. Several women were crying and hugging one another. I didn't necessarily take it that they knew the victim; sometimes people just cry and need comfort because they can't believe the horror in their midst.

I jumped from the car at the back of the crowd, pushed through as politely as possible, ducked under the tape and started up the walk.

"Whoa, sport," a burly uniform said, bringing his baton up to my chest. "Back it up."

"I've got to get in there, I'm –"

"Get behind the line."

A whistle pierced the air. We both turned and saw Waltz on the porch, fingers in his lips. "He's good, Bailey," Waltz yelled, pointing at me and shooting a thumbs-up before going back inside the apartment.

"Sorry," Bailey said. I headed up the walk, stepping inside just as the ME's people exited what I took to be the kitchen. Folger was in there, out of the way, leaning against a wall beside a print technician checking a latent. Waltz appeared at my side, wiping his face with a handkerchief.

"What is it, Shelly? What happened?"

"The kind of thing that makes me think about early retirement."

I saw the body on the floor just as the medical personnel were moving it to the compressed gurney. The face jammed in the belly was bright with blood. Gaping wounds rent her flesh, fierce dark slashes in stark contrast to her skin. The scent of blood and excrement was overwhelming.

"Watch the goddamn blood, it's everywhere," one of the med techs said, bending to grasp the corpse. Dead bodies aren't a tenth as maneuverable as they are in movies. They also fart, belch, gurgle, and slip from your hands at inopportune moments.

"Count of three and up," the tech said. "One, two . . . three!"

Grunting in unison, the two techs lifted the body. A heel of the tech nearest me stepped backward into a scarlet pool and skidded sideways. He went down hard, dropping the body. The concussion popped the head free of the abdomen and it tumbled across the floor and bumped the gurney. The open belly wound vomited intestines.

"Oh my God," a young woman from Forensics said, grabbing her mouth and sprinting from the room.

Someone moved in to bag the head and the body was finally placed on the gurney. I stepped outside and watched the onlookers part to let the ambulance take the body away. Bullard and Cluff worked the crowd, interviewing. I saw Waltz standing in the door of a Tech Services van, the height letting him scan faces in the crowd. He was looking for the face showing too much interest. Psychopathic killers loved to see the reaction to their handiwork. If there was a way to be at the scene, they would.

Cargyle had driven the van, I figured, the kid leaning against its hood, one of his phones in his hand, the other to his cheek. The victim's digs belonged to someone with a middle-class income and that almost invariably meant a computer. It would be Technical Services' job to disconnect the device and pertinent peripherals like backup drives, check for anything helpful. If the victim knew her killer, maybe. If not, Cargyle and his colleagues would shovel a lot of hours into the toilet. But it had to be done. There were a thousand things needing to be done in a murder investigation.

I saw Shelly step down from the van, knew by his face he'd seen nothing. He started toward the apartment and I stepped in beside him. We went back inside, where Folger was in a corner with one of the ME's people.

"I put on my running clothes, left the station, got home ready to fix real food for the first time in days. Now I may never eat again." She saw me. "Yeeee-hah, there he is. My favorite reverse carpetbagger. I'll bet the ME is going to find the woman's equipment got yanked out through the cut in the belly. He looked like he used a chainsaw on her. Ridgecliff's ramping up, Ryder. I probably don't need to tell you that."

I felt a flash of guilt that I hadn't yet read my brother's files. I knew *him,* did I need to read about his crimes?

Cluff stepped up, snapping through pages on his notepad. "Angela Bernal. New arrival on the block, a couple months maybe, no one knows much about her. Everyone says she was cheerful, pleasant. Christ, if I had a dime for every cheerful, pleasant corpse I'd –"

"Check for personal papers, find what she does," Folger commanded. "This looks like the home of someone with a decent job. Stable. Any indication of a man around?"

One of the other dicks shuffled up. "I only saw women's clothes in the closet and drawers."

Folger shot a glance inside the house. The Forensics people were darkening the walls and furniture with fingerprint powder. The television had been left as found: on, but muted. It was one of the 24-hour news channels. Folger started to turn away, but something on the TV caught her eye and she stared at the screen with a frown. All I saw was an insert of a weather pattern in the Caribbean, a satellite shot, time-lapse, white clouds spinning over blue water. When the insert disappeared, she turned to me.

"You're the one supposed to know about the crazies, Ryder. At least that's how the late Dr Prowse had you pegged What have you figured out to put us in front of this bastard?"

"I . . . don't have anything yet."

She crossed her arms, tapped her foot. Studied my face.

"Gee. Maybe I'm expecting too much here, but isn't it about time you started earning your keep?"

I turned to leave, feeling the heat rise to my face.

# ELEVEN

I bypassed returning to the station and went to the hotel, ashamed at allowing personal issues to freeze me into investigational impotence; stung by my inability to find the courage to read the reports on my brother's past crimes.

I opened the files and spread them on the table and phoned room service for the opening salvo of coffee. A cold shower blasted me awake. I pulled the drapes to blot the visual distraction of the city and sky.

Me and my brother's murders, alone at last.

I took a deep breath, opened the files, and read for four hours. It was a wrenching journey, a surfeit of grief. Twice during the reading I broke down, weeping like a child. For my brother's victims. For my brother. For my sick and broken family. For me.

I closed the last report at three a.m., retreating to the bathroom to wash numbness from my face, brush coffee from my teeth, a sonic montage of my brother's words banging through my head.

*"How did you lure the woman to you, Mr Ridgecliff?"* the interrogator asked, the transcript describing Jeremy's encounter with a victim taken from the river park in Memphis.

*"For that particular lady I used the Dear John Letter concept,"* Jeremy replied. *"Dejection is best displayed in the shoulders, so mine were slumped. I never overdid the tears angle – a crying adult frightens people – so I'd dab at my nose with a tissue. I liked blue tissues because they enhanced my eyes."*

And later, when the woman had been shown a knife and coerced to a secure and deadly location.

The interrogator: *"How did you kill her?"*

*"She needed the knife. It needed her as well, aching for her supple, coral skin. Jeremy watched her. She needed to display her love of the gleaming blade and had to talk to it before it talked to her . . ."*

I read another case in my head.

*"I wrapped my hand in a handkerchief spattered with red paint, fumbling with the handkerchief, like I couldn't get it wrapped. I said I'd cut myself on the fender of my bicycle. I'd picked up a battered old cruiser in a Goodwill store. The bike was so goofy it made her trust me even more: dangerous men don't ride purple bicycles. My props were always very well considered.*

*Pardon, sir? Was it difficult to lure her? It was easy to lure them all. I simply became the archetypal Sad Child or Hurt Child or Lost Child."*

And later:

*"Jeremy saw her crying, crying was natural, a purifying act. Then the knife entered the room and started looking for company . . ."*

Jeremy spoke in first person when describing the baiting of his targets. When it came to the killing, he jumped to third person, a detached voice. No more *I,* but *Jeremy.*

Odd. Or was it?

I thought back to my many prison interviews, both in college and as a detective. I'd heard point of view shifts before, especially in schizophrenics. But the shifts seemed random, dependent on whatever the mental voices or pictures were saying at that moment, lacking the defining line I heard with Jeremy. Luring, first person. Killing, third.

In every case, the separation.

I sat and pulled the reports close again, separating out the interviews with my brother. At places in the reading, I had skimmed the uglier parts, as if jumping over greasy puddles. There had been a rote sameness to the events: the luring mechanisms, the trip to the killing ground, the kill. Read one, you basically read them all.

"*I saw her pause and move in my direction, her interest in my feigned sadness clearly piqued . . .*

"*I saw no one near and dark was falling. I showed the knife and told her to follow me . . .*

"*She stepped clumsily into the garage. The woman was terrified, but it was the price of her betrayal. Jeremy saw the knife watching her . . .*"

In each instance, the shift in point of view was clearly demarked. The luring mechanism, first person. The trip to the killing ground, first person. For the kill, Jeremy always shifted to third. It was as if he'd walked through a door and changed at the threshold.

Plus there was the sudden personification of

the knife. It seemed a tool in the luring phase, but in the kill phase seemed to assume a strange conjoined personality.

Was Jeremy so subconsciously ashamed of his murders he had generated the distinction? Or was it something other than a linguistic quirk: Had he given birth to a secondary persona to handle the killing . . . an avatar of death?

It made a cold and perfect sense.

I yanked open the curtains and stared into the waning night, letting my thoughts roam between the buildings, across the light traffic rolling in the street below. What changed within Jeremy's internal structure to make him shift his descriptions during the interrogations? And if he was generating a secondary persona to handle the horror of his killing scenes, what was the persona like?

Where inside him did it hide?


"More cognac, sir?" the waiter asked, bottle in hand.

"*Satisfaça sim,*" Ridgecliff-Caldiera replied. "Please . . . yes. I would much."

The glorious liquid slid into the glass like thinned honey. Ridgecliff sat in candlelight at a front window table in the restaurant, spooning a dessert he'd invented with a little help from the chef, a goblet in which a chocolate torte had been placed, the torte overlaid with flaming Cherries Jubilee, white and dark chocolate shaved on to the cherries as they blazed.

Utterly delicious. He'd dubbed it *Cerejas e chocolate no estilo de Jeremy*: Cherries and Chocolate in the style of Jeremy.

He took a sip from the snifter and pulled a notepad from his pocket, flipped to a page labeled Tasks. He scanned to the small box he'd drawn beside the word, *Transportation*. Cabs were the most agile form of transportation, but every taxi ride was another pair of eyes on him. It was far safer to have a dedicated driver, and Jeremy had placed an electrically charged Latvian on retainer, ready to race to him if the need arose.

He checked the box, accomplished.

The next box was *Money*. He now had a grubstake, but it was New York, and he wanted a decent – no, make that decadent – lifestyle, so when the chance to earn more presented, he'd add to his account.

The box received a check. The next box was *Lodging*. Finding a decent midtown apartment had been easy. Money and the correct attitude had that effect.

Check.

Beneath *Lodging* were the words *Alice Folger, Lieutenant, NYPD*. They were underlined and encircled. Jeremy left the box unchecked. There were several sub-items needing attention before he could mark that chore off his list. He tucked the pad in the pocket of his suit jacket, happy with his progress, well ahead of schedule.

*With time to kill,* he thought, taking another sip of cognac and staring at a woman walking past the window. Like so many of the fashionable young women in Manhattan, she had a belly as flat and tight as a painter's canvas.

What a magnificent city. Truly a land of opportunity.

I was deep into sleep when a housekeeping cart rolled down the hall of the hotel and bumped into my door, hoisting me through filmy dreams. An eight a.m. meeting had been scheduled at the morgue. The autopsy on Ms Bernal wouldn't take place until a relative or relatives had been notified, but the pathologist would do a thorough visual and non-invasive check of the body to ascertain how the wounds compared to those of Ms Anderson. My alarm, set for seven a.m., hadn't buzzed. I yawned, pulled the pillow close, shot a glance at the clock.

Saw 8.36 turn to 8.37.

I howled and bailed from bed, raging at myself for forgetting the prime dictum of travelers: Never trust a hotel clock. Still dressing in the elevator, I sprinted into the street waving at the sea of cabs, all occupied. I ran for a block before a hack plucked me from the pavement.

It seemed wherever the cabbie turned, a traffic jam waited, vehicles welded to the street with horns blasting. I grabbed my phone, thought, then slid it back into my pocket. The inspection would proceed as scheduled, and calling wouldn't have made the difference of a raindrop in the Hudson. It took forty-five minutes to arrive at the morgue.

"The meeting about the Bernal victim?" I asked the guard as I scrawled my name in the log.

He shrugged. "That started an hour back. Folger's case, right? That lady's running on overdrive."

I ran down the hall. A section of the floor had been mopped, a cleaning cart straddling the floor as a warning. My shoes skidded on the wet floor and I grabbed the handle of the cart, barely kept from falling. I pushed through the door into the autopsy room. A morgue worker was rolling a draped body toward the coolers. A gray-haired pathologist snapped off his gloves, jamming them in the biohazard disposal. I figured by the look he gave me that I'd been a topic of conversation.

Waltz, Folger, Cluff, and Bullard looked up from comparing notes beside the autopsy table. "Good of you to show up, Ryder," Folger said. "Was it you I remember pissing and moaning about being included in every little everything? Or was that someone I forgot to invite?"

"It was one of those mornings." A limp and idiotic statement.

Cluff tapped his watch. "Don't worry, you're only off by an hour or so."

"Not a world-shaking event," Waltz said, downplaying my non-attendance. "It was pretty much like Ms Anderson. The womb was gone. There were more extensive injuries. Ridgecliff went wild with the knife, as you saw at the scene."

"I saw a lot of blood. They were loading the body when I arrived. I didn't get into the kitchen, I stayed in the hallway."

"Outside looking in," Bullard said. "I get the feeling that's a pretty regular occurrence for

135

you." He tongued something from a tooth, spat it to the floor near my shoes. He winked.

Folger stepped up. "Let's all go deal with the rest of the crap in our lives, then check back together this afternoon, three or so, see if anything's broken loose. That fit with your schedule, Ryder? Leave you enough time for your nap?

"I'll be fine, Lieutenant."

Waltz had to check the paperwork on another case and we made plans to meet later. I headed out the door, Folger and her two boyos signing forms saying they'd witnessed the procedure. I was twenty paces down the hall when Bullard's voice called behind me.

"Hey, Bubba, hold up."

I stopped beside the cart of cleaning supplies. It held bottles of disinfectant, a stack of rags, an empty two-gallon pail with a handle on a metal loop.

"What is it, Bullard?"

He stepped into my personal space. I felt heat from his body, smelled his breath and body odor. Overgrown bully types learn that trick early on, a wordless challenge. He tapped his watch. "Advice for the time-crippled. You can buy a Jap watch for twenty bucks. It'll tell you the time if you can't figure it out on your own. I mean it really tells you, you know?" He winked.

"I must be missing something."

"The watch talks. In a dumb-ass robot voice even you could understand." Bullard did an imitation: 'Hey, you hick pussy . . . it's eight-o-fucking-clock.'" He grinned like a Jack-o'-lantern carved from tallow, did the taunting wink again.

I feigned dumb hick amazement. "No shit, Bullard? What's your watch say?"

His eyes shot to his wrist. "Nine fort—" He realized what he'd done, said, "You're a smart-ass cunt. A little bitch."

Bullard hadn't liked me from the git-go. I'd not cared much for him, either, but so what? We had work to do. But Bullard was one of those keep-pushing guys, needing me to either hold up my hands in surrender or tangle ass, him figuring he'd win by four inches of height, two of reach, and thirty pounds of gym-bred meat.

My thinking was contrary. His pejoratives insinuated I was as low as a woman to him – not unexpected. I'd noticed him mocking Folger a couple times when her back was turned, pulling at his groin, licking his lips, grinning like the class clown. He knew crude jokes I'd forgotten in high school. *"Hey, you heard this one? Two whores and a gorilla walk into a bar . . ."* I'd filed Bullard into the class of men preferring women as receptacles first, arm candy second, companions and confidants, never. It gave me some buttons to push. I side-eyed the cart with the rags and pail, an arm's length away, gave Bullard a mocking look.

"Don't worry, Bullard. I'll be out of here soon. Back where there's more testosterone in the departmental structure, if you get my drift."

His eyes flashed. "What are you saying?"

I lowered my voice as if sharing a locker-room confidence. "I'm talking about sucking Folger's ass. Some guys can't climb the ladder on their own so they ride someone's shirt-tails. But it takes someone special to ride skirt-tails."

I figured Bullard for a groin-shot type, and he was: Faking a left shoulder roll as if loading a punch, then the foot snap toward my cojones. I blocked it with my thigh and he had to throw the half-spent punch. It caught my shoulder, spinning me away from the cart, not where I wanted to go. Grunting curses, he fired the right at my eyes. But he was power first and speed second. I ducked the punch and scrambled to the cart. I snatched the pail by the handle, flipped it over his head, and laid everything into a horizontal yank, firing his pudding face into the wall like a cannonball.

Thunk.

He spun from the wall with knees collapsing, a skater going into a drunken sit-spin. When his butt hit the floor I expect he saw a half-dozen versions of me whirling above him. One or two of them might have winked.

I put my hands in my pockets and walked away. When I turned, Bullard was limping in the other direction, heading for the restroom or the parking lot. I didn't expect he wanted to explain what would soon be a blue-ribbon knot on his forehead.

After my tussle with Bullard, I walked a few blocks until I came to a subway station, asked the woman in the cage what needed to be accomplished to get to Central Park. Not long afterward I was climbing into the sunlight at Lexington Avenue and 59th Street, continuing toward the oasis at the center of the city, arriving in a few minutes.

The scent of a vendor's cart caught my attention and I grabbed a soft pretzel, a Coke, and some spicy chicken impaled on a wooden spike.

I sat on a bench beneath an oak tree and ate, trying to fathom the sense of separation in Jeremy's files, the feeling that he had split into two entities.

A woman of perhaps twenty-five years of age stumbled by, gums so rotten they couldn't hold teeth, facial skin like wet fabric printed with sores – the effects of methedrine addiction. I heard frantic, overlapping sirens on the far side of the park, police vehicles racing to an emergency. I realized I was a few blocks from the Dakota apartments, John Lennon's home until a madman shot him dead outside the front door.

I couldn't finish eating. I tossed the cup and skewer in the trash can, mashing its point on the sidewalk so no rifling trash-picker would spear his hand. There was a fresh-looking newspaper atop the trash, and I pulled it out, shaking off congealed French fries. When I saw it was *The Watcher*, I nearly jammed it back in the can but remembered the crime reports and snapped it open to local news.

The headline grabbed my eyes.

*Slasher Kills Woman in Harlem.*

There was no shot of Waltz and me this time. Just a picture of Angela Bernal centered beneath the headline, a head-and-shoulder shot with an out-of-focus beach in the background. A breeze was trying to push her hair into her eyes and she was smiling as she held it back.

My breath stopped. I stared at her features, heart racing. I grabbed my cell, glanced down to dial, returned my eyes to the paper. I couldn't take them off the photo.

*This is Detective Sheldon Waltz,* the recorded message said. *I'm not able to take your call right now, but please leave your –*

I dialed my other NYPD contact number. It rang twice.

"Lieutenant Folger."

"We've got a problem," I said, feeling sick. Things had just jumped from bad to worse.

# TWELVE

"The victim's not Ridgecliff's type," I told Folger. "It's all wrong."

The full cast and crew had been assembled in a windowed briefing room with a whiteboard, a lectern, a dozen metal folding chairs. A bulletin board displayed photos of the victims, Jeremy, and a timeline. Half the chairs were taken by detectives working the case. Cargyle was multitasking in the corner, listening while repairing one of his phones. Bullard had shifted to jeans and an NYU tee, allowing him to wear a low-slung bandana over a bulge like a halved lemon. Whenever someone shot a curious glance, Bullard glowered back. Waltz watched from the doorway.

"Not his type?" Folger said, incredulous.

"You're talking like he orders them from a goddamn dating service."

"The women Jeremy Ridgecliff killed were stand-ins for his mother. He thought she'd betrayed him by not stopping his sadist father. All his targets were Caucasian because his mother was Caucasian. Bernal is Hispanic. Out of his cultural pattern."

"Cultural pattern?" Folger rolled her eyes. "I'll give you a pattern: The woman was re-fucking-arranged. Forensics found more hairs and fibers on the floor. The same internal organs are gone. What do you need, Ryder? Ridgecliff to leave a calling card?"

"You're not understanding, Lieutenant. I'm not saying Ridgecliff didn't do it. I'm saying he's jumped from his target profile."

Folger narrowed an eye. "You're saying he started out killing Mommy, but they're all Mommy now? Every woman out there might be setting the bastard off?"

"It's possible," I said.

"Jesus."

Leaving Folger shaking her head, I walked to the window, put my hands on the sill, and looked skyward into a sprawling advance of nimbus clouds, their purple underbellies gravid with rain.

The room was silent at my back, everyone digesting the news that our suspect was potentially at war with every woman in New York City.

The quiet was broken by Bullard's voice, loud and demanding attention.

"Everyone seems to have forgotten that Ridgecliff's first vic, Prowse, made a recording saying 'call Ryder' if she was found dead. Am I the only one that thinks that's real curious?"

Folger said, "How so, Detective Bullard?"

"Prowse was under Ridgecliff's total control, right? Who doesn't believe that? Show of hands."

No hands went up. Bullard continued.

"I saw the reports from the nut basket, the Institute or whatever. Ridgecliff's a whack job, but he's probably the Einstein of whack jobs."

"Your point, Detective?" Folger said.

"In the video recording, Prowse looks scared. What if Prowse didn't make the recording on her own? What if Ridgecliff was behind the camera flashing one of those knives he loves?"

"It's a possibility," Folger nodded. "Maybe a big one. And?"

"Then it wasn't Prowse that wanted Ryder here. Ridgecliff did."

I felt the sudden weight of every eye in the

room. Bullard's point was a damn good one, and I realized he might be a jerk, but he wasn't a dim bulb.

"Reflections on that idea, Ryder?" Folger asked, arms crossed. "That it's Ridgecliff who wants you here?"

"A good theory," I said, nodding to Bullard, credit where credit's due. "But if Ridgecliff's so smart, why would he want me in New York? I was the one who ID'd him, after all."

"He sent the blind guy to you," Bullard said. "Why?"

"Once he saw the picture in the *Watcher* and knew I was here, he had to make contact. It was pure hubris."

"Pure whatsis?"

"Pride," Waltz interrupted. "Sociopaths are ego machines, part of their delusion being they're smarter than everyone else." He paused. "Ridgecliff has some actual claim there."

"He was pissing on my shoes," I explained. "Rubbing my face in the fact that he knows I'm here and he thinks there's nothing I can do."

*But Jeremy always had a subtext. Was it my brother's way of saying good-bye, a last fond knock on the kid's head before he slipped into the persona that was consuming him? What, exactly, had my brother tried to convey through Parks's message?*

"We might also consider the opposite," Waltz said. "Let's say Ridgecliff believes you're the only one outside of Dr Prowse who knows how he thinks. Maybe he does want you here. He can't do a thing if you're in Mobile."

I stared, not grasping the implication.

"Don't be obtuse, Ryder," Folger said. "Waltz is suggesting Ridgecliff brought you here to kill you."

"What? Why?"

"Maybe he figures he'll be free from then on."

The door banged open. A dick named Perlstein ran into the room, breathless, waving a page of notes. "We got a fix on him. Ridgecliff. Or at least we know where Ridgecliff's been hiding. A homeless shanty town by the docks. Sleeping in a box. The precinct cops found people who remember him. Forensics just pulled his prints off a cereal box and a pop bottle."

"He's trying to blend in with the homeless," Cluff said. "He can add or lose clothes, fatten his shape or go skinnier, hide his face. He can eat at churches, soup kitchens. Panhandle money."

"I'll update the BOLO," Folger said. "What was he last seen wearing?"

Perlstein frowned at his notes. "It keeps changing. A green raincoat. A pair of overalls. A blue sweater and plaid pants. Black boots. Leather sandals. Purple running shoes."

"That covers half the homeless in New York," Waltz noted, not hiding skepticism.

"We've got a basic fix," Folger defended. "Check every bum on the street. The info on Ridgecliff keeps mentioning his big baby blues. If a bum's got blue eyes, hold him until he's cleared five ways from Sunday. Exercise extreme caution. This guy thinks fast, kills like a machine. If he even smells like he's gonna pull something, put three in his center ring, no regrets. Got that?"

Nothing but assent.

The news that Jeremy had been spotted scattered everyone in different directions. Folger went to update the info in the *Be On the LookOut* broadcasts. Cluff, Bullard and two others headed to the shanty town. That left just Waltz and me.

"What can I do?" I asked. "Give me something to do."

"Maybe you should leave the city. If this guy

147

feels some kind of bond with you, you're in more danger than you recogni—"

His cell went off. He checked the number, muttered, "Pelham's HQ." Put the phone to his ear. I listened unobtrusively, hearing the words *Doll?* and *When?* and *We'll be right there,* the last words spoken while looking at me.

"We received it today," Pelham's adjutant, the petite, square-jawed woman named Sarah Wensley said, looking over reading glasses at Waltz and me. "It came to Cynthia personally, but addressed to the campaign headquarters."

We were back in the small room to the side of the rah-rah phone-bank operation up front. A knock hit the door before it opened and Pelham scooted in, dressed in a red pantsuit, a white neck scarf billowing in her wake. She looked delighted to see a room with fewer than a hundred people inside.

"I'm just back from my third lunch today. If I push any more chicken salad in circles, I swear I'll go crazy. What's happening, people?"

Wensley said, "I'm showing the detectives the weird doll."

She pulled a rotund, vase-shaped doll from the bag. I was close and took it from her, latex gloves now covering my hands. The doll was maybe six inches tall. I opened the doll at the waist, empty. It should have revealed a smaller doll inside, and so on, for several dolls. I'd seen them in gift catalogs.

"It's one of those stacking dolls or whatever," Pelham said. "They're all over Russia. But usually there are other dolls inside."

I considered the cartoonish face. "Why no mouth?" I asked.

"That's what made it kinda strange," Wensley said. "Detective Waltz said call if anything was even a little odd."

"No mouth?" Waltz said, pulling on his own gloves. "Pass it over."

Waltz studied the flesh-pink paint below the nose. "The mouth has been painted over. Nice job of matching the color."

I said, "Do you have Russian followers, ma'am? Or enemies?"

Pelham shook her head. "I've been to Russia three times, junkets, trade assemblies. Part of a crowd of officials meeting a crowd of officials, everyone mouthing platitudes. I've never taken any sort of volatile position concerning Russia or member states of the former Soviet Union."

Wensley said, "There's something creepy about it."

Waltz and I traded glances. He thought so, too. That made three of us. He said, "I want everyone who touched the doll to get finger-printed. And I want Forensics to check it over."

"Why has the mouth been painted over?" I wondered aloud.

"Obviously, someone's taken her voice."

We all looked at Pelham. She started to say something else, but leaned against the wall and shook her head.


Jeremy Ridgecliff was crossing Canal Street, a steaming cup of coffee in one hand, two shop-ping bags in the other. He'd been to electronics marts, gourmet shops, and import outlets. New York had something for every taste.

"You, sir. Stop right there."

He turned to see a jowly uniformed cop leaning out the window of a blue-and-white cruiser. The fiftyish cop was looking over his sunglasses, brown eyes vacuuming in every nuance and detail. Jeremy felt angry that a stranger could so brazenly attempt to take his measure. He pictured the cop's head rent with a sturdy axe, a ten-pounder. *Crunch* went the cranium. The picture and sound calmed Jeremy's anger.

"*Que?*" Jeremy asked softly, stepping on to the sidewalk.

"Please stop walking, sir."

Jeremy halted and pointed to his motionless shoes, like *You mean this?*

"Yes, dammit. I mean, *si*." The cop exited the cruiser, an older guy, heavy. His equipment squeaked and rattled on his leather belt. Another cop, much younger, sat in the driver's seat looking between a photo on the computer screen in the car and Jeremy. He made a motion at his hip Jeremy interpreted as unstrapping his weapon.

The driver opened his door and stepped out, watching across the hood of the car, one hand dangling by his sidearm. The heavy cop kept a half-dozen paces between him and Jeremy.

"Please set the cup on the ground, sir."

Jeremy affected puzzlement, though he felt a sizzle of anger arcing across his gut. The cop jabbed a finger at the cup, then at the ground, meaning, *Set it down, now!* Jeremy complied, bending his knees, setting the coffee on the sidewalk, straightening. He kept his hands away from his body; Carson had said cops liked hands kept far from pockets.

151

"Now," the cop said, "may I see some ID? Slowly, please."

*Crunch*, the axe repeated.

"High-Dee?" Jeremy said, stretching puzzlement across his face. "Oh, iden-ti-ficacion. *Um momento por favor. Está em meu revestimento.*"

Jeremy reached toward his jacket, the cop watching the hand like a hawk focused on a field mouse. Jeremy retrieved his dog-eared passport, handed it over. The cop stared past Jeremy's glasses and into his eyes, then studied him and the ID with equal scrutiny.

*Crunch, crunch . . .*

Jeremy pretended to watch a burst of pigeons overhead, not overly concerned with the verisimilitude of the passport. His neighbor down the hall in the Institute, Ismael Rogmann, had been a forger in addition to his habit of collecting human hands. Rogmann knew his competition, naturally, a good businessman. He'd traded the name of another master forger for thirteen plaster renditions of Albrecht Dürer's *Praying Hands* sculpture. Rogmann had arrayed them on the floor and slept in their midst, a happy man.

The cop relaxed. Shot a *stand-down* glance at the driver. Handed back the Portuguese passport. "Thank you – I mean, *Gracias*, Señor Caldiera. We're just doing some checking."

"Chic-king? *Muito bom*."

The driver of the cruiser, who looked in his mid-twenties, shook his head, thumped the roof of the cruiser. "Come on, Pinelli. He ain't close to the Ridgecliff guy. Let's grab some chow."

The older cop grunted as he climbed into the car. "He fit the height and weight. Same face shape, too. Chances are Ridgecliff's fifty blocks away and looking like a bum, but everyone's guilty until I check 'em out."

"*Tarde boa, chefe*." Jeremy said, waving at the departing cruiser. He picked up his cup, tucked his axe away, and continued down the sidewalk deep in thought. It was a minor incident, but it had made him aware of the sudden increase in cops on the street. Some of them would be like the guy he'd just dealt with, a street animal, seen it all, suspicious of it all. Carson had said there were cops who could smell guilt on a perp's breath.

He decided it would be good to keep a weapon in reserve in case something or someone got in the way of his plans. Nothing so primitive as an axe, of course, though the hands-on aspect

153

was a pleasant thought. He needed something bigger, totally unexpected . . .

And as powerful as lightning.

I paced the floor for an hour until Folger, Cluff and Bullard returned from the homeless camp. Folger stripped off the jacket of her gray business ensemble, tossed it over a chair beside mine. I smelled a wisp of clean body warmth and perfume and caught my eyes studying the way her skirt hem slid across her geometrically perfect knees.

"Ridgecliff seems to have gone underground, Ryder. But people there claim to see him every night. He'll return to the roost sooner or later."

"We planted two dozen surveillance people planted in the area," Bullard crowed. "Plus two undercovers in the camp itself. He's nailed."

It didn't work for me because I knew my brother. He hated dirty people and cold cereal with equal vigor. I sat in the corner and pictured the brother I knew. I could see him visiting the encampment, tossing a box of cereal or two to the ground, then paying or otherwise convincing psychologically wounded people to claim to have seen him on a regular basis, loading their answers with misinformation. Given the people

Jeremy would select, they'd believe it themselves after several repetitions.

The cops were wasting their time. Jeremy delighted in sending people into mazes where every path led to a wall. It was on me to do something.

I stood, picked up a metal chair, banged it on the floor. All conversation stopped, every eye turned to me.

"He's not around the homeless camp," I said. "Not even close. He went there once, a misdirection. He's not coming back."

"You got a reason for that conviction, Ryder?" Folger said.

"Anytime you think you've got him figured out, it's a set-up. Jeremy Ridgecliff is playing you. And unless you stop running in circles and start listening to me, he's going to keep playing you."

"You've finally managed to get my attention," Folger said.

# THIRTEEN

I stepped to the front of the room, feeling the stares.

"First order of business . . ." I said. "Forget the homeless camp; he'll be a forever no-show. Then shitcan any searches in the other boroughs. Ridgecliff won't leave Manhattan."

Bullard said, "Total bullshit. The loony will hide wherever he can find a −"

"Zip it, Detective," Folger said. She shot a glance at Waltz, then dropped the big eyes back on me.

"Waltz told me your hunch that Ridgecliff would stay in Manhattan. I didn't believe Waltz then, I don't believe you now. Here's your chance to change my mind with actual proof."

"There is no proof with Ridgecliff, Lieutenant.

You get my gut instincts. Right now they're the best thing you've got."

Bullard slapped the desk. "We're the fucking NYPD, Ryder. We don't need your gut inst—"

"Shut up," Folger snapped at Bullard. "Tell me about Ridgecliff, Ryder. Have your gut sing me a song."

I starting pacing the floor, snapping my fingers, skin tingling, hairs prickling on the back of my neck, a hunger in my innards that had nothing to do with food. I had what Harry called the predator's rush, the mind energizing the body for the hunt.

"Ridgecliff will only leave Manhattan if he's cornered. He's not cornered, so he's here. To leave would be perceived as a loss of face."

Bullard said, "Makes no fucking sense. Why would Brooklyn or Queens be a loss of face?"

"It would be a retreat, signifying we had control."

"The ego thing," Waltz affirmed.

Folger said, "Refresh my memory. How much time did you spend with this guy over the years?"

I pretended to make calculations in my head. "Upwards of a hundred hours, Lieutenant. Enough to know how he thinks."

Bullard snorted. "How Ridgecliff thinks? Christ. How long are we to listen to this psychobubba bullshit?"

Folger said, "Get out, Detective Bullard."

"Huh?

"Out. Go work one of your other cases."

Bullard reddened, started to argue. Folger held her finger up like a warning flare and Bullard slunk away, shooting me angry backward glances, like everything was my fault. Folger closed the door at Bullard's back. She leaned against the green wall and crossed her arms, aiming the liquid browns at me.

"OK, Ryder, you own the floor. Give us your take."

"Forget the bum disguise, he'd consider it demeaning. Plus it positions him in a social stratum often targeted by law enforcement. He'll pick a social station above police work."

When Cluff grunted disbelief. I said, "Who would you rather roust: a skid-row crackhead or a guy wearing an Armani suit?"

Cluff nodded grudgingly. "The suit might have a wise-ass lawyer to make my life miserable."

"Ridgecliff knows that. And that dressing like money might buy him time to book."

"Or push a knife in your heart," Cluff noted.

Folger said, "So no blue-collar disguise either?"

"He'll be a businessman type. It's a broad category, but it'll allow him to dress upscale. There's another reason: Ridgecliff's been forced to wear variations on pajamas and sweatsuits for fourteen years, institutional clothing. He wants to look good."

"Ego again," Waltz said. "I'm beginning to get it."

For the first time since I'd landed at LaGuardia, I felt in control. Of my mind. Of my choices. Of my direction. Fear, guilt, sorrow, self-pity, all had somehow been pushed to the walls, and the electricity of the hunt danced alone on center floor.

"What color suit is he wearing right now?" Cluff asked, sarcasm thick in his voice. "Solid? Pinstripe?"

"How about double breasted?" Waltz said. "It worked for George Metesky."

Cluff frowned. "Metesky? The Mad Bomber?"

"It was 1956. The Mad Bomber had been on the loose for over fifteen years. The NYPD, completely lost, asked psychiatrist James Brussel to profile the Bomber. Brussel suggested the perp's approximate age, demeanor, origin . . .

even predicted the Bomber would be wearing a double-breasted suit when he got nailed."

Cluff held up his hands in protest. "You ain't gonna tell me that really happened."

"It didn't. When Metesky was arrested at his home, he was wearing pajamas."

Cluff said, "Ha!"

"It was before being taken to jail," Waltz added, "that Metesky slipped into the double-breasted suit he always wore."

Cluff looked at Waltz, then at me. He held up his hands again, but this time it was more like surrender.

Folger said, "Does your gut explain how Ridgecliff's paying for this little vacation, Ryder? We've been keeping an eye on credit-card thefts, can't tie anything to him. And I don't recall any big bank robberies lately. It's not like he can go to the ATM and take fifty grand from his account."

"The money isn't important, Lieutenant. He'll have come up with it. Probably through a scam, a con game."

"An insane guy can build a big con in a few days?"

I said, "You're thinking of a man who's crazy first, logical second. Ridgecliff's in reverse. He's logical, brilliant, a superb conversationalist and utterly charming. He knows people inside and out. Knows how to press their buttons."

"The smart guy gets what he wants, then the demon pops out and starts killing?" Folger said.

I nodded. "I think it's come to that."

# FOURTEEN

The tattooed man crouched beneath a stunted tree just east of FDR Drive. Behind him an orange-hued sunset turned the East River as bright as beaten copper. The man's head was shaved, his shirtless torso and arms a nightmare of upended crosses, flaming pentacles, weeping eyeballs. Muscles like titanium cords rippled when he changed position or paced the concrete bordering the river before returning to his crouch.

Jeremy Ridgecliff hunkered on a walkway above the street, studying though compact binoculars. He had followed the man for two hours, analyzing motions, gestures, facial expressions, studying the tattoos. He had watched the man wince when a Catholic church's bells tolled the hour. Heard him curse a street preacher passing out tracts. Seen him spit on the walls of a temple.

An hour ago the man had ended up here, either crouched in tense thought or performing machine-like repetitions of push-ups and sit-ups, veins pulsing across his engorged arms and shoulders.

A tourist boat on the river sounded a whistle. The man craned his head to the boat, bared his teeth, then returned to a dark place inside his head. Jeremy made a decision. He crossed west over FDR Drive and hailed a cab.

Near Times Square, he found a glittery novelty and electronics shop selling plastic Statues of Liberty, postcards, tee-shirts, and cheap, hi-tech gadgets. He scanned the display cases and found what he needed, hoping 130 lumens – whatever they were – would do the trick.

"Excuse me," he asked the clerk, "but would you also have a piece of strong thread? Perhaps two feet?"

The clerk sold him a pocket sewing kit for a buck, black and white threads, a needle. Jeremy thought a moment, then added a cheap fountain pen to his purchases. Outside the store,

Jeremy tested the thread between his hands, judged it strong enough.

The man was still there when Jeremy returned. FDR Drive was behind a concrete retaining wall, drivers thundering through the tight corridor. The sole light was from a flickering streetlamp a hundred feet away.

Jeremy crept through the shadow and leaned against a tree a dozen feet from the crouching man. He turned his head away, toward the river.

"That's interesting."

The man's head snapped to Jeremy. "What the fuck did you say?"

Jeremy kept his face averted. "I was listening to your thoughts," he said quietly. "I thought they were interesting."

The man uncoiled from his crouch like an angry rattlesnake, eyes narrowed, muscles rippling with every move. He lifted his clenched fist, preparing to drive Jeremy to the concrete. "Fuck your dirty lies," the man said.

Jeremy turned to face the man and began speaking.

"*Ari oha denda see . . . a mani a satano bayt manio . . .*" White light blazed from Jeremy's mouth. He spoke in a language from beyond Time. His teeth were translucent with inner fire, his tongue a squirming eel. His voice was the echo of a hell-bound train through a valley of ice.

"...*ronda nul beljus empet ... larati doma castara* ..."

The light from Jeremy's mouth illuminated the man's wordless terror. He dropped to his knees and lowered his head as if awaiting the guillotine.

"*Aro tomani memow ... synthicus wala pemb* ..."

Jeremy held his forearm low. Light from his mouth spotlighted a meaningless symbol scrawled below the crook of his elbow, a half-moon impaled on a spear. The man glanced at the drawing, spasmed as if seized by epilepsy, covered his eyes with his hands.

"W-What do you want?"

"I serve an entity," Jeremy intoned as he stood. "The entity directed me to you."

Jeremy fought to contain a smile. He could have used the word *spirit* or *demon* or *being*, but the word *entity* was magic. Half of these fuckers thought they were Swiss-cheesed with entities.

"The entity's name ..." the man whispered, "is it ... Asmodeus?"

Jeremy recalled Asmodeus as one of Lucifer's

demonic Kings of Hell, mentioned in *Paradise Lost*. His observations had been dead-on, he'd found a religious lunatic, a man toxic with broken saints and disgraced angels. A dangerous and disconnected man.

Perfect.

While the man cowered on the pavement, Jeremy turned away, pulled the slender thread hanging from the side of his mouth. The multi-LED key-chain light – smaller than a wine cork but guaranteed to be *130 Lumens! Brightest You Can Buy!* – slid from behind his tongue. He snapped it off and slipped it in his pocket. The idiot thing was about to gag him.

"Stand ye and act natural," he intoned. "Spies are about."

The man stood with reluctance, his corded muscles twitching. He kept his head canted away, as if a glance at Jeremy would be instant death. Jeremy lowered his voice. Tapped the symbol on his arm.

"Asmodeus sent me to show you his private name and convey his love." Dramatic pause. "He also sends a task."

"A task?" The man dared to look into Jeremy's eyes, unable to believe his good fortune. "Asmodeus sends a task for . . . me?"

"A task set for you in the timeless eons of the Before. A task awaiting you alone." *They love their frigging tasks,* Jeremy thought, his heart beating with glee. They'd wait their whole lives for some damn task, die for it. You just had to wind them up and point them.

"What does my Dark Lord bid me do?" the man said, tears of joy shining in his eyes.

Jeremy reached into his pocket. "Here is a special phone. When the time comes, the task will be revealed. Never use this phone, never lose this phone. It is your link."

The man took the pre-paid phone with hands cupped and head bowed. "On the hallowed name of Asmodeus, I promise."

Jeremy placed five Krugerrands beside the phone. "Gold. To buy what you may need for your task. The coins must not be seen by anyone. Do you have a hiding place?"

Hard fingers curled tight around the phone and coins. The man tapped his lower abdomen.

Jeremy nodded. "Kneel and be sanctified."

The man dropped to his knees. Jeremy tapped his finger six times on the man's sweaty, tattooed shoulder while chanting more nonsense. The man trembled as if on the verge of orgasm.

"Thank you," he whispered. "Thank you."

Jeremy turned and walked away, waiting until out of sight to grimace and wipe his finger on his pants. He crossed several streets and hailed a cab. Though he had much to do, he decided to take the remainder of the evening off and have a good time. Play a little.

The night was young and the city so alive.

# FIFTEEN

Charged, alert, feeling like a cop, I went back to my hotel and again read my brother's files into the night. No sweating, no weeping, no internalized histrionics: Just a laser-tight focus on the job at hand. Initially worried my perception had been wrong about the files and points of view, I found I'd been completely correct . . .

"*I was sitting on the grass, disconsolate. The woman kept shooting glances my way, wanting to take away my pain* . . .

"*Jeremy watched her learn the lesson of the knife* . . ."

Two separate personae. The first was a man-child lost somewhere between twelve and twenty-six, casting himself as a pitiful piece of bait to trap hapless and kindhearted women.

The second Jeremy was cold, colorless, almost an objective observer, seemingly emblemized by the knife.

And the second entity was in ascendance.

I fell into bed at two in the morning, awakening at six. I went outside and wandered, drinking coffee and watching trucks re-supply the city. When I got to the cop shop, Waltz had just entered and was filling a coffee cup.

"Let's suck in some caffeine and see what Folger's troupe unearthed during the night."

"Cluff and Bullard were here all night?"

"I think she lets them sleep until five, when she gets up. But they'll have read any reports generated last night."

I followed Waltz across the room. Bullard was drinking coffee at the small table in the conference room. My brother's face stared at me from a whiteboard, along with the faces of Vangie, Dora Anderson and Angela Bernal. The timeline on the board was mainly dots instead of solid lines, meaning nearly everything was speculation.

"Anything new come up on Ridgecliff?" Waltz asked. "Possible sightings?"

"Yeah, even after Ryder's gut instinct, here's what we got . . ." Bullard tapped his thumb and forefinger together, the big zero. Waltz nodded and turned away. Bullard *pssst*'ed me and when I looked his way he brought the thumb-finger O to his crotch, *Eat me*. The boy was back.

I shook my head and hustled after Waltz's back. He said, "Let's go see what's been dug up on Vic Two. Detective Cluff had a line on her this morning, backtracked her to her previous digs, was getting the skinny from there. We've still got to check her past."

Cluff was at his desk, blue shirt hanging on his skinny frame, weapon in a shoulder harness, sleeves rolled up. He was leaning back in his chair, teeth bared, scrawling on a wide expanse of white paper that ran off his desk to a roll of paper on the floor. I studied the scribbles, lines and arrows across the paper, dense on the left side, thinning out toward the right. The feeder roll on the floor was at least eight inches in diameter, a helluva lot of paper.

"Mind if I ask what's with the paper roll, Detective?"

Cluff grunted. "My own system. My brother-in-law owns a butcher shop on Long Island. He gets me butcher paper by the roll. I start on the left, writing all the crap I gather, every name, date, place, time. Everything. I cross off the stuff that doesn't seem relevant, circle repeated stuff, or crap that just seems right. I keep moving the more-solid info to the right. Repeat. By the time I work my way across a couple dozen feet . . ."

"Salient patterns emerge from the clutter?" I said.

"Shit shakes out."

"Of course."

Waltz walked up as Cluff rolled his chair back and threw his pencil down on the expanse of paper. "We just dead-ended on Bernal's history."

Waltz frowned. "Worked over at NYC Medical, right? Transcriptionist?"

"For five years she's been a model citizen, paying her bills and taxes and holding down as many as three jobs. Before that she's missing a little something. Like citizenship." Cluff put his hands to his temples, rubbed them in circles. "It's just gonna be a fucking slog for no goddamn reason. I'll spend the rest of the day with people terrified I'm going to send them back to Guatemala or wherever."

Waltz nodded toward his office, went in that direction, I turned to follow, stopped, turned back.

"*Buena suerte* in your endeavors, Detective Cluff."

He spun the chair to me, his eyes crinkled in anger. "The fuck's that supposed to mean?"

"Good luck tracking the lady's history. I hope you catch a break."

Cluff turned away. I saw a line of pinpoint boils on the back of his neck. I made it a couple steps toward Shelly's office when Cluff called from behind me.

"Hey, Bubba . . ."

I turned. He was studying me over his shoulder.

"What?"

"Bullard said he caught that big-ass knot on his head when a truck smacked him with its side mirror. But you laid that egg on his thick skull, right?"

I shrugged. Cluff turned back to the work on his desk.

"Thanks for your good wishes, Detective Ryder. Have a productive day yourself."

I caught up with Waltz by the door. He saw my face, said, "You look confused, Detective."

"I think Cluff was just nice to me. I didn't know whether to smile or duck."

"Cluff's OK. I forget you don't know his story. He busted a meth lab two years back. Damn thing exploded while he was cuffing the

173

perps, fire, chemical fumes, a bad mix. He damaged his lungs. He could get a medical disability, but being a cop is all he cares about."

I looked toward Cluff's cubicle. Nothing of a personal nature in his surroundings. No photos of wife, kids, dog, car. No goofy mugs or paperweights received as gifts. No drawings by the grandkids taped to the walls. Not even the photo with the fish. I'd seen the syndrome before. "He'd be dead three months after he retired," I said. "The department's all he cares about."

Waltz nodded. "A guy who can only pull three-quarter weight's a liability to a lot of people, no unit wanted him. Still, no one wanted to point him to the door."

"So Cluff was assigned to Folger by the brass?" I said. "No choice in the matter?"

"Nope. Folger requested Cluff."

I gave him a *huh*? look.

"Cluff's life is the NYPD, and Folger's making sure he's keeping that life. Not in some backwater precinct in an outer borough, but in Manhattan, right here in the high-profile center of the action with the rest of us. Cluff's not dead weight, he's a pro who's just slow by a couple steps. Folger stepped to the plate and saved him."

I heard a bray of voice and saw Folger on the far side of the room setting a desk jockey into action.

"So there's more to her than it looks at first?"

Waltz studied Folger with a mix of perplexation and admiration. "That lady keeps a lot hidden, I think."

Folger jumped back into her office, banged the door shut. I said, "What you got on for the day, Shelly?"

"My sister's birthday is tonight and she's decided I'm giving her some fancy-ass pot she saw in Macy's cooking department."

I held up my tattered paper bag of case materials.

"Macy's have briefcases?"

"They have about everything. Ever been there?"

"Years ago I came to New York with a girlfriend. She spent an entire afternoon in Macy's. I spent mine in the Museum of Modern Art."

"Contrasting ideologies?" Waltz said, slipping on his jacket.

"She liked upper Park, I liked Chinatown. She liked Le Benardin, I preferred Curry in a Hurry. We went home on separate planes."

Ten minutes later, Waltz pulled into a No

Parking zone on 34th. We made plans to meet in a half hour, Waltz bird-dogging his sister's birthday gift. I went looking for briefcases. I preferred the four-hundred-dollar model made of brown leather as soft as cream cheese, but had to be satisfied with an inexpensive fabric job.

I paid for my purchase, checked my watch, and was ambling toward the agreed-upon entrance when I noticed Waltz by the perfume counter. When I was a couple dozen paces away, I watched him lift a sample, spray his wrist, wave it dry. Sniff.

His shoulders slumped and he continued down the aisle. I picked up speed to catch him but, passing the perfume counter, stopped to lift the bottle Waltz had sampled. I spritzed a shot in the air. Inhaled. Then continued after Waltz, an odd notion in my head, and my heart running a half a per cent faster.

# SIXTEEN

Harry Nautilus slipped into the cottage in Gulf Shores, a white box with red hurricane shutters, part of a cottage community on the Intracoastal Waterway. He waved thanks to the Gulf Shores cop who'd overseen the fast access.

It was a typical vacation place, Nautilus noted: large windows to let in the view, simple furnishings, small, neat kitchen. There were posters for annual Gulf Shores shrimp festivals on the wall, bright and colorful. Outside on the water, a shrimp boat chugged along, its nets hung on outriggers and wafting in the wind.

Nautilus opened a door to the side of the main room and his heart skipped a beat. It was an office, small and spare and simple, but seemingly a place to see patients: Large desk and ergonomic desk chair, an overstuffed armchair in the corner, a couch, all seemingly de rigueur for a shrink. The room was greens and grays, the light through the window giving everything a relaxed and pleasant cast.

"Knock, knock, Vange," said a voice from the front door. "Permission to come aboard?"

"Come in," Nautilus said.

The voice was followed by a pair of eyes as green as the sea. The woman wearing the eyes must have been eighty, her hair as white as snow, her leathery, sunbrown face as creased as an antique saddle. She wore blue jeans and a tee-shirt advertising a local seafood restaurant.

"Who are you?" she demanded.

Nautilus ID'd himself. Felt compelled to explain the reason behind his visit.

"Oh, my lord," the woman said. She looked stunned and Nautilus moved to her side, helped her sit on the floral couch, got her a glass of water.

"Mind if I smoke?" the woman asked, pulling a half-crushed pack of cigarettes from her back pocket. "She keeps me an ashtray in the second drawer by the sink. And bring me a beer instead of water, please. It's in the fridge."

Nautilus retrieved a brass ashtray and a Bass Ale, set them beside the woman.

"I take it you knew the Doctor well, miz . . . ?"

"Helena Pappagallos. I've been living two cottages over since I retired as a ship's cook fourteen years back. Vangie's had this place for eleven years. I've seen her every weekend she could get down. I have a boat and sometimes we'd go fishing."

"Often? I mean her coming down, not the fishing."

"She tried to come down every weekend – it's only a three-hour drive – but work kept her visits at two to three weekends a month on the average. Sometimes she'd grab a few extra days, but she was a busy woman. This was her escape, mostly."

"Mostly?"

Pappagallos crushed out one cigarette, lit another. Took a bubbling suck at the beer bottle. Shook her head.

"She's consulted with a few patients here. It's been a couple of years since I've seen any. I could tell they were patients because they'd park their cars and skitter to her cottage like scared cats. She'd put a *Do Not Disturb* sign on the door. I once asked her why she saw patients when it was shrinking or whatever she was getting away from. She said she thought differently down here. I think she just loved what she did."

Nautilus felt his spirits fall. If Dr Prowse hadn't seen patients recently, an entire line of pursuit crumbled like a house built of spit and lint.

"So she doesn't see patients here any more, Miz Pappagallos?"

"I said *I* don't see patients here any more."

"What's the difference?"

"No one ever came or went that I saw. But every Saturday, from one to three, she put the sign on the door."

"Do Not Disturb," Nautilus said. "Her work sign."

"Like she was analyzing or whatever. Come to think of it, for the past three–four months or so, she's been here every Saturday. That's a record or something, first time in years."

"And each weekend the sign's been on the door?"

Ms Pappagallos nodded through a haze of blue. "Saturdays from one to three p.m. You could set your clock by it."

Nautilus walked Ms Pappagallos to the door.

Time to head back to Mobile, call Carson and pass on the latest. Not that there was anything solid, just a bag of smoke that grew larger by the day.

He headed back to the office to retrieve his briefcase. He was stepping out the door when he remembered he'd swung the office door open on his entry, hadn't checked behind it for a calendar, bulletin board, or the like. He recrossed the living room to the office, stepped inside, closed the door.

On the back side of the door was a photograph enlarged to poster size. Nautilus stared at it in disbelief. He closed his eyes and opened them again.

The photo was still there.

# SEVENTEEN

Waltz drove us to lunch at his favorite Indian restaurant, maybe three square feet larger than my living room. The air was perfumed with ginger, cardamom, cumin, cloves, coriander. When I die, I want my body marinated in those spices before I'm cremated, everyone downwind salivating instead of weeping at my demise.

The waiter arrived and I ordered saag paneer, Shelly the lamb vindaloo. We split an order of chapati. The food arrived in minutes, bowls of fragrant magic. We ate in silence to acknowledge the perfection of the selections.

"By the way, Shelly, whatever became of the hair and fiber samples vacuumed from the floors of the scenes?" I asked as the dishes were swept away and we nibbled at golf-ball-sized servings of mango ice. "Forensics run any tests?"

"No need, can't imagine what they'd prove."

"Because everyone knows Jeremy Ridgccliff is the perp?"

Waltz frowned. "You think otherwise?"

"No."

"If we're not going to get anything solid, then why process –"

"A friend of mine is a pathologist. Clair Peltier heads the Mobile-area office of the Alabama Bureau of Forensics. In her own field she's as reknowned as Dr Prowse. Her take on testing is that every answer is the answer you want."

Waltz thought a moment, tapping his chin with his forefinger.

"Because no matter what answer you get, it answers something?"

"Bingo. You think I could put Clair in touch with the NYPD forensics folks? I guarantee you they've heard of her. She's a heavy hitter in the path world."

Waltz pulled his notepad and started scribbling. "Hell, couldn't hurt. Have her call this guy. Meanwhile, I'll tell him to expect a call."

I took the number, pocketed it. I doubted Clair could find anything, but she'd worked miracles before. Waltz, meanwhile, settled into a pensive frown.

"Any idea why Ridgecliff's moving outside his initial target type?"

"All distinctions have become blurred. He's imploding."

"Do you think you're a target?"

"I think anything's possible, Shelly. I'm just happy Folger's listening to my input, whether she believes it or not."

"She's closer to your side than she's letting on."

I rolled my eyes.

"It's true, Detective. Two days ago I took the liberty of calling your supervisor in Mobile, Lieutenant Mason. I asked if he could fax a couple outlines of your PSIT cases up here. He sent three: A guy beheading men, a cult that followed a dead artist, and one that gave new meaning to the term 'family secrets'. I gave the outlines to the Lieutenant. She was suitably impressed."

"That a pair of yokels like me and Harry could find something outside the range of our asses?"

"Your successes were feats of experience and intuition. I think Alice Folger is a convert."

Shelly's phone rang. He spoke a few seconds. Snapped the phone closed.

"What?" I asked.

"That was Sarah Wensley at Pclham's HQ. They just got another doll in the mail, addressed to Pelham. The one that fits inside the doll they got the other day. Like a countdown."

"No mouth on the doll?"

"Painted over. Plus they have some new and nasty letters for me to look at." He threw his napkin on the table. "Ridgecliff's running amok, Pelham's got the loonies on full-pot boil. Ain't life grand?"

We were at Pelham's HQ fifteen minutes later. Ms Wensley hadn't touched the doll, but had left it in the box. It faced upward, so that whoever opened the box saw the mouthless visage when the box was opened.

"It's just creepy," Ms Wensley said, spinning on her heel and returning to her work up front with the phone banks.

Waltz called for a Forensics team to pick up the doll and take it in for vetting. The first doll had returned nothing: no prints, not even smudges. That in itself was a message; whoever sent the doll didn't want to be discovered. While we waited, Waltz scanned a sheaf of letters mailed to the headquarters.

"Anything real bad?" I asked.

"Once you carve away the invective it's mainly disagreement on various issues. About fifty per cent carry similarly worded passages, which come verbatim from talk radio and TV commentators. There's no real threat, just unhappiness with misspellings."

"Venting. But there's the stage above that, right?"

He tapped a much smaller stack of letters and phone-call transcripts he'd culled from the stack. "Women as bitches and whores and sluts. These people spend a goodly portion of their day frothing at the mouth."

I concurred. "I know the type. Guys who need an enemy in order to give them a life."

Waltz sighed. "What a full and happy life it is, hating gays, blacks, Latinos, environmentalists, Chevrolet owners, whatever." Waltz laughed without humor. "There's a bleak element in the anti-women contingent, the kind that fancies hooks and electrodes. Check this one out –"

I saw a poorly centered home-made letterhead proclaiming MEN UNITED! Beneath was a sour mishmash of hate and blame that rambled for seven pages, with particularly strident passages IN ALL CAPS TO MAKE A POINT. The writer had obviously gotten a bargain on exclamation marks.

I handed it back. "Seems them doggone wimmen have done him wrong."

Shelly tucked the letter into his pocket. "I've not heard of this particular group, so I'm going to visit our scribe. Want to come along? Maybe it'll be feeding time."

Whereas email correspondents tended to the anonymity of a handle like Ultiman or T'Rone34, J. William Blankley had opted for old-fashioned snailmail on letterhead complete with signature. J William lived in an apartment building near downtown Brooklyn, a decent but not posh address, according to Shelly. We exited the car to air smelling like impending rain, the clouds a low gray shelf. Thunder shivered in the distance.

Blankley answered the door. He was late twenties or early thirties. Not a bad-looking guy, semi-fit, five-eight or nine, tidy haircut, khakis and blue oxford shirt. Just a guy who might do your taxes or find a book for you at the library, until you noticed the tightness at the corners of his eyes. Scowler's eyes.

Waltz held up his badge. "Can we come in, Mr Blankley? We just want a few minutes of your time."

The small apartment was neat to the point of immaculate, resembling a photograph of a living room in an Ethan Allen ad. There was no color or sense of personality. Everything seemed beige, even the TV screen, an all-news channel, muted. A blonde anchorwoman moved her lips as Hispanics tumbled over a border fence superimposed at her back.

The only disarray was in a corner of the dining alcove, a computer desk and files, posters taped above the desk and work area. The word *Men* was prominent.

Blankley gave Waltz and me about six square feet just inside the door. Waltz held out the letter.

"You send this, Mr Blankley?"

"That's personal correspondence, you're not allowed to read it."

"The other party felt compelled to show it to me. That's allowed. I counted the word slut or sluts twenty-four times, bitch or bitches came in at thirteen, whore or whores hit the trifecta at seven. Your writing isn't overly joyful, Mr Blankley."

Blankley jammed his hands in his pockets

and strode away, stopped halfway across the room. "I'm supposed to be happy when men are under attack twenty-four seven?"

"I wasn't alerted. Have I missed something?"

"The feminist conspiracy to strip men of our gender-ordained rights. We're physically and intellectually superior, but treated like a disease because we lack the politically correct plumbing."

"Interesting. The, uh, upshot?"

He jabbed his finger toward a hand-drawn logo above his computer, either an artichoke on a stick or a raised fist, beneath it the legend, MEN UNITED!

"We're fighting the conspiracy to feminize America. Men are being treated like slaves, broken down, discarded. The insidious feminizing influences are everywhere."

Waltz said, "You've been feminized, Mr Blankley? I can't really tell."

"*I* haven't been. They've tried, but I've resisted. Are you here because I exercised my first amendment rights and wrote a damn letter?"

"We're checking out threats to conference participants. This letter verges on threatening."

"I'm the one that's threatened. My gender. My God-given maleness. Tell Pelham and her kind to stop threatening me, then I'll lay down my sword."

"How long has your organization been in existence, Mr Blankley?" Waltz asked.

"Almost five months. Our Ten Tenets of Male Awareness are as follows: One, to counter the pro-feminist agenda wherever we find it. Two, to create newsletters reflecting our –"

Waltz held up his hand to cut Blankley off mid-tenet. "You're the founder of the organization?"

"The Supreme Commander. And treasurer. Our third tenet is . . ."

I kept quiet as Blankley yapped. I'd seen guys like him before. Most had a pivotal moment or crisis that transformed them into ardent woman-haters, though they were quick to point out it wasn't all women, just the ones they disagreed with. And, of course, that women did it, too – hating men.

*Nyah, nyah, nyah . . . hated you first.*

Some transforming moments could be personal and harsh: the court siding with the ex-wife in a custody battle, stripping a caring father of rights or limiting them. It was ugly and it happened, but it was a problem with a legal system, not a gender. There were women who despised men, it was true, and sometimes for nothing but the need of an enemy. They were female Blankleys, often doomed to strident and unsatisfying lives.

But usually it was a personal failure transformed into someone else's fault. Sometimes the moments were seismic, others so small you wondered how they registered on the psyche, until one learned that inbred insecurities ripen a psyche for bruising at every turn. *Hit me*, these folks seemed to say. Once hit, they spent the rest of their lives whining about it and wanting you to pity their bruise. When it began to fade they hammered at it until fresh blood leaked beneath the skin.

I wondered if Blankley had such a transformational moment, and if that moment had registered in the legal system, occasionally the case. And could I use a little psychic jiu-jitsu to pop it out in the open?

I made a deal out of pulling the phone from my pocket, then faked a call. I pursed my lips and frowned, listening to nothing. I aimed the frown at Blankley, still declaiming his tenets. He looked at me looking at him.

"What?" he scowled.

I shrugged. "Nothing."

"I'm a tax-paying citizen and I've got a right to know."

"Seems you've had a problem or two," I generalized, starting to walk away, giving him rope. He jumped in front of me, his face demanding, accusatory.

"No way. Neither of them filed a formal complaint. How can there be a record?"

"There are two types of records. Official and call reports."

"It's ILLEGAL!"

Waltz picked up the thread. "Officers go on a call, they write down where and when and what."

Blankley's head snapped toward Waltz. "They lied."

"The officers lied?"

"The BITCHES lied. I wasn't harassing them. I was explaining how they could better themselves by listening to me instead of that righteous woman shit! They're all catty, manipulative, egomaniacal. Then they turn around and accuse me of being self-absorbed. I was trying to recover my manhood."

Waltz looked at Blankley's crotch, raised an eyebrow. "They stole it? Maybe you should have filed a theft complaint."

Blankley's chin quivered with anger. "You're trying to humiliate me. I'm filing a complaint with your superior!"

Waltz pulled out his cellphone, flipped it open. "I'll dial. You can complain. Her name is Lieutenant Alice Folger."

Blankley turned red and made a noise like a balloon losing air. He opened his mouth to unleash another rant. Shelly waggled his finger, *No*, like disciplining a puppy.

Rain was falling in earnest when we stepped outside and we ran to the car, jumped inside. Waltz sighed, brushed back damp hair with his palm.

"You ever get the feeling that only about twenty per cent of adults are adults, Detective Ryder?"

"Really, Shelly? I've always found it closer to ten."

We wrote off Blankley as no threat to the conference, just a sad boy with a small life. He'd had a couple of failed relationships and lacked the maturity to puzzle out what went wrong, deal with it, move on. It was easier when the women were at fault, or better, part of a vast conspiracy to de-male him in some way. No one de-males the J. William Blankleys, they do it on their own, almost eagerly.

We got back to the station and I found Harry had called. I went outside to the street, stood in the recessed doorway of an office building and phoned him. He sounded odd, tentative. Maybe it was the connection.

"The Doc's place took a Breaking and Entering a couple weeks back. Nate Allen responded. He said that about halfway through, the Doc got squirrelly, like she was nervous about having things looked at. She said nothing was taken. Nate thinks something unspoken was going on. Like maybe something got taken that Doc Prowse didn't want anyone to know about."

"Strange. Nate figure what that might have been?"

"No idea. Did you know the Doc had a place in Gulf Shores?"

"Sure. Her hideaway."

"Cute little place. According to a neighbor, the Doc sees the occasional patient there, but it's been a couple years. Unless the Doc was analyzing ghosts."

"How so?"

The neighbor says the Doc hung out a 'Do Not Disturb' sign like she was seeing patients, but the neighbor lady never saw anyone. This was every Saturday afternoon for two months."

"Sounds like Vangie's taking a nap," I said. "What else?"

"There's a posterized photo on the back of the door in Dr Prowse's home office. When the door's closed the picture's directly across from her desk."

"And?"

"It's a picture of a naked man."

Despite the circumstances, I couldn't stanch a chuckle. "Vangie was a young sixty-three, Harry. She's allowed."

"Uh, Cars, the photo's of your brother."

"Excuse me?"

"The naked guy is Jeremy. He's sprawled out on a quilt. It's, uh, real odd."

"Uh, listen, Harry . . . got to . . . there's a meeting up."

"Sure. Later."

I closed the phone, dropped it in my pocket, missed, picked it off the pavement. Vangie had a photograph of a nude Jeremy where she could see it as she worked. *Right across from her desk where she could look into his eyes!*

The horror of Vangie and my brother as lovers and co-conspirators made me physically ill.

Saliva flooded my mouth and bile spasmed to my throat. I covered my mouth, sprinted toward a trash receptacle, vomited before I got there. A car full of teenagers went past. They whooped, yelled, laughed. I leaned against a lamppost and watched the street tilt and whirl, like a ride at a carnival.

# EIGHTEEN

"Ryder. You OK?"

The voice was at my back. I turned, saw Folger approaching. Behind her, in a loading zone, was her ride. She'd obviously seen me at my less-than-best and pulled over to poke a little fun at the puking bubba. I waved her away, not sure I wanted to talk to anyone again, and certainly not her.

"No problem, Lieutenant. I'm fine."

She stopped two yards away, hands on her hips, studying me. "Sure, all the fine, problem-free people I know upchuck in the street. You been drinking? You look wobbly."

"Not a drop." I patted my gut. "A stomach thing, I guess."

She stared at me, nodded. "Come on, let's

go to a place not too far from here. I call it home. I'm bone-tired and calling it quits for today. I'll give you a cup of hot tea to get your delicate tummy right. I'll even put a couple cups of sugar in it. That's how Southerners like tea, right? Like syrup?"

"That's iced tea. Listen, Lieutenant . . . I'll be OK."

She looked at the trail I'd deposited on the pavement and jerked her finger over her shoulder at the cruiser. "Drop your butt in the car, Ryder. Or I'll run you in for littering."

She drove to a street on what seemed the south border of Chelsea, a mix of residential dwellings and small shops. I saw a tavern at the far end of the block, across from it a tailor shop. Folger parked in front of a slender brownstone shouldered against a line of others similar in style. Hers stood out, the only one with flowers sprouting from window boxes. It looked like a place with a nice personality, a house that liked walks in the park and tea on Sunday afternoons.

We stood on the stoop as she dug in her purse for keys.

She said, "You're lucky I drove today."

"What's usual?"

"Running. I've made two arrests on my commutes, one a pickpocket, the other a bike thief. The bike booster was so surprised he dropped a boltcutter on his foot and broke two toes. Made my week."

"No doubt."

"You look like you might work out a bit, Ryder. On your better days."

"I live on a beach. I enjoy running the shoreline. I also kayak and swim."

"Aha. That explains where the shoulders come from."

Inside, I saw spare and sleek furnishings designed in Sweden or Denmark, much like in my own home. There were enough plants to stock a small jungle, including a wide-fronded palm that owned an entire corner of the room. Light through the living-room window drew a golden parallelogram on the polished wood floor. I was taken by the sense of harmony.

"This is a nice place, Lieutenant."

"Don't sound so surprised. It's a small place, but it's in Manhattan. I rent out the top floor, live here."

Looking down a small hall, I saw two doors beyond what was obviously the bathroom. "Two bedrooms? That's nice."

"One's like an office. Or maybe a hobby room."

I glanced out the window. A pretty view of trees and the brick rowhouses across the way. Most cars on the street were upscale: Saabs and Audis and Beamers.

"I thought Manhattan was an expensive place to –" I caught myself, winced.

Folger kicked off her shoes, pushing them to the edge of a long blue couch. She tossed her purse on a counter separating the living room and kitchen nook. "To live? Too expensive for a NYPD dick, right? That's what you were thinking? Level with me, Ryder."

"You nailed me. It's exactly what I was thinking."

She walked to the window, stood beside me, hands on the sill, looking out. A wistful look crossed her face. "It's freaking insanely expensive to live in Manhattan, anywhere halfway decent. I have an angel."

"Pardon?"

She turned from the window, went and sat on the couch, crossing bare feet beneath her. I sat in a matching chair. A table of some blonde wood rested between us, on it a stack of *National Geographic*s and a couple of magazines called *Weather*.

"Six years back a lawyer comes to the door of my thousand-buck-a-month rathole in Brooklyn. Shows up out of nowhere. He's an ancient Jewish guy, stooped over, carrying a briefcase that folds like an accordion. He offered me half a million dollars. Free money."

"Get to the punchline, Lieutenant."

"The working day's over, you can call me Alice. And it's no joke. There was just one catch. Mr Ancient Lawyer said it was a conditional grant. I had to use the dinero to improve my living conditions. Not buy a car, not invest in alpacas. No Dior gowns. I had to buy a home, and it would be purchased under his supervision to make sure I got it right."

My skepticism was blatant. "How much is it you want for the Brooklyn Bridge?"

She smiled gently. It was so pretty as to be disarming. "I still don't believe it myself sometimes. But that's exactly how it went down. After taxes, I ended up with enough to make a heavy down-payment here. Plus I get rental income from my tenant upstairs, Julie Chase, an accountant who's even quieter than me. The upshot is I own a home for less than the rent on my old apartment, where steam pipes knocked and greasers smoked dope on the fire escapes."

"Any idea who made the grant?"

She pursed the full lips, thinking, like the question was something she puzzled with a lot. "I'd just made detective after four years in uniform, doing my damndest to nail 'em and jail 'em. I figure somehow I impressed or helped someone rich. He, she or they wanted to move me out of my former shithole, pardon my Iroquois."

I'd heard of such munificence. Though, in general, folks helped by cops made donations to the department or a specific unit, like a kidnapping squad who'd returned a family member. It was rarer for a gift to be made to an individual. Rarer still for it to be anonymous.

"You told the department about the grant, I hope?"

"From nowhere a brand-new detective gets a half-million bucks dropped in her lap? God, yes. I'd have been suspected of being on a pad for either the Mafia or Donald Trump. Turns out the lawyer, Mr Solomon Epperman, esquire, was a heavy hitter in his day, still is when he wants to be. Mr Epperman had a talk with the brass, convinced them the giver would remain anonymous, no strings."

"Not someone who could pop up one day and pressure you."

"Yep. Like, 'Look, hon, I laid a half mill on you, now fix my parking ticket.'" Folger slapped her forehead. "Duh, I was going to make you some hot syrup with tea in it. Fix up your tum-tum."

"Beer is remedy of choice for the Southern male."

"I can do that."

She bounced from the couch, went to the kitchen area, yelling at me over her shoulder. "Bathroom's first door down the hall if you want to wash up and gargle. I'd advise both."

I headed to the bathroom, shoulder-tight, with all the usual fixtures. I turned the hot-water faucet, let it run. A mirrored medicine cabinet was over the sink. My eyes were veined from upchucking, my hair in disarray. There were several disturbing flecks sticking to my chin.

I filled the sink with hot water, palming soap into it, slapping the froth on my face. I emptied the sink, did the same bit with cold water, sans the soap, my rinse cycle. I fought the impulse for a ten-count, then, under cover of running water, opened her medicine cabinet, scanning.

All typical stuff, over-the-counter analgesics and nostrums, a couple prescriptions I recognized as a stomach-acid reducer and an allergy relief med.

Two hard knocks hit the door a foot from my ear. "Ryder!"

I whipped the cabinet closed. The magnetic latch clicked, sounding as loud as a pistol shot. I saw my grimace in the mirror.

"Uh, what . . . Alice?"

"There's nothing interesting in the medicine cabinet. But there's a new toothbrush in the closet. You can have it if you promise to buy me a replacement."

My heart pounding with childish guilt, I turned off the water and started to respond, but her footsteps were moving away. I gratefully accepted the brush, using toothpaste and mouth-wash in deluge quantities.

When I emerged, much refreshed, she was in the kitchen area. The last few feet of the hall was bookshelves, books of all sorts. I looked closer and noted the two bottom shelves, ten running feet altogether, were devoted to meteor-ology. I slid one out: *The Physics of Climate Change*. It seemed the sort of text one studied in college, maybe even post-grad. I slipped it back, pulled another. A biography of someone named Carl-Gustav Rosby.

"Who's Rosby?" I asked.

She turned and saw me with the book. Her neck colored. "He, uh, was a pioneer of high-atmosphere meteorology." She walked over, hiding embarrassment behind a sip of wine. "I really like reading about weather. I know it seems weird."

I took a bottle of Sam Adams from her hand and nodded toward the shelves. "Makes perfect sense to me. I fish and kayak in the Gulf. The last surprise I want is high surf or lightning. I'm a Doppler devotee. Did you know that Mobile is the rainiest city in the country?"

"Followed by Pensacola, New Orleans, and West Palm Beach." She looked at me as if trying to make a decision. "Would you like to see my station? My weather station?"

"Lead on."

I followed her down the hall to the back room. There was a desk and a Mac Pro computer connected to a large flat-panel display. More books on shelves. Two big snake plants on the floor and ivy leaves tumbling from a wall sconce *cum* planter.

She pointed to the Mac. "I've got a sensor

station on the roof. The physical readings happen up there, wireless info bursted to the computer every two seconds. Air temp, wind speed and direction, solar radiation, relative humidity, barometric pressure, precipitation. Plus I've got my weather program and input networked to eighty-two remote stations across the country, sites run by amateur meteorologists through related software. I helped create the net. I could tell you what it's doing in Paducah, Dubuque, Ypsilanti . . ."

I crossed my arms and posed a challenge. "How about Fort Wayne, Indiana?"

"Why Fort Wayne?"

"An old friend lives there. Can you do it?"

She sat and commenced a furious ticking of keystrokes, conjuring charts, graphs, numbers, a maelstrom of American weatherness. Her interest was infectious, and I leaned over her shoulder and watched the screen, unable to ignore the scent of perfume from her hair, something warm and sunny.

"Here we go. The station in Fort Wayne is operated by a Duanine Eby, I don't know if that's a him or her, but it's raining – a tenth of an inch so far – baro pressure is 1016.36 millibars and rising over the past two hours.

Wind is northwest at present, shifted from north-northwest this morning, holding steady. Let's check a bit south, Indianapolis. Wind is west, baro's higher, so Fort Wayne's about to catch the edge of a southerly high pushing up from the Gulf, now centered around Memphis. In two hours the rain will disappear, the wind will pick up for a couple hours, then presto, your friend in Fort Wayne will be in a new system. Blue sky, nothing but blue sky . . ."

"Alice?"

"What?"

"This is great."

She looked over her shoulder, skeptical. "You really think so? You enjoy meteorology that much?"

"I enjoy your enjoyment."

The embarrassment again, manifesting in a pause and a cleared throat. "I've loved the weather since sixth grade. My father took me to the Jersey shore, Cape May. I watched storms forming, clouds merge, darken. Curtains of rain connected the clouds and the ocean. It took my breath away. I got books on weather from the library and built a hygrometer made from three of my dad's hairs, a dime, and a plastic milk carton. I kept daily accounts in a notebook called Alice's Weather Observations. Every night at dinner I'd solemnly forecast the next day's weather."

I laughed at the sight of a young Alice Folger holding forth at the table.

"What did your parents think about all this?"

"I was an only child. I could do no wrong."

I saw a photo at the far side of the desk, a big, lantern-jawed officer in dress blues, his arm around a solid woman in a white gown, sweet eyes in a plain face. They were in their middle-to-late thirties, I judged, and resembled a pair of happy potatoes.

"These are your parents?"

A pause, as though she had to switch gears. "On their wedding day in 1963. Myrtle and Johnny at Niagara Falls."

"Your dad was a cop."

She looked at the photo. "It seems like everyone I grew up with was or became a cop. Every male, at least. A lot of women, too. Mainly support work."

"You have siblings? Oh, you said you were an only child. I guess you were expected to carry the blue banner forward, right?"

Two long beats passed. "My choice. Mine alone."

"Sure."

"It's all I ever wanted to do as far back as I remember."

In the span of a minute something had changed. It was small, a shadow in the corner of the room, weightless, but detracting from the overall light. She turned from the wall, pushed a smile to her face.

"Hey, you look like you're feeling better."

I held up the beer. "What the doctor ordered. Listen, I'll be heading on back to the hotel. I'm studying the Ridgecliff files. I might be able to close in on what part of town he's operating from."

"It's good to have you out of your shell, thinking. You need a ride to the hotel? I can run you in the –"

I waved my hands and shook my head. "I think a little air is necessary. I'm going to take a walk, see what's happening in the neighborhood. Thanks for taking pity on a guy leaning against a lamppost, Lieutenant."

I was half a block away before I realized I'd left everything to do with the cases at the door when entering Alice Folger's house, and she'd done the same, at least for thirty minutes.

My nicest half hour in New York since I'd arrived.

# NINETEEN

I went back to the hotel that night reflecting on my brief time with a living, breathing, happy Folger. I had felt an attraction to her, I realized, a roiling in my guts that I didn't in any way need.

For a year or so, I'd kept close company with Clair Peltier, the head of pathology for the Alabama Bureau of Forensics. Our early fires had banked into warm coals these days, as we discovered we were closer as friends than as lovers. Still, the physical relationship was something we'd had to experience in order to discover we were destined to be friends. New Age-y sorts would call us soul mates I suppose, beings who have crossed several lifetimes together, and who can now communicate about everything through a glance and a gesture.

I'd called her earlier to see if she'd speak to Waltz's NYPD forensics guy. Our conversation made me recall how comfortable we were, and that the relationship was what I enjoyed at the moment.

Still, thinking of Folger made my heart race. So I pulled on my running shoes and shorts. Time to switch my head off, wear my body down. I did a few minutes of cleansing breathing, trying to regain the calm I'd felt at Alice Folger's house, then beat feet from the hotel aiming south, picking up speed, feeling the night slide by like cool water.

My calves gave out about the time my breath did and I pulled up short on a slender street somewhere in the East Village or Lower East Side. My hands were on my knees and I was sucking hard breaths when my phone rang.

"Yeh-he?" I wheezed instead of spoke, sounding like Cluff.

"Ryder? Is that you? I didn't hear what you said."

"Folger?" I gasped.

"You OK? You sound –"

"Running. Winded. Gimme sec."

"Where are you?"

"South of . . . hotel somewhere. Zig-zagged all over. Probably lost."

"Check a street sign. Hurry."

I half jogged, half limped to a pair of street signs. "I'm at Prince and Elizabeth. I see a church spire a block down."

"Old Saint Pat's, northwest of you. Can you grab a cab? There'll be cabs on Houston, north of Prince."

I saw a flow of headlights and taillights a block away. "I see the traffic. Could you tell me what this is –"

"Hustle, please. Here's the address . . ."

Folger answered my shave-and-a-haircut knock dressed in exercise shorts and a filmy sleeveless top. Brown leather moccasins on her feet. There was a nine millimeter semi-auto in her hand, aimed at the floor.

"You always arm yourself for company?" I said.

She put her hand on my back to usher me into the living room, then leaned out the door, her eyes scanning the street in both directions before ducking inside.

"I saw a face at the window. Someone was looking inside. When I checked, no one was there. But look . . ."

212

She set the nine down and picked up a high-intensity flashlight from a small table. She opened the door and steadied the beam on the deadbolt. I scoped out the left keyhole, saw scratches cut through the faux-antique finish.

"Lock pick, you think?" she asked. "Sure looks like it to me."

I slid my fingernail over the scratches. Fairly deep, considering the hardness of the finish. "What were you doing when it happened?" I asked.

"Checking the weather before taking a shower and tottering off to beddy-bye. I've been tracking an ENSO and it's –"

"ENSO?"

"El Nino-Southern Oscillation episode, a disruption of normal tropical precipitation that . . ." She caught herself, shifted back to the problem at hand. "I had the Weather Channel on. When I shut down the computer and turned off the TV, I heard the scratches. I heard someone yell, 'Hey you! I see you!' A deep, hard voice. Scary. I went for my weapon, crept low toward the windows. Looked out and saw nothing. It took thirty, forty seconds for me to get from the desk to the door."

"You see who called out?"

"No. A guy with a big voice. Probably saw someone at the door, yelled. Didn't want to hang around and get involved. Good for him, anyway."

"Why didn't you call your people? Bullard. Cluff. Anyone. You've got the whole NYPD at your beck and call." I paused, had one of those cartoon-lightbulb-over-the-head moments, smiled gently. "You didn't want to seem upset in front of your people, so you called the Mobile Police."

"No . . . I mean, yes. It would have been embarrassing. There's been strangeness happening for a couple of weeks." Her eyes studied mine. "You've got the sense, right? The tingle when things aren't what they seem?"

"The cop sense? I have my share."

The cop sense is when you know things by the feel of the air. Or a shiver in the spine. Or a twitching in the gut that says *something's off*. Harry hears a distant siren in his head.

Folger's long bare legs scissored across the room to the window. She was dressed for lazing around the house, braless, her tidy breasts bobbing beneath the thin fabric. She studied the street, turned to me.

"I've had a screwy feeling. Like I'm being watched."

"Found anything to back it up?"

"I saw a parked car someone might be watching from, but it zoomed off. I feel eyes. But when I turn my head, nothing." Folger spun a finger at her temple. "Maybe I should run you back to your hotel before they lock me in the loony bin."

"You never saw anyone?"

"Just shadows. A few days back I was running in the park and the feeling was strong as it gets. I lost my cool and acted like an idiot. When I spun and saw a big guy jump behind some bushes, I ran over and dragged him out."

"What happened?"

"Guy had a terrified look on his face and a leash in his hand. His mutt had jumped at a cat, broke the leash clip. The poor bastard was trying to find his dog." She hung her head. "I'm not kidding, Ryder. Maybe I am going nuts."

"Thinking you're going crazy is the best protection against going crazy. You recently have a tough breakup with a significant other?"

She pushed a loose lock of dark hair behind an ear and laughed without humor. "I vaguely recall dating. Isn't there a movie involved? Dinner?"

"You piss off anyone in the line of duty?"

"Almost daily. Perps and colleagues both. But

I racked my mind on perps and ruled it out. That leaves going bonkers."

She sat on the couch heavily, dropped her chin in her hands, sighed. I sat beside her, on my own separate couch cushion. As per Old South tradition, one could have fitted a Bible between our respective thighs, making it proper. A stack of holy tomes, however, would have done nothing to blunt the scent of her perfume as it mingled with the scent of her fear, an olfactory cannonball that blasted me into dizziness. I turned my eyes from her hands, her thighs, her lap, spoke to the far wall.

"Shelly tells me you're very smart and intuitive. I think you'd know whether or not you're being followed."

"That's sweet of Waltz. I think he's amazing. I just wish he seemed happier."

I told her Koslowski's story about how a laughing Waltz used to brighten a bar by walking through the door.

"What made him so unhappy?"

"Koslowski didn't know, just that the Waltz of long ago was a lot happier than the Waltz of today."

She put her feet up on the coffee table, shifted her body an inch my way. "I guess everyone has secrets," she said. "Even Shelly Waltz. Speaking of secrets, I don't expect to hear anyone talking about my weather obsession. Thanks in advance."

"You just lost me," I said.

"After you left this afternoon, I realized how goofy it must have seemed – me chattering about frontal systems, getting lost in the weather. I figured you'd tell people on the force. Like, 'Hey, guys, you won't believe what Folger does at home. She's queer for clouds.' Then I realized you're not like that. I misjudged you and I apologize."

"You didn't know me. And love of weather isn't an obsession, Alice. It's cool."

She tipped my way another inch or so. "You really, truly don't think it's weird?"

I picked up her hand, held it between mine. "You're fascinated by the science of climatology. Weather's everywhere."

She looked at our hands. Her body tipped closer until our shoulders touched and I felt her warmth, smelled the wild spices of her body. Her lips softened. "Whoops. Here's honest-to-gosh proof I'm weirding out."

"What's that?" I whispered.

Her lips parted and moved toward mine.

\* \* \*

Jeremy Ridgecliff leaned forward and tapped the taxi driver on the shoulder.

"We can go now, Ludis. I think it's time for a repast."

"Re- what?"

"I'm hungry. I'm so very hungry lately."

"YOU SEE WHAT YOU WANT HERE AGAIN? FOR YOUR MOVIE?"

"I think some pivotal scenes will be shot here. Take me to a restaurant. Italian. Candlelight."

"We drive in LITTLE ITALY! Look in restaurant windows for candles, how that work? Maybe see PRETTY GIRLS. I know you LOVE looking at the girls."

Ridgecliff studied the streets, shops, houses, entranced at what was there for the seeing.

"Beauty, Ludis. There's so much of it out here."

"WHAT YOU MEAN? Out here where?"

"On this side of the wall. No, don't ask. Find me some candles."

As the cab pulled from the curb, Jeremy Ridgecliff took a final glance at the brownstone with the lovely window boxes. His stomach growled, and he laughed.

# TWENTY

Seven a.m. found me sitting at Alice Folger's kitchen table, coffee perking merrily. I heard a throat cleared, turned. She was in the doorway wrapped in a thick terry robe, white, her face a cross between apology and embarrassment. A sincere but strained look. She might have also attempted cheery bravado, another common mask for a morning meeting with someone you've had an unplanned night with, a night where conversation was often monosyllabic.

I held up my hand like a Hollywood Indian. Instead of *How*, I said, "Don't."

"Don't what?"

"Don't apologize or be embarrassed or do or say anything that isn't perfectly you, which is perfectly magical." I pointed to the coffee pot. "You ready for some brew, Weather Lady?"

Embarrassment turned into a smile, the smile turning wry, escalating to a grin. She shook the robe from her shoulders to the floor.

"Eventually."

We reconvened at the kitchen table a half-hour later. She toasted bagels and set out cream cheese and lox, and we ate like confirmed Manhattanites. She licked pink lox from a matching thumb.

"We probably shouldn't walk into the station together this morning. Wagging tongues and all that."

"I'm hitting the hotel for a change and a shower. I've been thinking about Ridgecliff, want to run some more ideas past y'all today."

"You seemed like you made a breakthrough or something yesterday, like information about Ridgecliff was pouring into your head."

I looked away. "It's the way it felt."

"Keep that faucet turned on," she said, kissing my forehead.

The sun was fresh to the blue eastern sky as Harry Nautilus pulled into the white sand drive of Evangeline Prowse's cabin. He had been an idiot yesterday, letting Jeremy Ridgecliff's photo stun him into stumbling from her cottage without taking the photo. Carson would want to see the thing. And the picture wasn't the sort of item to be left for anyone to find.

Maybe the Doc had some kind of strange relationship with Ridgecliff, but after twenty-plus years as a cop, Nautilus realized when it came to vagaries of the heart, anything was possible.

When he entered Prowse's cottage the place felt more haunted than yesterday, something jingling Nautilus's alarm system. He opened a closet by the front door to see a shiny, store-bought sign saying, DO NOT DISTURB, red letters over black. Helen Pappagallos had for-sure seen a sign.

He tossed it back into the closet and went to the office, rolling up the Ridgecliff photo. Something continued to register on his alert system, faint, like the pulsing of a distant siren.

Nautilus checked out the window behind Prowse's desk. He turned to see a red light blinking on her answering machine. *Blip, blip, blip*. The message was setting off his alarm; he didn't know how these signals worked, was glad they did.

Nautilus sat in Prowse's chair – comfortable, a Herman Miller – and pressed the Play button. The phone beeped and dated the phone call as having arrived last night at eight. A voice appeared in the air.

*"Doctor Prowse, this is John Wyatt. It's been a few months and I was wondering if you found everything you needed in the files I sent. I guess I'm also wondering if you're working on something related and interesting. Hell, everything you do is interesting, at least to folks like me. Anyway, keep me cued in and if you need anything else, just give me a yell."*

An interesting message. Nautilus dialed back.

"FBI . . ." an assured female voice said. "Behavioral Sciences Division."

"This is Detective Harry Nautilus with the Mobile Police Department. I'm returning John Wyatt's call."

"One moment please."

The phone picked up seconds later. "This is John Wyatt, Detective Nautilus. I don't recollect calling you."

"You didn't. I'm returning the call you made to Dr Evangeline Prowse. I'm in her office and just found your message. I'm very sorry to have to tell you that Dr Prowse is dead."

A three-beat pause as the information was absorbed, contemplated, accepted.

"My God. What happened?"

"She was murdered in New York six days ago. No one's sure why, but there's a suspect in mind. I'm looking into things on the Southern end and found your phone message. Might I ask what you sent the Doctor?"

Wyatt sounded rattled. "Let me get my head back. What a tragedy . . . she was a great lady, brilliant. Uh, let's see if I can give you a chronology. Dr Prowse called me about a month back and asked for information on the DC snipers. You know of the pair, of course."

"John Allen Muhammad and Lee Boyd Malvo. Killed ten people back in 2002. At random."

Nautilus saw a mind-picture of the fortyish, good-looking Muhammad with his arm around the much younger Malvo, a bright grin on the kid's face, like he's about to float away into Joyland.

Wyatt said, "Doctor Prowse wanted everything the Bureau had on the pair, especially psychological work-ups and personal histories – how they met, ages at the time of meeting, relationship with one another . . ."

Nautilus one-handedly slipped a notepad from the pocket of his lime-green jacket, began taking notes.

"Just Muhammad and Malvo?" he asked.

"Yep. Oh, and she wanted the information ASAP."

"That was unusual?"

"Very. Dr Prowse generally needed Bureau info for a scholarly article or a presentation at a symposium, that kind of thing. It was always 'Send it when you find a spare moment.' But she wanted me to send the DC snipers material as fast as I put it all together."

"Which you did."

"Anything Dr Prowse wanted, she got. She came as close to understanding psychopathic minds as anyone I've ever known; an empath."

"She say why she was so interested in the pair?"

"I took it she was studying the hold John Muhammad had over Malvo. How it got started, how strong the hold was. She did mention something about 'looking into someone's past'. I thought she was referring to one of the snipers, but in retrospect, maybe not."

Nautilus wrote *looking into someone's past* in his notepad, paused, underscored *someone's*.

"The kid, Malvo, was what age at the time of the shooting rampage – sixteen?"

"Seventeen," Wyatt said. "Muhammad was forty-two. An ex-Marine with the highest classification in marksmanship. He passed the sniper skills on to Malvo." Wyatt sighed. "My father taught me to hunt rabbits."

"The kid take to the skills willingly, or was there coercion?"

"Willingly. But Lee Malvo was under a bad star from the git-go, lived poor in Jamaica, no steady male influence in his childhood. His mother abandoned him regularly. Muhammad befriended Malvo's mother, stayed with Mommy and son a while in Antigua. Muhammad probably seemed a stable influence in the kid's life. An authority figure."

"A drifting kid finds an anchor," Nautilus said.

"Fast-forward a decade to Bellingham, Washington. Muhammad enrolls Malvo in high school, telling everyone he's the kid's biological father."

"Muhammad's closing the deal."

"The little lost boy finally has a daddy, big and strong and protective. I figure Lee Malvo was so desperate for a father he would have let

225

Charles Manson put him on a leash and walk him on hands and knees over broken glass, as long as he could call Manson 'Papa'."

"Unfortunately, Daddy's a psychopath."

"A big drawback. When Muhammad and Malvo got caught, they were planning to murder a cop, plant an IED at the funeral, make more corpses. The ultimate plan was to blackmail the government – they'd stop the carnage for ten million dollars."

"Incredible."

"Here's the post script, Detective. They planned to use part of the money to find and recruit other emotionally devastated young boys. Muhammad hoped to train them, set them loose across the US."

"Murder missions," Nautilus whispered.

"You got it, Detective. A cadre of robot sons killing to please Daddy."

# TWENTY-ONE

Alice dropped me at the hotel on the way to work. I went upstairs, showered, put on a fresh new shirt and pants.

Recalling that I hadn't talked to my favorite boss in a couple days, I called and gave Tom Mason a broad overview of events, pledging to return as soon as possible. Though my absence left Tom a slot short in his roster, he seemed proud one of his cops had been called to New York to work a case. Or maybe me being gone made his life easier. I was about to ring off when I recalled the PSIT cases Tom had sent Waltz, making Folger decide maybe I was a pretty decent detective, even if I wasn't NYPD.

"Hey, Tom, thanks for sending the case outlines to Detective Waltz."

"Wasn't nothing. He said you'd mentioned the hundred per cent solve rate and he wanted to pass details to some lady lieutenant looking to break your whatevers."

"My whatevers are fine, Tom. The Lieutenant and I are seeing eye to eye now."

Tom sighed. "Yankees."

"You know they actually named a baseball team that?"

"Go figure."

"What'd you think of Shelly Waltz?" I asked.

"He seemed a gentleman. Interested in how you got on the force, made detective. Real impressed with your history here in Mobile. Even wanted to know a bit about your upbringing."

My internal ears pricked up, hearing the alarm that sounds whenever my past is a topic.

"Upbringing?"

"Where you grew up, family ties, that sort of thing. You kind of moved around as a kid, right? No daddy, your mama an army nurse? I couldn't really remember."

*Because I suggested a false story of my past once, Tom.* Then never mentioned it again, wanting only the impression to remain.

I faked a yawn. "Not a whole lot to tell."

"No close relatives, anything like that?"

228

"Hmmp? Shelly ask that, too?"

I heard Tom sip from the coffee mug ever-present in his hand. He yelled something across the room, listened to the response, came back on the line.

"Just family stuff. You from a big family, little family? Tight or scattered around? Any brothers or sisters that went into law enforcement? The usual questions about what made a country kid want to become a city cop."

"What'd you tell him?"

"That I never recalled you mentioning much about family and I thought you might have been an only kid. That's right, isn't it?"

It's strange the allowances I make to retain a semblance of integrity. I didn't lie, I suggested. I never led down the primrose path, I let someone make assumptions. I never dodged, I distracted.

"Aw crap," I yelped, looking at my watch, a method actor.

"What?"

"I just looked at my watch. Late for a meeting. I gotta go."

"I heard about them New York minutes. You take care and don't let 'em run you ragged. Oh, Carson?"

229

"Yeah, Tom?"

His voice dropped into serious. My mind's eye saw concern furrowing his brow. "You're gonna nail that sumbitch, right? That Ridgecliff fella?"

"Ridgecliff's all I think about, Tom. Day and night."

"Get him, boy. Take him down."

We hung up. Though the room was cool, sweat peppered my forehead, drew my shirt tight to my sides. Shelly's questioning Tom Mason about my history was in all likelihood totally innocent, two cops talking about the only thing they had in common: me. But any questions involving my past sent my heart rate soaring, and now was no exception.

I hit the street at a run, making it to the precinct house at nine fifteen. The crew was in what had been dubbed "the Ridgecliff Room", the conference room displaying the timelines and photos. Bullard and Cluff were drinking coffee and pushing sleep from their faces. I shot a look at Alice Folger, got a smile back, a split-second wink. Waltz was sifting through the night's reports. He looked up.

"You took over yesterday, Detective. You felt strongly about Ridgecliff, obviously."

"Things started to come together, Shelly."

"You're fully convinced Ridgecliff's looking upscale? Everyone else had him pegged for low end."

"He thinks he's being slick, but he's also programmed in several ways."

"Like wanting *GQ* clothes and shoes after years of uniforms and slippers?"

"Not wanting, needing. He needs to be the opposite of what he was in the Institute."

Bullard said, "I don't see how Ridgecliff has a choice in the situation." He shot a glance at Folger to make sure his tone was suitably professional.

I waved it away, *no*. "We have to stop thinking of Ridgecliff's situation as controlling him. We have to figure he's controlling the situation."

Bullard grunted dissent. "He can't control the situation when we're on his ass."

"You kept the surveillance in place at the homeless camp, right?"

"I wasn't going to take your word that –"

"He didn't show, did he?"

Bullard reddened and looked away. Cluff stepped into the circle. "You're saying . . ."

"We have to picture Jeremy Ridgecliff as a rich man on vacation in New York. That's the life he's living."

Bullard shook his head. "Except now and then something makes him want to cut a woman apart?"

"Yes."

Bullard was reaching his limit again. "I don't give a fuck how smart Ridgecliff is, he's still a loony. Where's he getting money? We checked Prowse's accounts, no major withdrawals in the past six months. Ryder says Ridgecliff's scamming the money, but won't say how." He jutted his chin at me like a challenge.

I said, "You've never known anyone like Ridgecliff, Detective. He's a different order of magnitude."

"What? He pulls gold coins out his ass? How's he paying for all these fancy suits and Park Avenue apartments and whatever else you think he's doing?"

I froze. *Gold coins?* A conversation from days ago played in my head, the two dicks in Property Crimes discussing a paranoid schizophrenic.

*"Seems Gerald came home last night, snuck in the husband's office safe and grabbed forty-seven grand's worth of Krugerrands the investment guy had stashed . . . Said he was buying his freedom from the CIA."*

"Don't move," I said. "I'll be right back."

I sprinted to Property Crimes, eyes following like I'd frazzled my wires. Two minutes later I was back, a puzzled cop on my heels, Sergeant Brian Hedley.

"Tell them, Sergeant. About the investment guy who got ripped off by his paranoid brother-in-law."

A bemused Hedley reprised his tale of the paranoid conspiracy theorist who had been convinced to steal tens of thousands of dollars in Krugerrands and cash by a man posing as a fellow object of governmental harassment.

Waltz said, "You're saying Ridgecliff is the perp here?"

Bullard grinned and clapped his hands. "We can check this one out, Ryder. The limb's gonna bust off under you, and I'm gonna laugh the loudest."

"It won't take long to verify," Waltz said, grabbing his hat.

# TWENTY-TWO

A rolled photo under his arm, Harry Nautilus strode into the morgue, more correctly the pathology department of the Alabama Forensics Bureau, south-western region. He waved at Vera Braden, the creamy-voiced receptionist, saluted Fred Tomlinson, the elderly security guard. Tomlinson returned the salute and went back to reading the newspaper.

Nautilus found Doctor Clair Peltier behind her massive wood desk, a crystal vase on her desk overflowing with flowers from her garden. Given the competing scents in the morgue, Nautilus was happy the Doc was a gardener.

"So what is it, Harry?" Peltier asked. "Your call wasn't exactly a font of information."

Nautilus leaned back to look out Peltier's

door; no one in the hall. Still, he closed the door. "I wanted to show you something, Doc. Just between us."

Puzzlement clouded Peltier's arctic blue eyes. "Sure."

Nautilus unrolled the photo. He stood across from Peltier's desk and held it up. She studied the shot.

"He's a damn good-looking . . . wait, is that? My God, Harry, is that . . . ?"

"Yep. Jeremy Ridgecliff dressed only in his own skin. A recent photo."

Peltier pulled her lanyarded reading glasses to her face, studied the photograph. "I've only seen photos from Ridgecliff's arrest. He looked like a kid, though he was twenty-six. He still could pass for early thirties." She dropped the glasses back to her waist. "Any specific reason you wanted me to see this?"

"Because you're one of the few who know the secret about Carson and Jeremy Ridgecliff. And you know Carson. Put your glasses on again. Look at Ridgecliff's expression."

She pulled the half-glasses to her face. "And?"

"The look on Ridgecliff's face . . . isn't that almost the exact expression Carson gets when

235

he's . . ." Nautilus let the words hang, wanting to be no further influence.

Peltier's mouth fell open. Her hand flew to cover it.

"When he's about to confess something he's been hiding. Half-frown, half sad-ass smile. Teeth tight together. Jeez, Harry, now that you mention it, that's Carson's Ready or Not, Here it Comes look. I once told him I could hear that look in the dark."

"The boy'll never be a poker player. I'm glad you agree. I thought maybe I was going nuts."

"You're not. Who the hell took the picture?"

Nautilus re-rolled the photograph. "Uh, it looks like the photographer was Evangeline Prowse. It would have been taken at the Institute."

Peltier raised a dark and slender eyebrow. "Carson's trip to New York. It's bad? He's been real close-lipped."

"He's walking a fine line. I get the feeling the less we know, the better. I think he's trying to keep me insulated for a couple reasons."

Peltier prodded a small clear bag on her desk. "I just received my own piece of New York. A sample of hair and fiber evidence collected at two Manhattan crime scenes, heavy on the hair follicles. You heard? Gathered from New York salons and barber shops, mixed with a ragpicker's sampling of fibers. The NYPD forensics folks think it's useless, especially since they're convinced it was gathered by Ridgecliff, and he's already the prime suspect . . ."

"Gotcha. So why is it here?"

"Carson wanted me to see if there was anything I could discern from the material."

Nautilus sighed. "Carson being Carson. What're you planning to do? Wait until he forgets about it and fixates on something else?"

"I'm going to load it all in the gas chromatograph. I'll burn it, then the toxicologist and I will read the combined results of the hairs from several hundred heads."

"Isn't that stuff usually run a hair or two at a time?"

"It's all I can do. It's like dropping a net over a thousand horses."

"Won't the result be a net full of horses?"

Peltier folded her arms and stared at the bag of hair like it had challenged her to a duel.

"Unless I somehow see a zebra."

Nautilus held his confusion in check. He tucked the photo under his arm. "I'm out of here. I've actually got a Mobile case or two to deal with. Then I have to call Carson and fill him in on what I've been digging up."

"Anything big?"

"A mish-mash of weirdness with no common denominator. There was the photo, of course. Plus an invisible client of Prowse's, and from nowhere a mention of the DC Snipers. What happened to the good old days of drive-bys and domestic shootings?"

"Thanks for showing me the photograph, Harry. That look on Ridgecliff's face is amazing and kind of scary. It truly is Carson's confession look."

"They're brothers," Nautilus said. "Same blood, same genes. Carson said that when they were kids, one could start a sentence and the other would finish it without missing a word."

"Like twins, born six years apart."

"A few differences, thankfully," Nautilus said. He flicked a wave and walked out the door.

Peltier suppressed a shudder that came from nowhere. She stared at the bag of evidence from the NYPD, then filled out the request for a gas chromatograph mass spectrometer test, underscoring the word immediate.

*     *     *

Rebecca Weinglass stood beside her Krugerrand-appropriating brother, Gerald Orman, a - mousy-gray, fortyish man in a faded cardigan, gray slacks, leather slippers. Orman hunched low in a plush chair in the center of the condo's expansive living room. The furniture, Oriental carpets and objets d'art said we were in a place where large amounts of gold were at home. So did Ms Weinglass's dress, a designer something-or-other that did a good job of disguising her stout frame. Since we hadn't called ahead, I figured she wore the diamonds every morning at breakfast.

Ms Weinglass's stubby and bejeweled fingers squeezed Gerald's thin shoulder. He winced at the touch. Gerald looked as if he would have been more comfortable at the Spanish Inquisition, the effect of a half-dozen cops staring at him.

"Gerald has been taking his medications," Ms Weinglass crooned. "It's brought him back to us. He's promised to keep taking his meddies. Isn't that right, hon?"

Gerald didn't look so sure. A fair amount of those with delusions and hallucinations think the meds make them dull and robotic, and they prefer the rush of internal voices and colors that sing.

Waltz stepped closer to Gerald. "We think we may have a lead on the man, Mr Orman. We'd like you to look at a photograph. You recall him, don't you? The man who made you take the money and gold?"

Orman squinted and blinked rapidly. If he'd had whiskers I'd have tossed him a chunk of cheddar.

"Not . . . very well. It was dark. And I was terrified. At first I thought he was going to kill me. He was very frightening."

"Poor dear," Ms Weinglass recited, patting Gerald's shoulder. He winced and sank lower in the chair.

Waltz slipped the trifolded photo from his jacket pocket, unfolded it. Everyone leaned a little closer. Waltz held the photo a foot from Gerald's nose.

"Ever seen this man before?" Waltz said.

Gerald closed his eyes and began twitching all over.

"I'll take that as a yes," Waltz said.

When we got back to the station I was The Man. Even Bullard stayed quiet. The whole Ridgecliff team, main and peripheral, followed me into the conference room. Cargyle was pulled in by the hubbub, carrying a broken monitor, yammering into a phone, tools slapping at his side. Even two janitors got caught in our forward motion, grinning in the corner and watching the show.

Folger took the lectern, clapped her hands to get attention.

"Listen up, people. I want everyone to start showing Ridgecliff's photo at toney eateries. Other suggestions, Ryder? Your gut's got the floor."

"Ridgecliff has dark hair. Black probably. I'd bet on a mustache, too. He'll be disguised as a . . . a . . ."

*It wasn't my gut talking. It was years of life with my brother. A brother who had always lamented his pale yellow hair – my father's hair – calling it the color of phlegm, always wishing he could trade it for my head upholstery, brown almost to black.*

I froze and saw my brother in my mind. Listened to his words over the years. Heard him speaking a few phrases in a foreign language.

"Aloiso is a good man, Carson . . . *um homem bom. Tem problemas, mas nós todos temos problemas.*"

I went to the window and looked out, yet

saw nothing but the movies in my head. I made mental tallies of data, subtracting what didn't fit. I felt my pulse quicken and sweat prickle on my forehead.

Everyone stood back and gave me room to pace, afraid of breaking the spell. I painted a picture of my brother in my head, added a shift in eye color via tinted contacts – simple with money – tossed in three bucks' worth of hair color, and perhaps a couple visits to a tanning salon or using a skin toner to ameliorate his pale skin.

"Come on, Ryder," Cluff prompted. "What?"

Images whirled, facts aligned. The answer fell into place as perfectly as if whispered in my ear.

"He's a Portuguese businessman," I said.

"No way," Bullard spat.

I said, "One of the patients at the Institute is Aloiso Silviera. He and Ridgecliff were buddies."

Aloiso Silviera was a rapist-murderer of Portuguese descent who terrorized Boston for seven years. Jeremy had always spoken of Silviera with a sort of condescending camaraderie.

"*Aloiso's unhappy in love, Carson. But he has a primitive charm, a love of beauty,* um amor da beleza."

242

Cluff winced. "Friends? Silviera?"

"Less a friendship than an alliance. Ridgecliff forms alliances with people he can take something from. I've heard him speak Portuguese. Small phrases."

Cluff said, "That's hardly enough to pass as a –"

"You don't understand, Detective. Ridgecliff wouldn't have used any Portuguese phrases unless he felt fluent in the language."

"Why the hell not?"

"He'd consider it presumptuous."

Cluff's pencil hit the desk. "I'm not buying into –"

"Shhh," Folger said. "Keep going, Ryder. If Ridgecliff speaks Portuguese, it makes sense he'd use it in his disguise. Your gut tell you why he's here?"

"To kill," Cluff said. "That's obvious."

"Maybe. Ridgecliff would see the prospect of killing in Manhattan as a supreme challenge. The ultimate high-wire act."

Folger gave me a look teetering between belief and doubt. "Bottom line: Jeremy Ridgecliff is a dark-haired, well-dressed Portuguese businessman living in an upscale neighborhood? That's the way you're seeing him?"

"I think it's a strong assumption."

A call came for Cluff and he slipped away to take it. I fended off Devil's Advocate questions about my conclusion, strengthening my own belief along the way.

Cluff returned, held up a page of fresh notes. Cleared his throat. "Maybe we should keep looking other directions as well."

"Why's that?" Folger asked.

Cluff flicked a page. "I finally got some background on the Bernal vic, the one without a history? Looks like she worked at Bridges."

"Son of a bitch," Waltz said. "Bridges."

"Bridges?" Cargyle said, looking startled. "She, uh, worked on bridges?"

"*At* Bridges, kid," Cluff said. "Bridges Juvenile Center. Over in the Bronx, medium to high security, tough cases. Bernal was a housekeeper at Bridges for four or five years. It stopped five years back when Bernal got citizenship, started climbing the ladder to better jobs."

Waltz looked at me. "Juvie detention. With Dora Anderson working in Child Welfare in Newark back then, there was some overlap. We've got a possible connection between Anderson and Bernal. Troubled kids."

They were running down the wrong path again. I shook my head, *no, no no*.

"Pure coincidence," I said. "Ridgecliff was in the Institute when the two women worked in the juvie system."

Cluff raised an eyebrow at Folger, "Your call, Lieutenant. Should I keep digging on Bernal?"

Folger shook her head. "Not now, but I reserve the right to change my mind."

"Woman's prerogative," Bullard said. He could have said it funny or shaded it toward sarcastic. He leaned it the second way. Folger's eyes narrowed in his direction.

"What'd I say?" he wheedled. "Jeez, sorry for fucking living."

Folger clapped her hands for attention. "Here's the drill: Suspend background checking of Anderson and Bernal, we don't have the time. Get Ridgecliff's pic doctored like Ryder says and start pushing it past maître-ds and rental agents and the like."

Everything I suggested was done. The detectives hit the streets with updated photos and new avenues to find their quarry. Waltz had testimony on a case, went out the door practicing his lines. It was past lunch and I hit a Thai restaurant a few blocks down the street.

When I returned an hour later, Waltz was back at his desk. "How'd the testimony go?" I asked.

He put his hand high above his head, snapped it down. "Slam dunk." He was in a good mood like everyone else on the case, the effect of seeing light at the end of the tunnel. It wasn't much, a half a lumen maybe, but it was supernova bright compared to all the dark we'd seen.

"Cool. Anything showing up on Ridgecliff?"

"We may be working our way up court on that one, too. Perlstein dug up a waiter at Chez Pierre, a la-di-da place on 64th. The waiter said the guy's face resembled the pic of our new Ridgecliff, with the dark hair and eyes. The waiter said the customer barely spoke English. He ordered by poking his finger at the menu, asking, 'Is this a food?'"

*That fit Jeremy's sense of humor.* "What did the customer order?" I asked.

Waltz leaned out his door and barked, "Perlstein!"

The heavy junior detective arrived a minute later, out of breath from his sixty-foot waddle. "Yeah, Shelly?"

"The customer at Chez Pierre. You ask what he ate?"

Perlstein puckered liverish lips, pulled a notepad from his pocket, flipping through pages. "Uh, lessee, he drank some kind of white wine, Chateau pauf de dawdle or something. I ain't good at French. He had the house salad, and dinner was tornadoes Rossalini."

Perlstein flapped over another page. "For dessert the guy wanted something special . . . chocolate mousse with chocolate syrup, chocolate shavings over that, and them shiny candy cherries over everything."

I said, "It's Ridgecliff."

Waltz gave me perplexed.

"Ridgecliff loves chocolate with cherries. He'd have me bring him chocolate-covered cherries on my visits."

"Visits?" Waltz frowned. "Candy? You make it sound like a Valentine's Day date."

"I did what it took to keep him talking, Shelly."

On my way out I wondered if I'd sounded as defensive to Shelly Waltz as I had to myself.

# TWENTY-THREE

I booked from the station to a small park six blocks away. There was an attached dog park, a half acre of fenced-in gravel where folks exercised their pets. I was amazed at the variety of canines: poodles, Great Danes, coonhounds, Jack Russells, beagles, and several trendy types I couldn't name, shnitzidoodles or whatever.

I sat on a bench and phoned Harry. He'd left several messages in the morning but I hadn't wanted to call from the station, afraid of being overhead.

Harry filled me in on his findings. He'd been busy.

". . . message on the Doc's phone, Agent John Wyatt at the Bureau's behavioral unit inquiring about files he sent. I called back and . . . What's

248

all that barking? Are you calling from the city pound?"

"I'm near a dog park. It's like a playground for dogs."

"I don't want to know. Anyway, it appears that three months ago, the Doc turned a hard eye toward the DC sniper cases. You know the story."

"For sure, bro. Pathetic, discarded kid with no father figure, in steps a willing male adult, a father. Kid idolizes the father figure – a psychopath, unfortunately. Kid wants to show Daddy he's a man too, and all hell breaks loose."

"You remember Muhammad's plans for an endgame, Carson?"

"Turning a group of lost boys into his own personal army of hate. Did Agent Wyatt say why Vangie wanted the information?"

"Only that she wanted it fast, like overnight. And it fits into the time Prowse told Traynor about a confidentiality problem with a private patient. It's also when the 'Do Not Disturb' sign showed up. Her invisible patient."

"I don't see it as part of anything up here, Harry. But I'll mull it over."

Harry and I talked a few more minutes. He

was delighted I'd doped out the Silviera and businessman angle. I returned to the precinct at five, found three more possible sightings: at an upscale Italian restaurant on Mulberry, lunch at a place on Mott, and a clerk at a high-end Park Avenue shoe shop who had sold a pair of black loafers to a thickly accented man who mentioned his birthplace as Lisbon.

Showing photos to rental agents proved more problematic. Unlike restaurants and shops, agents moved around and did things like take vacations. But someone had helped my brother get his digs.

When we found the agent, it would be over.

Everyone on the case was charged. Double shifts were run as detectives hit establishments that might attract a wealthy man vacationing in Manhattan. Folger orchestrated the commotion, sending teams hither and yon, keeping files current. I figured her late father would have been proud to see the cop gene in action.

I was coming from a bathroom break when I saw her alone in the Ridgecliff room, the first time in hours.

I said, "Doing anything tonight, Weather Lady?"

She shot a sideways glance at the detectives' room, dicks on phones, circling desks, yelling at one another. She gave me a sad smile and a sigh.

"I'm probably here half the night, dead on my feet when I get home. Think we can sneak in a meal and . . . whatever . . . tomorrow evening?"

I licked my finger, held it in the air.

"Conditions are perfect for warmth and conviviality."

We puckered our lips at one another and I headed out, switching to detective mode when I hit the street, hoping Jeremy was somewhere studying a plate of food, and not on the street, studying the faces of women.

*Eat up, brother,* I thought. *Your menu's running out.*

I showed up fresh and ready in the morning, juiced by success. Waltz was on the phone, and I waited for the crew to assemble.

Before falling asleep I'd tumbled my conclusions through my mind. A Portuguese businessman was a potent disguise in Manhattan. I admired my brother's ingenuity for thinking it up, mine for figuring it out.

Waltz hung up. I wandered over, cup of coffee in hand. Waltz looked up from reading the night's reports. "Another possible sighting at a luggage shop on Lex, a place where a suitcase costs more than I make in a week. The clerk thinks he sold Ridgecliff a messenger bag. He thought the customer spoke Spanish, but that's easily confused with . . ."

We heard a grunt at the door and looked up to see Bullard's mug. He looked angry, tie pulled aside, sleeves rolled up, jacket jammed beneath his arm.

"Where the hell's Folger?" he said.

"Why?" Waltz asked.

"She and me were supposed to meet with the dicks up at the 25th about that drive-by last January. The case is going to court."

"Folger never showed?" I said.

"Why the hell would I be asking why she didn't show if she did show? And why are you talking to me when I'm talking to Waltz?"

"You call her cell?" Waltz asked.

"About eighty fuckin' times. I got nada, voice-mail. There were half a dozen dicks and a captain waiting at the 25th. They were pissed. I told them Folger was probably having one of those *women*'s moments when nothing's real clear.

252

Think you might ask if she could pretty-please be there tomorrow at ten if she's not too busy having her period?"

Bullard thundered away.

"The Lieutenant missing an appointment?" I asked Waltz. "That unusual?"

"Not for Alice Folger," Waltz said, frowning. "It's unheard of."

I closed the door. "Folger and I were talking a couple nights ago, Shelly. There'd been scratching at her door and she thought she saw a face at the window. She'd also felt like she was being watched the past couple weeks, but never saw anyone watching."

"You and Folger were talking?"

"She's easier on me these days."

"Cluff's in Tribeca showing Ridgecliff's picture. I'll get him to run over to Folger's digs. Maybe she overslept."

Waltz punched the speaker volume on his phone so I could hear. Cluff answered.

"Shelly Waltz here. You know where the Lieutenant lives?"

"Sure," Cluff said. "I was at her Christmas party. She lives five minutes away. Why?"

"She missed a meeting this morning. How about you check it –"

"On my way," Cluff said. The phone clicked dead.

I had the creepy-crawlies but didn't know why. Waltz looked even less happy than usual. I tried small talk.

"How are things with the Pelham project?"

He raised three fingers. It took a second for the message to sink in.

"Three dolls?" I asked.

"Another arrived yesterday. No mouth, no prints, no nothing."

"How many are in a grouping or whatever?"

He shrugged, not really caring at the moment. "Five or six."

I wiped my damp palms on my jeans, checked my watch. When I looked up I saw Shelly was doing the same. Six minutes crept by, then seven. Waltz said, "Cluff's got to be there by now. I'll call and see what's —"

The phone sounded. Waltz's hand hit the button mid-ring, cobra speed. The line crackled as the connection wavered. Followed by Cluff's voice in full gasping wheeze.

"Jesus, Shelly . . . it's a bloodbath over here. She's . . . on the floor. I called for the medics, but . . . Folger's dead, Shelly. She's been torn apart."

# TWENTY-FOUR

We were outside Folger's house in minutes, running to the door. The ME's van was rolling up, the bus – ambulance – already there. Cluff was at the door, shaking his head, his voice labored, squeezing past pain.

"I got here . . . the front door was open about an inch, I called inside. Nothing. Then I stepped in, found . . ."

I stuck my head through the door. Blood. On the floor. On the walls. The air was thick with its reek. I saw Folger's body on the floor, clothes awry, legs splayed, red with blood. The head was still attached, but the rage had been cut deep into the flesh. What remained of the face was turned toward the door, the teeth pink with blood and clenched in the rictus of misery.

There was nothing to be done.

"Get back," a voice said. "Coming through."

Two technicians from the Medical Examiner's office pushed into the room, one stripping the wrapping from a new thermometer. I grimaced as he plunged it beneath Folger's ribs, deep into her liver, the temperature helping to determine time of death.

Shelly was beside me, wanting to run to Folger, his cop instinct holding him back, letting the techs work before the dicks took over. I heard him sucking air, hard, as if hyperventilating.

"Steady, Shelly."

"I can't take much more," he whispered. I turned to him, saw faraway eyes in a ghost-white face.

"Shelly? Are you all right?"

His eyes rolled up and his knees collapsed. I managed to grab around his chest and slow his fall to the floor. "Need help over here!"

A paramedic appeared beside me, fingers against Waltz's neck, ear tight against Shelly's chest. "Pulse is reedy but steady. No arrhythmia. I think it's syncope, fainting. Probably stress and anxiety."

Waltz's hand whipped by my face, trying to

push away my shape. He was disoriented, but returning. Tears poured into his eyes and he smeared his sleeve across his face, leaving tears and spit and mucus across his cheeks.

"It's a nightmare," he moaned. "A fucking nightmare."

"Just rest, Shelly. Stay calm."

He covered his face with his hands, muttered, ". . . all a nightmare," and lay still, gathering himself.

I sat back and watched the tech pull the thermometer from the liver. A breast slipped from beneath a torn strip of what had been a blouse. I stared at it, heavy, the aureole large and brown. I rose, stepped around the red pools. My foot slipped in a patch of excrement and I slid sideways, grabbing the shoulder of the tech, nearly tumbling across the corpse.

"Easy," the tech said.

I lowered myself to a crouch and gently lifted a clot of blood-soaked hair, the head following like a puppet. I slipped my gloved fingers under the chin and spun the face to mine.

I turned to Waltz. It would later haunt me that a person's death could give so much relief.

"It's not Folger, Shelly. It's someone else."

*   *   *

Within twenty minutes a dozen detectives and evidence techs filled Folger's house. The usual banter was gone, replaced by brutal efficiency, as if a fuse was burning. Or a clock ticking on a bomb.

The front door opened and Bullard entered. "I just heard. What's the word?"

Waltz put his hands in his pockets, walked to Bullard. Something in Waltz's eyes set off an alarm in my head and I followed.

"It's just a woman's moment," Waltz said to Bullard.

Bullard was confused. "What you talking about, Waltz?"

"It's what you said when she didn't show up at your meeting this morning. She was having a 'woman's moment'. You know, Bullard, one of those times when things aren't real clear."

I stepped closer. Re-thought things. Stepped back and put my hands in my pockets.

"You're babbling," Bullard said.

"Folger was having her period, you said. That's why she was late."

"Hey, I didn't mean anything. I was just havin' fun."

"Me too," Waltz said, driving his fist into Bullard's sternum.

Bullard dropped to the floor, gasping. Every eye turned to the action. No one moved. After a few seconds everyone went back to work as if nothing had happened. Two dicks grabbed Bullard under the arms and ushered him from the house, not gently.

Shelly returned to worrying and watching the investigation progress. Records and photographs found in the upstairs apartment showed the corpse was that of Julie Chase, a forty-two-year-old accountant for Morgan Stanley. A stairway connected the up- and downstairs. The connecting door was open.

"There's blood spray into the stairway," one of the dicks said. "Like the vic heard something down here, came to check."

"Got taken down when she walked in?" another asked.

"Slammed."

"So where's Folger?" Waltz asked.

No one said a word. The crew moved to Folger's bedroom and Forensics began bagging the bedclothes for inspection for hairs, semen and other physical evidence. At the same time the print techs were pulling latents from the headboard.

I winced, cleared my throat, looked at Waltz.

"I, uh, suspect y'all might find a few of my fingerprints around the place, Shelly. Probably a little something on the sheets as well."

Every head turned to me.

I retreated to the stoop. The techs had stopped talking to me, the dicks regarded me with wary eyes. Waltz stepped outside a few minutes later. His eyes were steady, hard.

"Four million women in this city and you hit on Folger?"

"If the past week has told you anything about me, Shelly, you know it didn't fall like that."

He rubbed his eyes with his fingertips. "Sorry. It's a shitty day, it's been a shitty week. You're both adults and it's none of my business."

"It surprised us more than anyone. There's about five more sides to her than most people see."

"She's one smart girl. Tries to hide it, be one of the guys, but I've been around intelligent people. It's in the eyes, something you can't describe . . ." His voice trailed away.

"We'll find her, Shelly."

"What's with the *we*? You're officially a suspect. You're done in the department. Nor can you leave town. You're in limboland until you're cleared."

"A suspect? That's nuts."

He looked at the sky and scratched his chin. "Let's see . . . a missing woman. Everything in her life was hunky-dory until she got a new boyfriend a day ago. How do you do things down in Mobile, Detective Ryder?"

"I'd be suspect number one," I said. "Maybe two and three as well."

"Then you know what to do."

I left my prints with one tech. Gave another a cheek swab for a DNA sample. I couldn't do anything on Folger's disappearance, and couldn't hang around the cop shop, so I went back to the hotel. Waltz called an hour later, his voice low, verging on bitter.

"Hairs and fibers at the scene. It's Ridgecliff. Looks like he got interrupted while abducting Folger, killed the tenant. We checked every resident on the block. No one saw a thing, of course. The guy across the way thought he saw a cab lingering outside the place a few times in the past week. A cab in New York City, there's a clue."

# TWENTY-FIVE

*"What do you want from me, you bastard?"*
*Alice Folger said.*

*"I need you to take off your panties and hose."*

*Alice Folger glared up at her captor. He stood above her with a bright knife as she sat on the floor with her fingers laced behind her head. She appeared to be in the home of someone with money, the floors polished wood, the furniture tasteful. There was art on the walls and in curio cases. The only light was coming from a dozen or so candles arrayed in the three rooms she could see.*

*"Fuck you," Folger said.*

*Her captor nodded as if understanding, then his arm became a blur, the knife slashing an inch from Folger's eyes.*

"TAKE THE GODDAMN THINGS OFF!"

Glaring defiantly through her terror, Folger wriggled from her trousers, slid off hose and panties, leaving a hand over her pubis.

"Stand up."

She stood, hand in place. Knife tight in his palm, the man circled her, staring at her legs and buttocks. She closed her eyes, tried to still her racing heart. The man stepped behind her.

"Open your legs."

She put her feet a few inches apart, knees shaking.

"WIDER!"

She stepped out further and heard the floor creak at her back. It sounded as if he was crouching and studying her. After a long minute he walked out in front of her and pulled a folded brown bag from his pocket, bending to grab the garments on the floor. He stopped, frowning. His eyes scanned the room until seeing a broom in the corner. He grabbed it, using the handle to push the clothing into the bag. He rolled the bag shut, flashing a glance at her crotch.

"Get something over that before the smell makes me sick."

*"I can put on my pants?"*

*"Either that or weld a plate over your . . . thing."*

*Folger almost gasped with relief. She pulled on her trousers with shaking fingers.*

When I arrived at the hotel, I patted my jacket for the electronic key, but it seemed to have disappeared. I recalled my stop for coffee, how I'd slipped the jacket off. It seemed the slippery plastic card had fallen out.

I'd run back inside the shop for a couple minutes to grab a refill, leaving the jacket in the adjoining chair, but a thief would simply have taken the jacket. The card was probably laying beneath the chair, useless without the room number.

No harm done. I had the deskman generate a second key.

Sickened by events I hid in my room and wondered why Jeremy had targeted Folger. It was apparent that at some point when Jeremy was following me, he had seen Folger. She had flipped his switch.

It was my fault. I hadn't figured he'd tail me.

What did he have planned for Folger? Was she already dead? And why had he killed the tenant so brutally? She, it appeared, had flipped his switch as well.

Jeremy was falling apart at a terrible rate.

I turned on a muted television for quiet company, something to keep me from being alone with the horror of my thoughts and culpability. I watched until the news show focused on Cynthia Pelham's campaign and the rancor it aroused in many. Faces screaming soundlessly are even uglier than with sound. I turned off the idiot box, pulled the blackout curtains, and lay in the dark.

Several minutes passed and I became aware of an indefinable presence I could not identify, like a sound just past the edge of hearing. The sole light fell from the red LED clock numbers. I listened into the room until I fell into sleep.

Sometime later my eyes snapped open. I heard my last snore in the air. My heart was racing. Why? I looked for the clock but couldn't see its display. The room was as black as a coal mine. My open eyes saw little more than my closed eyes.

I felt something in the room. A presence.

*It's standing by the bed,* said my child's mind.

*Nothing's there,* the adult countered. You've felt this before. There's never anyone there.

*It's coming closer*, gasped the child. *It's above us!*

I held my breath, ready to attack what I could not believe was there. Then, softly . . . a sense of movement. Followed by the most terrifying whisper I'd ever heard, hatred shredded through broken glass.

"A gun is aimed directly at your heart. I have night-vision goggles. Move and you die."

"I'm not moving an inch," I whispered.

"I'm going to restrain your arms," the voice said. "Roll over and put them behind your back. This is the most dangerous moment in your life."

I complied. Tape wrapped my wrists, ankles, my legs at my knees. I heard a chair pulled close to the bedside. The chair squeaked under weight. Another voice appeared in the air, light and conversational.

"Jesus, Carson. Can you believe the price of a good steak in this town?"

*Jeremy.* The room went silent save for the traffic on the street. I strained my eyes in his direction, but the room was lightless. I wondered if he was studying me through his goggles, making an inspection.

"I want to help you, Jeremy," I said, as calm as I could muster. "The police might kill you

266

on sight. You've got to go in and . . . talk with them. I'll go with you, keep you safe."

I felt his warm voice at my ear. "For sure you're going to keep me safe, little brother. Timmy's in the well."

"Timmy's in the . . . would you please make sense?"

"THINK ABOUT IT! Do you remember those old Lassie re-runs we used to watch? Lassie's owner, that idiot Timmy, was always stuck in a cave or falling down a well. Little Timster depended on Lassie to bring help. Arf."

It took scant seconds for the realization to sink in. "Folger's dependent on you for food and water. Maybe even air."

"I don't get to her for a few hours . . . goodbye Alice."

"What if something goes wrong and you can't get back to her? I don't want her to die, Jeremy."

"Dear Carson, ever the hero on water and land." His fingers scruffed my hair. "Obviously, it's incumbent on you to keep me free."

I heard his feet start away.

"Jeremy?"

"*Si?*"

"You held something over Vangie, right? Leverage?" Hoping against hope.

"Her idea, start to finish. Prowsie needed me to be her Sirius, Carson."

"What are you talking about? Her serious what?"

"S–I–R–I–U–S. The brightest star in the heavens, Sirius. After all these years, Old Prowsie took the hots for her prize subject, wanted a big fling in the Big Apple."

"I-I don't believe that."

"It's what she croaked to me on the plane: 'You're my Seeeer-rius, Jeremy. I neeeeed you.' Not that I'd have surrendered my virtue. I can't imagine anything more disgusting than grunting over Prowsie's ancient body. It would be like fucking a corpse."

I heard the door open. Close. He was gone.

I struggled twenty minutes with the tape, stretching it enough to work free. My devious brother had swiped the key from my pocket. By the time I'd returned to the hotel and had a second key generated, he was already in my room, beneath the bed.

I fumbled toward the light switch, tripping over something on the carpet. I flicked on the lights and found a brown paper package, a folded-over grocery bag. I upended the bag over the desk.

A woman's panties and panty hose tumbled out.

They were followed by a cheap postcard like ones sold across the city. It displayed a photograph of the Empire State Building. Above the building, in balloon type, were the words, WE'RE HAVING A FUN TIME IN NEW YORK CITY! On the reverse was a line written in purple ink. It said, simply,

*Do what he says. Please.*

Below that,

*Alice*

I held the postcard in my hand and stared out the window as the sun turned the sky to orange behind the skyscrapers. Alice Folger was alive. I had to hope Jeremy was in control enough to restrain his urges for now. His visit was to tell me that his capture meant Alice Folger's death. My brother never made idle threats.

I dressed and went to the station, arriving at seven. I saw Perlstein doing paperwork at his desk.

"Yo, Perl . . . how's the hunt for Ridgecliff?"

"Cluff finally bought in to your rich guy view.

He pushed your hoity-toity take on Ridgecliff up a notch, thought Ridgecliff might be artsy. Guess what? We saw a guy looked a lot like a Portuguese Ridgecliff waltzing past a security cam at the Guggenheim yesterday."

"That's great," I said, my mouth going dry. "Smart move."

"We're gonna shoot this fucker dead on the street, Ryder. Thanks for pushing us on to the right path." He shot a thumbs-up and turned back to his reports.

Thanks to me, the cops would soon be breathing down my brother's neck. Had I been smart enough, or less frightened, I'd have told Jeremy his disguise and habits were known. But all I'd been able to think about was his relationship with Vangie. It wasn't until he was gone that I realized my plight. Folger's plight. I had to somehow let my brother know the NYPD was on to his disguise.

Why hadn't he told me how to make contact? It seemed an omission on his part.

I wandered out to the street to pull some energy from the sun now filling the streets. I passed a newsstand as a bundle of early-edition papers slapped the pavement beside the rickety kiosk. The papers had been tossed from a delivery truck, a flatbed piled high, a man on the back offloading bundles of the *New York Watcher*.

"Hey, buddy," I called to the guy on the truck. "You know where the *Watcher*'s offices are located?"

# TWENTY-SIX

Benny Mac slapped toast crumbs and clots of scrambled egg from the front of his shirt. The goddamn shirt had shrunk, buttons tight, belly hair pushing through the puckered openings. He was sitting at a small round table outside a coffee shop adjoining the entrance to the *Watcher's* headquarters, the table his de facto office in decent weather. A half-eaten plate of bacon and eggs, pancakes and fried potatoes sat in front of him, as did two cellphones, three pens and a notepad.

He paused in shoveling food into his mouth to observe the approach of a skinny black man in a blue uniform and crocheted Rasta hat. The man grinned from the pavement side of the low wrought-iron fence separating the tabled section from pedestrian traffic.

"Hey, Jimmy Warbles," Benny Mac said through a mouthful of egg. "S'up?"

Jimmy Warbles ran the cleaning services at City Hall, was one of Benny Mac's best sources of hot political dish. Benny wiped his mouth with a piece of buttered toast, lowered his voice.

"You got anything, Jimmy?"

Jimmy Warbles set his elbows on the fence, leaned forward, eyes making sure there was no one near. "I t'ink a lady in archives is makin' it wit' another lady in archives. T'ey bote married ladies, sure enough. They go in a supply room. Close t' door."

"Muff divers!" Benny said, eyes widening. "You sure?"

"Ever'body know 'cept the two ladies, who don't know anybody know."

Benny Mac considered the situation. "Tell you what, Jimmy, you figure out when I can get in with a camera."

"It can maybe happen. What it wort'?"

Benny Mac saw a 120-point headline on the cover of the *Watcher*: "LESBO LOVE NEST IN CITY HALL".

"If it makes the front page, Jimmy, you get five hundred. Inside gets three."

Jimmy Warbles snapped his fingers and

grinned yellow teeth that would have done a horse proud. "Be back atcha, my man."

Benny thought a second, amended his proposal. "Tellya what, Jimmy. If I can get a shot of 'em kissing, you get a grand."

*A pair of lesbos kissing in City Hall. Magic.*

Warbles's fingers flicked across Benny Mac's palm, deal. He pimp-walked away, hands in his pockets, the bright hat bobbing like a multi-colored mushroom.

Benny Mac returned to his breakfast, eating with renewed vigor. He finished, set the plate on the clean table at his back. He looked at his phones, hoping a story would ring in. The lesbo deal wouldn't pay off for a while. It'd been a slow news week and unless something came up, he'd have to hit the *Watcher*'s photo archives, make up another fucking space alien story.

Benny Mac sighed, turned his eyes to a man pulling out a chair at a nearby table.

*I know that guy. Jeez, wasn't he the one I took the picture of . . .*

"Hey, buddy. I know you. I saw you at the crime scene of that real estate lady. You were with my good friend, Shelly Waltz. Come over to my table, lemme buy you a cup a coffee.

274

Hey, you don't sound like you're from around here."

*You sound like a mush-mouth hickarooni . . .*

"Really? Inner-departmental loan, sent up to learn from the NYPD? I'm sure you have plenty to teach us as well. You want something with that coffee? Bagel? Danish? And is it officer or detective? Hey, those ladies that got cut wide open, Detective . . . How the cases going? Tough ones huh? I know, you can't talk about it.

*This hillbilly knows something . . .*

"I know, bud. NYPD sees stuff most departments never will. A lot of my friends are NYPD dicks. Shelly Waltz and me are like this. He's always telling me stuff on the QT. When I finally write the story I always run it by the NYPD first. I could do a rough draft on the belly slasher story, fax a copy to Shelly and you this very afternoon. How do you spell your name? No, I don't have to use it if you don't want . . ."

*Come on, spill it . . .*

"Oh sure, the United Nations can be a big problem. The immunity thing. It's true, a person could commit a crime and nothing can happen. It's like they're always in their own country. Sick. They come here to rape and pillage and then glide home scot-free. You can't dynamite

275

them out of the homeland. The only way to get at them is the free press."

*Is Bubba suggesting someone with diplomatic immunity killed the woman? Please, what embassy? Please oh dear God . . . I can keep this on page one for a fucking month . . .*

"That's the way it is up here. If the guy hops a plane back to his home country, it'll take a helluva legal wrangle to get him back over here, if ever. Happens all the time. Gotta watch the airports, that's crucial."

*Did the hick just say NYPD's staked out TAP Airlines? THAT'S PORTUGAL!*

"It's a sad thing the way these foreigners take advantage of our good nature. Hey, gotta run buddy. Nice seeing you again. Enjoy your stay."

*You idiot hayseed . . .*


Every Southerner knows the thicker your accent, the more you're viewed as a naïve bumpkin by anyone north of the Mason-Dixon. After using my most cartoonish twang to shovel shit into Benny Mac's nonexistent lap, I walked the streets to burn off energy. I went up Lexington, crossed to Central Park, spanked pavement down Eighth Avenue to Greenwich Avenue – passing within two block of Folger's house – walked Greenwich to Sixth and into Tribeca. I angled east to the Lower East Side and turned back uptown. I was only a dozen or so blocks from the precinct when my phone rang: Clair Peltier's cell.

"Hi, Clair."

"I tested the hair and fiber evidence from the NYPD. It's strange and I don't think it's what you expected."

Boom. That was Clair in work mode. Direct and focused, science all the way. One of the reasons she was one of the top pathologists in the country.

"Uh, expected what, Clair?"

"You said the hair and fibers found at the woman's crime scene were from New York?"

"Local shops, salons, barbers. At least that's what everyone figured. What's wrong?"

"Let me walk you through it. We took what you sent and burned it all in the gas chromatograph mass spectrometer."

"I don't underst—"

"Hush your head and listen. NYPD was right, testing on an individual basis was out of the question, unless you've got a hundred technicians or a couple of months. So our top tox guy, Ward, loaded everything in the GCMS, flashed it, and we checked the results. It's almost bizarre."

"How?"

"We got an amazing spike on arsenic. A few of those hairs were loaded. We think it has to be the hairs, unless someone had spilled arsenic on a rug, say, the rug fibers then included in the fibers left at the crime scene. But there were a lot more hairs than fibers. On a weight comparison, I'd put it a hundred-to-one hair over fiber. So I think a hank of hair inside the bag was thick with arsenic."

"Got you."

"I checked with the CDC in Atlanta. There was an arsenic poisoning in Key West nine months back, a husband loaded his invalid wife's meals with the stuff. But, being an invalid, would she have gotten her hair cut outside her home, where someone could gather her hair? There's that to consider. Anyway, that's all I found in the whole country. At first."

I held my breath. "And?"

"An hour ago I got a call from the CDC. They found a case that hadn't reached the official records yet, still being documented. They put me in touch with a county coroner who said that his department had just recently uncovered an arsenic poisoning, homicide. A woman had loaded her abusive husband's vitamin supplements with an old but potent agricultural-grade rat poison. The guy was a bodybuilder type, fit and powerful."

"So it took a lot of arsenic."

"The guy got sicker and sicker but thought he wasn't adjusting his carbs and fats or whatnot – a head case. So wifey keeps upping the dosage until the guy could probably kill rats by sneezing on them."

"But he got a haircut during the poisoning, right?"

"Every week. He wanted to look tidy if the Mr Universe pageant called."

My grip tightened on the phone. Maybe the hairs could provide a starting place to find the killer.

"The poisonings were in the New York area, right? Or maybe New Jersey?"

"No, Carson. Not quite."

"Where, then?"

"A little town southeast of Jackson, Mississippi. Right here in our own back yard, so to speak. Does that change anything in your cases?"

I hung up a minute later, head spinning. There

was no proof the hair in the NYPD evidence bag was from Mississippi, it could be a local poisoning in progress. But the Mississippi case was scant miles across the border from central Alabama, an hour's drive to the Institute, to Vangie's house, to the area where my brother and I had grown up . . .

It made no sense. Nothing made sense. I didn't have long to ponder the anomaly. My phone rang. This time it was Waltz, brusque: "Get here now."

I grabbed a taxi and was in his office five minutes later. He threw the afternoon edition of the *New York Watcher* my way. I snatched it from the air, saw the headline.

PORTUGUESE DIPLOMAT SUSPECT IN SLASHER SLAYING.

The accompanying photo showed a hapless member of the Portuguese legation denying everything. The story was attributed to "an unnamed source close to the NYPD".

"Oh Jesus," I said, hoping my face registered appropriate horror. "Where the hell did it come from?"

"'Close to the NYPD' usually means some janitor or civilian passing through the detectives' room heard the words 'slasher' and

'Portuguese' and ran to the *Watcher* to trade the words for a hundred bucks." Waltz sank into his chair. "The local TV and radio are gonna land on it like flies on horseshit. You know what this does, don't you?"

I handed the paper back, nodded.

"It'll push Ridgecliff underground."

Waltz tossed the paper in the waste can. "Do you think this will set Ridgecliff off? If Folger's alive, will this make him kill her?"

"If he's kept her alive there's a reason. Having his cover blown shouldn't affect that reason."

He walked to the open blinds and drew them tight. He turned to me.

"Nothing makes sense about why Ridgecliff is in New York. It's a goddamn carnival of mirrors. You sure you're telling me everything about him?" Waltz stared, as if studying my reaction.

"Why would I keep information under wraps, Shelly?"

"Did you ever talk to Ridgecliff's people? His relatives? That kid, the one who disappeared – Charles. Did Jeremy Ridgecliff like him, hate him?"

"Jeremy Ridgecliff was adamant that he saved Charles's life."

"How?"

I frowned, as if sifting through hazy memories. "Jeremy Ridgecliff's father was falling into pure madness. Harsher abuse, more frequent. The father had initiated the physical abuse when Jeremy Ridgecliff turned ten, like the kid reached some sort of point where the old man's anger turned physical."

"I'm not getting it."

"A few days before his tenth birthday, a friend gave Charles a hamster as a gift. The kid hid it under his bed. On the night of the kid's birthday, Mama and kids are in their usual tense state, no one knowing what Daddy's gonna do. The cake is presented, Daddy gets a big-ass grin on his face, and runs off. He reappears with the hamster in his hand."

Waltz shook his head. "Oh Lord."

"Daddy screams, 'I told you, no filthy animals in the house.' He winds up like a major-league pitcher and fires the hamster into the wall. It falls to the floor, still alive, squeaking and twitching, blood coming from every opening. Hamsters scream . . . Ridgecliff told me that."

Waltz could only shake his head in horror.

I said, "Daddy goes full berserk, smooshes Charles's head into the cake. Mama disappears into her room to sew, like she always did. A week later, Ridgecliff kills his father."

Waltz studied my eyes. "You never told me any of that."

"Uh, I just remembered it, Shelly. But it's what Jeremy Ridgecliff's always told himself: He killed the father to save the brother."

Shelly offered an enigmatic smile.

"Wonder what the brother thinks?"

I shrugged, spun away quick, an odd tingle rising up my spine. I left Shelly to his work, hoping Jeremy had received my message.

# TWENTY-SEVEN

It was late afternoon and the streets were filling with people heading home from work. I was walking quickly, dodging bodies, when my phone rang. I pulled it out, jumped into the recessed storefront of an electronics store to keep from being trampled. Cameras, binoculars, flashlights, cellphones, and every kind of MP3 player filled the window at my back.

"Hey, Carson, Tom Mason."

"Hey, Tom, great to hear from you again. What's happening?"

"I got a call from Rick Saunders up in Pickens County, State Police. He said some guy's been calling around about the Ridgecliff case. Pickens County is where the family was living when the kid killed his old man. The family rented a farmhouse in the middle of nowhere."

My home, a million years ago. Fear rose to my throat like a lump of iron. A crowd of Oriental tourists walked to the window, pointing at the glittering electronic booty. I turned away and cupped the phone to my ear as Tom continued.

"The caller was that Waltz fellow. He was real interested in the family. I take it there was a younger kid, Ridgecliff's brother, who seems to have fallen off the face of the earth."

"Probably just Shelly checking loose ends, making sure Ridgecliff hasn't holed up with relatives."

"Doesn't sound like there are any, 'cept this one kid. Guess he'd be in his mid-thirties or so."

"I imagine he put a lot of gone between him and the family, Tom. I would."

"Can't blame him. Anyway, what I was gonna tell you, since things are a bit slow down here, knock wood –" I heard Tom rap his desk – "if you need Harry to take some more time and check out the Ridgecliff history a bit, don't hesitate to ask. You can pass that on to Waltz as well."

"Got it, Tom, though I expect it was just another shot in the dark."

"Stay safe, see you soon."

When I closed the phone, I couldn't walk and leaned against the store for support. I must have been breathing, but I couldn't feel any air in my lungs.

Shelly Waltz was digging in my past.

Jeremy Ridgecliff's pre-paid cellphone rang. He set aside the newspaper and pulled the phone from his pocket. Folger was supine in a box, bound with tape, a pillow beneath her head, eyes wide, watching. Her mouth was stuffed with a washcloth, the cloth secured with bands of tape. The box was hand-painted with the legend, *Antiques: Handle With Extreme Care. This Side Up*. An arrow denoted the Up side.

Jeremy brought the phone to his mouth, leaned over the box. He frowned at Folger and switched to a nasal Yankee voice, an older homosexual man, what they used to call a queen.

"Mr Matapang? Of *course* I'll give him a reference. Honesto is a *darling* man, rents our cabin in Vail every year. We do an exchange with him now and then, he stays in our *cottage* on the Vineyard, we use his, get this . . . *villa* in

286

*Manila*. He collects parrots . . . No, not *real* ones, cloisonné parrots, ruby eyes, that sort of thing, *stunningly* pricey and just to *die* for. He's absolutely a *sumptuous* find."

He hung up, set the phone on the table, waited. It rang.

This time he answered with his new voice and identity, a gay Filipino male in his forties. According to the newspaper, Senhor Caldiera had been discovered. Carson, no doubt. Snitch.

". . . Yes? Wonderful Mr Dammler. I can't wait to get settled in. You have my money order? Splendid. Could you leave the key at your office? I'll send a driver by to pick it up. I'll be in residence in an hour or so, just have to –" he shot a wink at Folger – "pack a few things and call the movers."

He hung up and studied his eyes, darkened by eye-liner, and adjusted the wig, silver-blonde, short haired, the hair layered. His new alias was Honesto Matapang, an excruciatingly gay and wealthy Filipino. He'd rubbed mascara into the creases around his mouth, eyes, and neck, then rubbed most away, accentuating his wrinkles, aging himself by years. Two sweat shirts beneath his silk tunic added twenty pounds. When outside, he stuffed tissue between his gums and cheeks to pooch them outward. From tinted hair to slipper-like shoes, he resembled a badly aging roué, a Nero-in-progress.

He hung up and winked his aged eyes at Folger. "Isn't it wonderful, Miss Alice. There's a whole network of fruity professionals just waiting to help us find new digs." He cackled wickedly. "I was getting so tired of being a cauldron."

Jeremy reached down and folded a length of tape over Folger's eyes, pressing it down into her skin. He studied her bound body for a quiet minute, then picked up a hammer.

I sat on a bench in a green space beside a bank. If Waltz discovered the truth, I'd have to be ready to deal with it. It would be an exceptionally dangerous moment.

A tall and imperious woman walked by, breaking my concentration. She clicked on heels as slender as ice picks. When she was a dozen feet past, I smelled her perfume, delicate and strong in equal measure.

The potency of the scent reminded me of a thought I'd tucked away a few days earlier, less a thought than what Harry called a "flag moment", when a conversation or event raised a tiny flag in the mind. Most were coincidence or misreading a person's words or actions, and checking every tiny flag would be futile. It was when flags started to cluster that they became worth a look. I'd seen several since my arrival, a bouquet of poppy-red pennants.

Fifteen minutes later I was at Macy's fragrance counter, looking among the dozens of perfumes out for sampling . . . *there*, the small crystal bottle that Shelly had sniffed the day I bought the briefcase.

The salesperson, a sixtyish woman with white corkscrewing hair, sidled over with nose lifted, as if spying a skunk in the lily patch.

"Can I help you?"

"This fragrance, is it common?"

"None of our fragrances are common, sir."

"I mean, do you sell a lot of it?"

"It's quite expensive, and rather individual. A very subtle blend."

"Can I take that as meaning you don't sell a lot of it?"

She thought a moment, scarlet nail tapping the mole.

"You may."

I thanked la grande dame and left the store, unable to stop sniffing my wrist. As the scent faded, my memory of it grew stronger, a strange phenomenon. I pulled my cell from my pocket, punched the number.

*"This is Harry Nautilus, please leave a message at the . . ."*

When the phone beeped its need for a message, mine was brief, and carried a furtive prayer beneath the words.

"Harry, it's Carson with a huge favor to ask, bro. If it pans out, it just might save me from something real bad. Here's what I need you to do, and at the speed of light, if possible . . ."

I returned to the hotel. I'd turned off my cell to give my head some space. The hotel phone blinked that a single message was waiting. I heard Waltz's voice, neutral in tone.

"Hello, Detective Ryder. Listen, you've never been to my home – an omission on my part. Can you stop by this evening at nine? I'd like to talk about something."

A tornadic wind was blowing toward my house of matchsticks. I set my cellphone on the table and prayed that Harry would call with the news that the pennants in my head were flying in a countering wind.

# TWENTY-EIGHT

I jumped from the cab into a hard-blown rain, pulled my hat low and sprinted to a trim blue house on a broad Brooklyn avenue of other trim houses. Shelly had the door open as I leapt up the steps.

"Come in, Detective. Welcome."

"Anything on Alice?" I asked.

He shook his head no. I looked to a dining-room table stacked with papers.

He saw my glance. "I've been looking through files your partner sent. As well as some others. It's the only use I've found for the dining-room table, since I eat at the kitchen counter by the TV. The joys of bachelorhood."

"Were you ever married, Shelly?"

A pause. "Once it seemed possible, but in hindsight it was never an option."

Waltz went to grab himself a drink. I hadn't known what to expect from his digs, thinking either neat as the proverbial pin, or as disheveled as a frat house. It turned out to be both: open and orderly rooms with dark carpet and a peach hue to the walls, solid furniture, a long shelf of books in the living room where I stood. The other side of the equation held in a small room to the side, centered by a table bearing stacks of books, magazines, a small fan that looked ready for repair, a shirt still in the wrapper, a box of candy, a handful of neckties, and so forth. The corners of the room were nests of items: spinning rods with red and white floats on the line, a vacuum cleaner, old shoes, a tennis racquet.

The home felt like Shelly Waltz. There was general order, but with a section of items awaiting categorization or some form of decision. An overstuffed chair, well worn, owned one corner of the room, and I pictured Shelly ruminating over the items from the chair, tented fingertips tapping pursed lips, sad eyes scanning the disorder in hope of a solution.

The light in the house was a low, warm

yellow. Thunder shivered the windows as Waltz returned with his beer, nodded me to sit on the couch. He sat opposite in an armchair. On the low table between us was a manila folder, pages peeking from the edges.

"Pegging Jeremy Ridgecliff as a Portuguese businessman was a damn interesting piece of intuition, Detective."

"It was just a hunch, but it felt right."

"You play a lot of hunches, I take it."

"They seem to work a fair amount of the time."

He paused, as if gathering thoughts into a bundle. "Have you put any thought into contacts Ridgecliff might have in the area?"

"We'd all pretty much eliminated that line, I thought."

"The Ridgecliff family never came up north, you said. Or if they did, it wasn't long enough to leave traces."

"True."

"Not leaving traces," Waltz said. "Isn't that interesting?"

I smiled politely and nodded. But Waltz wasn't done with the subject.

"Though it's useless to us, there's Ridgecliff's bit with the hair, obliterating

293

traces. And while he was on his spree years ago, he managed to obliterate all traces of himself, at least until viewed in hindsight after his capture. Perhaps obliterating traces is a Ridgecliff trait."

"Umm, I suspect so, Shelly. Guess you hit a dead end."

He crossed his legs, opened the file, set it on his knee. His finger tapped the pages. "I'm not sure. Ridgecliff has a brother. His name is Charles. They grew up together."

"Sure. We've all seen the files. Charles disappeared."

Waltz flipped open the file. "Charles went to college for two years in Mobile, edge-of-expulsion grades. A party boy, I'll bet. Then Jeremy Ridgecliff gets nailed. Shortly after that, bang: Charles Ridgecliff disappears, leaving an empty bed and a lot of rumors. A guy who bunked with him for a while heard the guy ran off to a commune in Oregon. Others heard Charley-boy got wanderlust, headed to sea on a freighter. You studied at University of Alabama, right? Psychology? What year you start?"

My palms dampened. I pretended to stifle a yawn, told Waltz the year.

He nodded. "The year Charles turned to vapor."

I feigned confusion. "Am I missing something here, Shelly?"

Waltz shifted pages in the folder. I tried to catch a glance of what he was looking at, but he held the edges high.

"There's no ID photo of Charles in the college files. There should be, but back then hackers could dive right into databases, rearranging info, adding, deleting. But in checking with the university, I discovered Charles had been a member of the swimming club. I had a club photo sent up, a fax of a copy. It's murky, but have a look."

Waltz passed the photo over. I was in the back row of the twenty or so swimmers standing at the edge of the pool. I hadn't changed much.

"You're Charles Ridgecliff," Waltz said.

I handed the photo back. It was shaking. "I'm Carson Ryder."

"Let me re-phrase, Detective: I believe that for the first twenty-one years of your life your name was Charles Ridgecliff. What is it preachers like to say . . . Can I get an Amen on that?"

I closed my eyes. "It's not like you think. It's –"

Waltz's voice turned to a whisper. "Are you here to fuck up the case, sabotage it? Did you pass the information to the *Watcher*?"

"No to the first question."

"And the second one?"

I held Waltz's eyes. "Yes."

Waltz slammed the file to the floor, pages scattering like white leaves. He stood, shoulders forward, hands clenched into fists, his eyes like jets of flame.

"Get the hell out of my house."

"I'm trying to bring Jeremy in, Shelly."

He stormed to the door, opened it. "You hid the fact that the perp we're after – a man who's killed three women in a week – is your goddamn brother! Then you tipped him off that we were on to his disguise."

"I also told you what the disguise was."

"Because you're probably as sick as your brother and get off on pulling our chains. Get out of my house. Expect a visit from the NYPD tonight. You better damn well be at your hotel."

I looked into the controlled chaos of Shelly's room to the side, my mind racing. I had one card to play. I pulled it from smoke, from nagging moments of the past few days, from red flags unfurled in far corners of my mind.

I looked Waltz in the eyes and threw my card on the table.

"You knew her, Shelly."

Hesitation, a millisecond. "What the hell are you talking about?"

"Vangie. You didn't just know who she was, you knew her personally. She was a friend of yours. Or a relative."

"*What?*"

"The tape from LaGuardia. You picked her from the crowd while her face was a blur, even though I couldn't make her out. Several times while talking about her, your throat 'got dry' or you claimed an allergy, wiped your eyes. Talking about Vangie nearly broke you up, you needed to reach down and hold it together."

"That's laughable. Preposterous."

"You refer to Bernal and Anderson as vics or victims. You refer to Vangie as 'the lady' or 'Dr Prowse'."

Waltz's face was scarlet. "This isn't about me, this is about you withholding infor—"

"Three days back, Shelly. At Macy's. You were at the perfume counter, sampling something. It seemed to hit you hard. When you walked away I sniffed the scent. It was familiar but I wasn't sure, so tonight I sent my partner

297

to Vangie's house to check. It was the perfume she wore."

His index finger jabbed anger at my face. "Don't muddy the situation with your wild accu—"

"DON'T LIE TO ME, SHELLY! Look me in the eyes and tell me you didn't know Evangeline Prowse. LOOK IN MY EYES!"

He didn't meet my eyes. His shoulders slumped.

I lowered my voice to a hiss. "You spill my secret and it's over for me. But I'll spill yours and you'll be gone, too. When the NYPD brass hears you hid a personal relationship with a victim, your ass gets kicked off the case. Bang! No chance to find Vangie's killer. No chance to help Folger. I know things, Shelly. Folger is alive. My brother sent a message to that effect."

I pulled the postcard from my pocket. Handed it to Waltz. He saw Folger's handwriting, read her words.

*Do what he says. Please. Alice.*

"We can avenge Vangie's death," I pleaded. "We can save Folger. Help me, Shelly."

Waltz never met my eyes. Thunder rumbled across the night sky, flickered the lights in the house. He retreated into the shadows of a dark hall. I heard a drawer open in a back room, then slowly shut. His footsteps started back down the hall, and he emerged from the shadows with eyes filled with pain.

And a revolver in his hand.

# TWENTY-NINE

It was a big gun, a .357 Colt Python, blue steel, the bluing dulled with age. I hefted its weight in my palm, then handed it back to Waltz, who gently set the weapon on the table.

"This was Vangie's father's service weapon?" I said. "He was a cop?"

"Sergeant John Edward Prowse. Killed in action in 1962 when she was seventeen."

"She never told me," I said, suddenly feeling as if parts of Vangie had been in code.

Waltz reached in his shirt pocket, pulled a badge polished as bright as a new dime. "And this was her father's tin."

"She gave you his badge?"

"To help keep me safe, she said, a second shield to cover my back."

"When did this happen?"

"In 1973, when I made detective. We'd grown up in Queens, neighbors, though I was just a scruffy kid to her. At least until we grew up."

"You and Vangie were . . . lovers?"

A catch came to Waltz's voice. He pushed past it. "The most beautiful years of my life. Then it sort of ramped down into friendship."

"But you still held the torch?"

The misery in his eyes told the story: *Then, now, always.*

"Did you know she was coming to New York?"

He stood, wiped his eyes with a handkerchief. "No. And that's totally out of character. She always called. For a few days we'd be together and I'd pretend I wasn't heartsick that she'd go away again, back to that damned Institute."

Waltz hung his head. Rain hammered the window.

"I never knew much of her history," I said. "Because of my past, I never ask people about theirs."

"Her father was ambushed by a sociopath when she was in high school. Her mother had died years before, the Big C. She and her father were all each other had, always there for one another, a team of two."

"His death must have been devastating."

"She retreated inside herself for a month. When she emerged, her first reaction was to join the force, follow in his footsteps."

"What happened?"

"She pulled all her courage together and went to the jail to visit her father's killer. To spit on him, she later told me, and to claw out his eyes if she got the chance."

"Sounds like her."

"She thought she'd find some hulking, tattoo-stained monster with bloodlust in his eyes. She found a forty-three-year-old actuary with a wife and three kids, house in the Connecticut 'burbs. He barely acknowledged her, too busy listening to the voices between his ears. A drooling, gun-slinging doper she could understand – and hate – but a white-collar guy who said a dragon lived inside his spine? That she couldn't fathom."

"Vangie didn't join the force, I take it."

"She had been considering biology before her father's death. She shifted to Psych, immersed in it – this was a senior in high school, mind you, reading all night, writing papers of professional depth. She got attention, grabbed a full ride at Princeton."

"And pretty much re-invented the field of aberrational psychology," I said.

"She couldn't not do it," Waltz said. "She was amazing."

"What happened when you saw the body was Vangie's?"

I needed to ask, did it quietly. Waltz closed his eyes.

"It was an explosion of cold in my face. My knees nearly went, the room swooped around. I realized if our history was known, I couldn't work the case. So I reached inside and grabbed on to something, you know?"

Like the day I found out Jeremy was a mass murderer. I said, "Yeah, I know."

"We found the recording saying contact you. I chilled the investigation and pulled every sting I had to get you here, to find out if you could help. Someone killed one of the best people on the planet and I need justice."

I stared into his eyes. "We can get justice, Shelly. But you've got to believe in my ability to find the truth."

Waltz walked to the window and parted the drapes, looking into the wind-blown ghosts of rain.

"How do I know I can I trust you?"

"Because Vangie did."

He closed his eyes, nodded, said, "Tell me the whole story."

It took a half an hour. I'm not sure how many of my conjectures he bought, but he asked no questions until I'd finished, starting with the one he found the most troubling.

"You say your partner, Nautilus, saw a photo of your brother in Evangeline's office? Naked."

I nodded.

"It couldn't be. She wouldn't have entered a relationship with a . . . with a . . ." Words failed and his face dropped.

"Jeremy said Vangie had called him her Sirius. Like the Dog Star. It jives with the reference in Vangie's recording. That she needed a 'serious' . . . then she stopped."

"Dog star?" Waltz frowned. "Needed a Sirius . . . ?" His face went white and I thought he was headed to the floor again.

"What is it, Shelly? What?"

Waltz grabbed his coat from the back of the couch, started pulling it on. "I've got to take you somewhere."

Rain whipped the window. Lightning flashed.

"Outside? In that?"

"Get your goddamn coat on."

We ran to his car, drove from Brooklyn into Manhattan, wipers fighting the rain. I knew by the streets and buildings we were near where the Twin Towers had stood. Waltz U'ed in the street, pulled up beside a small fenced-in area bathed in the yellow glow of streetlamps.

"This is a dog park, right?" I said, perplexed.

"A dog run. It was named after an explosives dog that died on 9/11. The dog's a local hero."

"Explosives dog? You mean a bomb-sniffer?"

"Exactly."

We got out of the car. The rain had dropped away to a chilly mist. Waltz pulled me by my sleeve to a metal plaque on the gate of the run. I couldn't read the words. He got out his flashlight, snapped it on. The plaque showed the outline of a retriever followed by a dedication date and a few lines of type. Above the dog and inscription were three simple words . . .

SIRIUS DOG RUN

"My God," I whispered. "The bomb-sniffing dog's name was Sirius."

Vangie had grown up in NYC. The first years of her career had been here. She visited often, subscribing to the *New York Times*, the *Post*, and the *New Yorker* to keep a foot in the old neighborhood. Surely she'd seen news stories on the incident, the park dedication.

If so, *"I need you to be my Sirius, Jeremy,"* equated to *"I need you to sniff out a bomb, Jeremy."*

But Jeremy wasn't tuned to explosives, he was calibrated for mental dysfunctions. His life among the violently insane, his intellect, his supranormally tuned senses, his self-awareness, all combined in the ability to detect pathological mental conditions in others, to know how those people would act in a range of conditions.

Question: Why would Vangie want my brother to find a madman?

Answer: Because something unspeakable would happen if the madman went undetected.

Waltz had arrived at the same conclusion. He touched my arm.

"Do you understand what may be happening, Detective Ryder?"

"I think so, Shelly."

"Where do we go from here?"

# THIRTY

The tape snapped from Alice Folger's face. Jeremy Ridgecliff plucked the washcloth from her mouth. She gagged, then accepted the water he dribbled across her lips. She was in a bed, canopied with red velvet. She was tied tight, but with a pillow beneath her head. Ridgecliff had lifted her from the wooden box; it must have taken tremendous strength. Where did he store it in that lanky body?

She heard another rumble of thunder outside. It would rain until the leading edge of the incoming high-pressure ridge pushed the low out to sea. The rain would dissipate tomorrow afternoon. She'd at least like to die on a sunny day.

Ridgecliff said, "Do you need to drain?"

"No. I'm fine."

"Food?"

She shook her head. Her last meal had been bits of leftover duck scented with cognac. He'd allowed bathroom visits in both locations, all carefully controlled. So far he hadn't hurt her.

He started to replace the tape. She shook her head. "Wait . . . I can help you in this unfortunate situation, Mr Ridgecliff, We have a friend in common, a Mobile detective named Carson Ryder. You used to speak to him when you were at the Institute. He speaks highly of you, says you're exceptionally intelligent. In fact, he thinks –"

"Are you fucking him?"

"What?"

"Are you fucking Ryder? You'd be attractive to him and he'd love to swim the ol' weenie around in you. Are you fucking him? It's a charitable thing to do."

"I don't think we should discuss my personal life, Mr Ridgecliff, not when there's so much to talk about –"

Ridgecliff began chanting like a schoolboy. "Heard it, heard it, heard it in your voi-eece. You've been fucking Ry-der."

"Mr Ridgecliff . . ."

"I hear these days women will fuck anything without a second thought: other women, Dalmatians, pumpkins, Carson Ryder . . ."

"I won't lie to you Mr Ridgecliff. You're in trouble. There's a chance you could get hurt –"

"Do tell."

"I'd like for you to consider me a friend. Someone who can help you get to safety and –"

"STOP TRYING TO HUMANIZE YOUR-SELF! I'VE FORGOTTEN MORE OF THAT FRESHMAN-LEVEL PSYCHOBABBLE THAN YOU'LL EVER KNOW."

It was the most terrifying voice she'd ever heard. That it was coming from a plump man in eye liner and shag wig made it more fright-ening, like a kitten opening its mouth and having a cobra's fangs.

"I'm . . . sorry Mr Ridgecliff. I didn't mean to make you angry."

"DON'T GET ON MY UNHAPPY SIDE."

"It was a mistake. I learned from it. I'm sorry."

Your contrition is accepted, Miss Alice. Unless you misbehave, I have no plans to hurt you."

It took several seconds for his words to register. "Wait, what? You don't plan to . . . kill me?"

"It's messy and I wouldn't get my deposit back on the house."

"Then why did you abduct me, Mr Ridgecliff?"

"To protect you."

"Protect me?" Folger asked. "From what?"

He pushed the tape over her mouth. Started away, but turned. He put his lips beside Folger's ear, his breath warm and wet.

"My past."


In the morning I met Waltz for breakfast in a coffee joint three blocks from the cop shop. The last of the storm was blowing through and all the vendors on the street had magically produced boxes of umbrellas in two color choices: black and blacker. I closed my new black umbrella and went inside, saw Waltz at a lone table by the window, staring blankly into rain plummeting over a multihued sea of traffic.

I bought coffee and a bialy and we huddled close across the small table. We had both walked out on to a tightrope no wider than a thread. We didn't know where it went. All we knew was that any fall would be long and irreparably damaging.

"What are we going to do?" he asked. "We didn't discuss much of that last night."

"We have to operate on the assumption that Vangie brought Jeremy here to find a madman. That finding the madman would avert a disaster. If the investigation starts closing in on Jeremy, we, we . . ."

"We fuck it up, temporarily," Waltz growled. "If that's going to keep Folger safe, that's what we do."

"I've got to redirect my investigation toward Vangie. Try and figure out what she fell into."

"How will you start?"

"By changing my entire mind-set, Shelly. Inverting my prime assumption: that Jeremy is decompensating."

"He is. You said it a dozen times."

"Maybe. But the new assumption has to be that Jeremy is as bizarrely rational as always. Though he may not be making sense to us, he's making perfect sense in his world."

"I wonder how much sense he made to Evangeline?"

I shrugged. It hit me that now might be the time to ask something that had been on my mind since last night."

"Shelly, the Evangeline Prowse I knew never

wanted anyone to call her anything but Vangie, was almost strident about it. She didn't care for Evangeline. Yet that's what you call her."

Waltz turned away and looked out into the rain. It rippled and shifted down the pane, turning the streetscape into a scene from a kaleidoscope filled with shards of light and broken shadows. His finger touched at the window, like he could change the shapes he saw.

"She loved the name Evangeline, actually. Loved its rhythm and poetry, as did I. But she said from the moment she went to Alabama, she would tell everyone that her preference was Vangie. Only one person would ever again call her Evangeline."

I started to speak but couldn't find the words. Waltz turned back to the window and that's how I left him.

I hustled back to the hotel. The stacks of files and information supplied by the NYPD had grown daily. Pads of paper covered the bed. I had sticky notes on one entire wall and had forbidden the housekeeping staff from entering lest some crumb of note-taking be disturbed.

I arm-shoveled pads to the floor, turned on a muted news channel and stared at the ceiling.

Vangie's reason for bringing Jeremy to New York was to avert a disaster. But had she encountered the threat during a visit to New York? Or in her daily work?

How did this connect to Jeremy's assertion he and Vangie were . . . what? He'd never used the word lovers, choosing innuendo and bombast, which he often used to disguise a lie.

Was there any connection to the invisible patient? The confidentiality problem to which Traynor had alluded? The break-in at Vangie's house?

My mind felt like a myopic eye trying to track a thousand comets through the night sky. Facts swirled across suppositions, names danced around places, theories disappeared down black holes. I'd absorbed too much information and it had jumbled. How to make sense of an onslaught of the senseless? I mulled the thought for two minutes, then called the concierge.

"How fast can you get me a roll of butcher's paper?"

I was intrigued by Cluff's methodology. Pour your mind on to a white expanse and study the facts in a spatial setting, adding underscores, arrows, impromptu timelines. Decide what's wheat and chaff and keep unrolling paper. If an

313

idea goes nowhere, you still have a quarter-mile of thinking ahead.

I sat and poured both fact and supposition on to the paper, crossing out, adding, tearing away paper and starting anew.

I transcribed the duality of voices at Jeremy's murder scenes. I saw my notes on Harry's conversations with Dr Traynor at the Institute, how my brother's underlying motive – primal judgment? Was that what they called it? – had never been ascertained by Vangie. She must have ceaselessly attempted to uncover Jeremy's "Fire that lights all fires" as Traynor also called the seminal moment of transition to murderer.

My pen paused. Was it irrelevant? Of all the cases presented to Vangie over her career, my brother's would have been one of the most enigmatic. Apparently, however, he had never confessed his original pinion point: What drove him to kill the first woman?

I heard Vangie pick away at the lock as Jeremy jittered and danced, bobbed and weaved, letting Vangie close, but never in the final door. He would have been irritating, frustrating and angering. A total challenge from the day he entered the Institute.

*Challenge.*

The word echoed in my mind. Why?

I studied trails of words and arrows on my eight-foot-long mural of death. Where had I seen the word? *There*, in my longhand notes of Harry's discoveries. Traynor had told Harry that if Vangie had a private client, he or she would have to pose a tremendous challenge. Saturdays, one to three p.m., Vangie had – according to her neighbor – kept hours with a client. But the neighbor had never seen anyone enter or exit.

Maybe there wasn't a client. Perhaps it was Vangie's way of grabbing some quiet time to write or take a nap.

Or . . .

Could it be because the challenging client couldn't be there? Except perhaps, as an avatar, a symbolic representation.

A photograph on the door.

Had Vangie been searching for Jeremy's primal judgment? Had she uncovered a transforming moment in his past that had kindled today's crimes?

I re-read all police reports, moving backward in time, ending with Officer Jim Day's notes on my father's murder scene: clear, precise, insightful, with a concluding judgment that stepped outside objective reportage:

"...  *the entire scene was drenched in anger and release. It seems some pivotal mental barrier was broached, a threshold crossed, a major decision acted upon.*"

Pivotal mental barrier? Day seemed to have discerned a subtext in my brother's murderous actions. Had Day noticed anything else? And if he had, would he remember?

Was he even alive?

There was nothing I could do from here. Not with any efficiency. I pulled my phone and called Harry. As I dialed, my eyes drifted to the far-left end of the butcher paper, where I had started by encapsulating the details of my father's death. The details had been supplied by Officer Jim Day, his name in a wide swathe of black ink.

Day. Where my brother's records started. Where everything started.

"Nautilus," my partner answered.

"I need to talk to a guy, Harry. He may be hard to find."

# THIRTY-ONE

Nautilus listened into his phone, heard pages flipping back and forth as the county police clerk checked her records. "I got it that Officer Jim Day worked here for three years and two months and, uh, six days. That was twenny-five years back."

"There's no current address for Officer Day?"

"Nope. If he'd worked here long enough the state'd have a pension account address, where the check is sent, but he didn't do that."

"Is there anyone who'd know where Officer Day might be?"

"I expect Sher'f Reamy might. He was around back then, only retired a few years back. If anybody kep' touch with Officer Day, it would be the Sher'f. Or mebbe he knows somebody who knows somebody, that kind a thing. You got a pin or a pincil?"

Nautilus dialed Reamy's number. Heard the phone pick up.

"If this is another goddamn call for burial plots, I ain't gonna be the one needing 'em."

"Is this Sheriff Reamy?"

"Not if you're selling something, it ain't."

"This is Detective Harry Nautilus in Mobile. It may seem odd, but I'm trying to locate Officer Jim Day, need to talk to him."

"The subject?"

"A killing over twenty years ago. Earl Ridgecliff."

"If there'd be anyone to ask, I guess it'd be Jim Day. The case weighed down a corner of his desk for a long time. He had a thing about it."

"A thing?" Nautilus asked.

"An interest. Probably just simple curiosity."

"Were you there as well, Sheriff? At the scene."

"Yep. Looked like people had been fighting with red paint and buckets of meat."

"Do you know where I might get in touch with Mr Day?"

"No I don't." Reamy paused. "I'm not sure I'd want to."

Nautilus canted his head at a sound in a far corner of his head. A siren.

"Can I run up and talk to you, sir?"

Hollis Reamy, retired sheriff of Pickett County, Alabama, stepped to the porch. He pulled off a white hood, showing a wide, sun-browned face and intelligent gray eyes. His hair was more salt than pepper. Reamy patted sweat from his forehead with a red bandana and gave Nautilus the cop appraisal.

"You're a husky fella, ain't you?"

Nautilus tugged at the lapels of his orange jacket. "It's interesting. I grew just big enough to fill my clothes."

"And right colorful ones they are, Detective. Gimme a moment and we'll talk about Jim Day."

Reamy set aside the beekeeper's hood and hive-smoker he'd been carrying, resembling a coffeepot drizzling smoke from its spout. He yanked off gloves and jammed them in his back pocket. Pulled off a sweatshirt. He wore a starched white shirt and red suspenders braced his khaki pants. Nautilus looked into the side

319

yard and saw the hives, a dozen white boxes, the surrounding air alive with black dots. He hoped the dots returned to the task of making honey. Reamy nodded to a pair of wicker chairs in the corner.

"Drag them chairs into the shade while I fetch something cool to drink."

Reamy disappeared inside the home, a beige modular with green shutters on several acres in the heart of farmland. The acreage was studded with water oaks, pecans and towering longleaf pines, cones the size of shoes at their bases. Reamy was back a minute later with two glasses of sweet tea.

"Some folks like Red Diamond tea," Reamy said. "But I prefer Luzianne. I sweeten it with two parts white sugar, one part turbinado sugar, one part honey. I balance it off with a little mint and lemon."

Nautilus took a sip and pronounced it delicious. Reamy nodded appreciation and sat his chair in reverse, arms crossed over the backrest.

"So the gist is you're trying to find Jim's Day's personal take on the killing of Earl Ridgecliff all them years back?"

"My partner thinks it might be important."

"And he's way up in New York?"

"Yes."

Reamy sighed and stood. "Let's take a drive, Detective."

They drove out the main highway, turned on to a tight road bordered by piney woods. Reamy swerved from the road and drove through three hundred feet of woods, branches squealing against his pickup. He stopped in a quarter-acre clearing surrounded by arrow-straight pines. The two men exited, walking a carpet of pine needles.

"This is where it happened?" Nautilus said.

"I remember it clear as yesterday. A guy out hunting squirrels found the body, what there was of it. Hadn't been dead more'n three hours, what the coroner figured." Reamy raised an eyebrow. "The guy that found the body? He never went hunting again, said it got ruint for him."

Reamy's boots crunched over a deadfall. He paused and surveyed the scene. "Day was closest and got here first. Probably here ten minutes 'fore I arrived. We both parked on the road, afraid of messing up potential evidence, tire tracks, whatnot. I came down a deer trail yonder."

He nodded to a dirt path tracing through underbrush.

"The path's soft with needles and Day didn't hear me coming. He was standing in the middle of all that human wreckage, not moving, like he was hypnotized. When he heard me, he snapped out of it and waved. It was a strange moment, but Jim Day was strange. Then the rest of the crew showed up, the Staties, the Medical Examiner and so forth."

"Day wrote the official report, not you."

"Because he had an eye for detail and a dictionary vocabulary. He took the photos that day, went through twenty packs of film. Shot every bit of meat, every organ, every possible angle. He climbed that tree over there to get pictures from above. Couldn't get enough pictures."

"How much involvement did your department have with the case?"

"Interviewing the locals, mainly. The State Police and ABI did the heavy lifting. But Day always kept them bloody pictures up on his desk like the case was his alone. Kept the full stack of reports, too. All the updates. One day, about a year after the killing, he put them away like the case had been magically solved, though that was still eight years away."

"You never had an inkling who did it?"

"The Ridgecliff kid was never a suspect. A skinny, smart-brained and good-looking young fella who never spoke much. When the truth came out you could have dropped me with a feather."

"When we spoke yesterday, you gave the impression of not caring much for Day."

Reamy looked down, kicked a pine cone. "Seemed like a super choice when he got hired, the best scores ever seen from a recruit. But he never quite fit in, a loner when it came down to things, I guess."

"I know a lot of guys who go their own way. Good cops."

Reamy followed the cone a few feet, punted it into the trees. "Once I asked him to clean the gear in the ordnance cabinet. I was working third shift, about three a.m., and come in from a patrol. Day was cleaning the pieces when I passed by, didn't know anyone was there. He had maybe twenty weapons disassembled, rifles, handguns, shotguns, specialty weapons, all laying on newspaper on the floor around him . . ." Reamy pulled off his cap, scratched his forehead.

"And?" Nautilus prompted.

"I'm pretty sure he had an erection."

"What'd you do?"

"I never asked him to clean the ordnance again. But like I said, he did what he was asked and got it done. No one disliked him, no one liked him. He was here three years and when he left, the whole place seemed happier somehow."

They climbed back in the car. "Could you drive by the house where the Ridgecliffs lived?" Nautilus asked. "If it's not out of the way."

"Ain't far. I got nothing else to do but play with my bees."

They drove three miles down the road, the air rippling with heat as though the land were a thin crust atop a raging furnace. Reamy turned a corner, pointed.

"That's the one. Looks pretty much the same, abandoned out here all by itself."

They drove by the white two-story farmhouse, windows boarded over, one side of the porch swing still dangling on its chain. Nautilus's head replayed stories of occurrences within the house and he held his breath as they went by, like a kid passing a graveyard and afraid of inhaling ghosts.

# THIRTY-TWO

"You were right," Waltz said. He'd called and we'd met in a subway station near the precinct house. A train swept to the platform, wheels squealing.

"About what?" I yelled.

Waltz waited until the train pulled away. "Ridgecliff. The uproar at the Portuguese Embassy was threatening to ramp into a major brouhaha, so the NYPD put out the word that we were looking for a Portuguese businessman, but no relationship to the Embassy. All a mistake."

"I saw the clarification."

"Anyway, a rental agent, Jessica Stambliss, was visiting family upstate, When she heard, she ran to her nearest precinct, all whipped up.

Turns out she had leased a place to a Mr Caldiera, a Portuguese businessman."

A train swept to the opposite side of the station. "What happened?"

"We got to the leased condo, a sublet. Empty. It's staked out now, but he's gone."

Relief washed over my body.

Waltz said, "There was fresh food in the fridge, take-out entrées from a four-star restaurant. A chocolate cake, too. Covered with cherries and nuts, like a sundae. There was torn duct tape beside a bed. And an empty roll. How's he moving her?"

I'd given it a lot of thought. He was using his special ability.

"All he needs is a schizophrenic driver, Shelly. He can convince the guy of anything. Maybe he enlisted a psychotic with a taxi."

"Jesus. He's got a thousand potential accomplices."

Waltz's phone rang. He took the call, shaking his head. He closed the phone and muttered a curse.

"Gotta go."

"Something with Folger?"

"The Pelham problem. Another damned doll just showed up."

"How many does that make?"

"Four."

"How many in a set?"

"It's all over the board. Some have a dozen. Five or six is typical."

I thought a moment. "Can you take someone along who knows the things? Got any Russian cops in the precinct?"

Waltz frowned. "Not at the station. Wait, there's a guy fills the pop and candy machines, Alex something or other. I can probably get hold of him."

I accompanied Waltz to Pelham's headquarters, knowing her nibs would be happy to hear a friendly accent. Especially given the phalanx of screaming anti-Pelhammers across the street from her HQ. Waltz figured the two of us could handle the doll gig, get back to our little problem with my brother.

Sarah Wensley was in her usual position in front of the table with the brown box, the doll nestled inside, face up. I'd seen the first doll, but not the two recent additions. They had gotten smaller and the doll I was looking at was four inches tall.

Waltz peered into the box. "It's from the same series or whatever as the other. Mouth's gone."

Pelham wandered into the room, waving at a departing news crew.

"I'm thinking when we get to the last doll, it'll have one of those party snakes in it, y'know. The ones on a spring?"

Wensley shivered. "I'm not opening it."

Waltz had his gloves on. Shook the doll. "Sounds empty, like the others."

One of Pelham's Secret Service handlers pushed through the door, looked at Waltz.

"There's a guy out front says he's a consultant to the NYPD. He's a bit odd."

"Fat? Got a thick Slav accent?" Shelly asked.

The agent nodded. "And pockets full of candy bars."

"Send him back."

Alex Borskov entered the room like a liberator, handing out chocolate bars. I figured he was real popular with kids. Pelham smiled, took a Snickers. When his pockets were empty, Borskov grinned.

"Am understanding I am come here to consultate?"

Waltz said, "These people have been receiving some dolls, Mr Borskov. They've gotten four, starting with one six inches tall, now they're down to this . . ."

Borskov eyed the doll, his face breaking into a wide grin.

"I KNOW THEM WELL! Every Russian know them well. They are matryoshka dolls."

I tried the name. "Matra-matree . . ."

"Matryoshka! The word comes from the name Matryona."

"Does that mean something special?" Waltz asked.

Borskov pumped his hands over his chest to indicate large breasts. "Matryona is by tradition a buxom, earthy peasant woman – the mother."

"The dolls are especially symbolic of mothers?" I asked.

"Many kinds of nesting dolls. Hundreds. Matryoshka is only one for symbol of perfect mother-woman. Strong lady, Matryona. Very powerful."

"They're more than funny dolls," I said to Waltz. "They're matriarchal symbols. Womanhood symbols. And who's the most powerful woman in the country right now?"

We both looked at Pelham.

Waltz dispatched the doll to Forensics for more useless testing, then pulled me into the men's room, locked the door.

"Your brother hates women, kills them. He likes symbols and strange little pranks like those damn dolls. We've got to give the Secret Service a heads-up. If we tell them he's a danger to Pelham they'll put full Secret Service resources into the hunt. We could use them."

"You want to doom Folger?"

Someone tried the door. I yelled "Occupied!"

"What if your goddamn brother kills a presidential candidate and it comes out we knew the possibility in advance?"

"It's not him, Shelly."

"That's from your new assessment, right? Where you're assuming he's not on a spree, he's on a mission or something."

"It why Vangie brought him here. Sirius, remember?"

"It's a theory! What if she didn't? What if she was . . . mixed up or something?"

He'd given me my leverage. "You knew Vangie best, Shelly. It's your call."

He closed his eyes and turned to the wall, slowly tapping his forehead against the white-painted brick. "They're just a few damned empty dolls, right? A joke by some sorry geek. Still, I'm gonna make sure the SS boys have every photographic permutation we made of

Ridgecliff. There's no way even your brother could get past both the NYPD and the Secret Service."

Waltz headed to the station to see if he could pour surreptitious sand into the gears of the Folger investigation until I could get us ahead of my brother. I bought some Chinese take-out and went back to my bunker for more research, rolling out another meter of white paper.

My phone went off. When I saw Harry's number on the screen, I figured he'd tell me one of two things: either he'd found Officer Day's number for me to call, or he'd been unable to find the man.

I hadn't considered that Harry would tell an eerie story about Jim Day.

"Day was real interested in my father's death?" I asked.

"Obsessive, to hear Reamy tell it, keeping the photos on his desk, the reports."

"It just stopped one day?" I asked.

"A year or so later. Not long after, Day resigned. Grabbed his letter of reference and blew town, Reamy thought."

"About the time Jeremy headed to college," I noted, not sure if it meant anything.

"From getting aroused by guns to keeping the scene photos on his desk, Day smells a little off to me. I booked a room at a local motel so I can hit the county courthouse tomorrow, try for the three snapshots."

When Harry and I needed an immediate scan of someone, we tried to find people who knew the subject in childhood, youth, and adulthood. Three fast views: snapshots.

"You're the best, Harry. I owe you more than I can ever repay."

"Won't stop me from trying. Get some sleep, Carson. You sound half-past dead."

I turned on the TV for background, saw live coverage of Cynthia Pelham campaigning near Central Park, the cops cordoning off several hundred protestors. The camera panned the anti-Pelham crowd: angry faces, fists in the air, bibles being quoted, epithets hurled.

I'd never seen so many adult faces that looked like angry children. I thought I noticed Blankley in the crowd waving his idiotic logo; it figured. I turned off the hatred and fell into bed drifting into a restless sleep haunted by mouthless dolls.

# THIRTY-THREE

Harry Nautilus arrived at the Pickens County courthouse forty-five minutes before it opened. He cupped his hands around his eyes and peered through the door. Lights were off, the halls empty. He sat on the steps to review his notes. The door opened at his back.

"You here for the view?"

He turned to a woman pushing – or maybe pulling – seventy years of age, her dress a rage of color, her too-black hair stiffly coiffed and geometrically perfect, her blue eyes alert with curiosity.

"I'm here to look at some records. It's an official visit of sorts."

He pulled his badge wallet, held it up. She lifted neck-strung reading glasses and leaned close to study the ID. Nautilus could smell her perfume, something at odds with her age.

She looked up from the ID. "Mobile? Aren't you a little out of your jurisdiction, Detective Nautilus?"

"Actually, ma'am, I'm working on a case in New York City. It's a long story."

"I'd imagine." She gathered him inside with the crook of a finger and he followed her down the hall, almost jogging to keep up with her clicking high heels. "You're in luck, Detective Nautilus," she said over her shoulder. "I'm Loretta Quint. I own this here place."

"Ma'am?"

She led him into a windowed room filled with file cabinets and empty desks, the records division.

"Been working here since I was twenty-seven. That was back when a computer was a man who ciphered numbers in his head and type-writers were powered by fingers. I know where everything is, and if I don't know, it's only because I'm pretending to not know. You get my drift?"

Nautilus grinned. "Indeed, ma'am. You are the most gorgeous woman I ever laid eyes on. I live to breath in the air you breathe out."

334

She laughed, more percussive than melodic. "I already like you better than three of my five husbands. You tell me what you want to see, and I'll point where to go. How's that work for you?"

Under the supervision of Quint, Nautilus accomplished his mission in forty minutes, racing through a round-robin of files, copying pertinent information, cross-checking, and finding more than he'd hoped, leaving with a notepad of names, addresses and numbers.

The regular clerical staff, a dozen women between thirty and sixty – a collection of some of the plainest and most drably dressed women Nautilus had ever seen – were arriving at their desks as Ms Quint escorted him to the door of the courthouse. She held his arm tight and leaned against him as if suddenly frail. He feared his requests had worn her out.

"I'm fine on my own, Miz Quint," he suggested. "You don't have to see me to the door."

"I surely do," she whispered, wrapping tighter against his arm. "Since you was here when they all arrived, I'm wanting the others to wonder if you might be my new boy-toy and we just spent the night tusslin' on someone's desk. I got

335

to do something to amuse myself around all these turnips."

Nautilus fought a laugh. They continued to the door, a dozen pairs of eyes recording the voyage. Before leaving, he shivered his knees as if they were failing, kissed the woman's forehead, and said – just loud enough to carry down the hall – "Oh baby, you just about wore me down to a nub."

He swore he heard gasps from down the hall. Loretta Quint squeezed his wrist and winked.

The air was fifteen degrees hotter as Nautilus got in the car than when he'd left it an hour before, the solar furnace ramping up toward Alabama summer. He flipped open his notepad, deciding where to start. In checking property records on the Days, he found the lot and house across the street had been bought for $34,000 by an Elbert and Carla Joiner when the Days had lived on the street. It was now owned by Carla Joiner, the only property on the street with continued ownership. Nautilus also discovered that Elbert and Carla Joiner had divorced two years later, suggesting Ms Joiner received the house as a settlement, never felt compelled to move.

The neighborhood was down a crumbling

highway several miles from the main road, the horizon distorted by heat shimmering from the dry land. Arriving in the wide-scattered cluster of houses, he saw the lots were large, the houses small, built in the twenties and thirties for blue-collar families. There was a pervasive sense of decrepitude, both in appearance and smell, like a suppurating pond was nearby. Nautilus figured anyone with a decent income had long ago moved to the tidier post-war 'burbs along the highway.

He drove by the house where the Days had lived, a two-story frame at the back of a half-acre lot. A broken-down pickup was in the front yard, as well as several tires and a rusting outboard motor. A sad-eyed hound was tied to the outboard motor amidst piles of excrement. It watched Nautilus without interest.

The Joiner house was a tiny mildewed bungalow a hundred feet from the street, one side of the porch slanting, imperiled by rotting underpinning. The granules had crumbled from the shingles, the roof dusty gray. No grass grew in the front yard, only spindly weeds pushing from crusty dirt. The car parked in the front yard was an 80s-vintage Detroit rumbler, the tailpipe wired to the bumper with a coat hanger.

Nautilus surveyed the desolation and knocked gently on the doorframe, afraid a hard knock would bring the house down. He saw a curtain shift at a window and he stepped several feet back from the door and tried to look pleasant.

After a minute, the door opened and a woman in her middle sixties appeared. She had a high-mileage face, the skin lined and loose, eyes bagged and burdened with too much make-up. The hair was tinsel-bright blonde with an inch of brown roots. She wore a faded yellow house-dress and poufy mules with three-inch heels. Nautilus heard a loud TV and smelled fried food, cigarettes, and root beer.

He said, "Miz Carla Joiner?"

"Whatever you're selling, mister, I can't afford –"

Nautilus held up his badge. "I'm asking around about a man name of Jim Day."

"Never heard of him."

She said it too fast as she pushed the door closed. It stopped on the point of Nautilus's right forefinger. He flicked his finger and the door swung open.

"Maybe I should have said I was asking about a boy name of Jim Day. You would know him as a boy, since records show you living here when the Days lived across the street."

She shut her eyes, trapped. "I don't remember hardly nothing. We weren't close. It was a long time ago."

"Still, may I ask you a few questions?"

She sighed theatrically and motioned Nautilus inside with a ring- and bracelet-laden hand holding a promotional glass from a fast-food restaurant, a grinning clown painted on the glass. The glass was empty, save for cubes of ice and an ounce of brownish fluid.

Nautilus stepped past the woman, smelling something stronger than root beer on her breath. He walked to the television, crossing a room filled with the sort of furniture advertised at truckload sales, seven pieces for three hundred ninety-nine bucks. The stuff was one step above cardboard. He nodded to the blaring TV, the tips of its rabbit-ear antennae bulbed with foil.

"May I turn the sound down for a few minutes?"

Joiner shrugged. "Ain't but shit on anyways."

She sat on a tattered couch and fired up a cigarette, nodding for Nautilus to sit on a wooden chair across a low coffee table piled with celebrity-focused magazines and three full ashtrays. She crossed legs so white they could have been bleached, blue veins pressing hard against the skin.

"What can you tell me about the Day family?" he asked.

"I said I didn't know that woman and her kid. I can't help you with nothing."

"I'm just trying to find out a bit about the boy's history. What his past was like. Childhood."

He saw the spider webs at her eyes tighten at the word "childhood". Guilt distorted her face before she turned it to the mute television, trying to find a place for her eyes to hide.

*She knows something*, Nautilus thought.

"Miz Joiner? Hello?"

Her face turned to him, her teeth clenched. "Ain't you listening, mister? I hardly ever saw them folks. How can I tell you what I don't know?"

Nautilus considered the available options. After over twenty years of interviews, he had interesting choices, ranging from acting like a clueless nitwit to hulking over skinny white guys and squeezing his hands together as if fighting to keep his fingers from wrapping a neck.

He settled on a tactic that had often worked

in such situations: granting Carla Joiner the anonymity of a fictional middleman. He leaned back and laced his fingers behind his neck.

"Let me ask this, Miz Joiner . . . did you know anyone more acquainted with the Days? Someone that might have told you little pieces about them? That happens a lot, people talking across fences."

Carla Joiner pursed her lips, thinking about the notion, accepting it with a subconscious, almost imperceptible nod. She looked at the ceiling, tapped her lips with a chipped and bitten crimson fingernail.

"Come to think of it, there was a lady lived next door to the Days for a while. She told me things now and then. I don't carry no gossip. But it ain't gossip if it's the Lord's truth."

"Did she tell you much about Jim Day's upbringing?" Nautilus asked. "This other woman?"

Joiner looked at her glass, saw it was empty. "I need a little something to wet my throat."

Nautilus watched Carla Joiner pad to the kitchen area, set the glass on a counter littered with used dishes. She opened the fridge and dropped three cubes of ice into the glass, pouring it half full of store-brand diet root beer. She turned the corner and was out of sight for a ten-count. When she returned the glass was full. Vodka, Nautilus figured, stifling a grimace at the thought of vodka and root beer.

"Can I git you something?" she called from the kitchen.

"A glass of ice water would be nice."

Given Carla Joiner's lax sense of house-keeping, Nautilus didn't want her glassware near his lips, but any interaction softened the sense of interrogation. Nautilus had once been trying to pry information from a man painting his house. The guy had looked away and grunted until Nautilus picked up a brush and started slapping paint. Ten minutes later the guy was beating his gums like an auctioneer. The afternoon-long conversation had ultimately solved a pair of shootings, which was good, since Nautilus had painted the guy's entire front porch.

Carla Joiner set a plastic tumbler of tepid water beside Nautilus. He thanked her warmly and took a sip, trying to skinny his lips between a lipstick smear and greasy thumbprint. She sat, found a place in the overflowing ashtray to stub out her cigarette, then lipped and lit a new one. Blue smoke plumed from her nostrils. Nautilus leaned forward, resisting the impulse to wave the smoke from his face.

"Now, what did the lady who knew about Jim Day's upbringing tell you?"

A mirthless laugh. "It wasn't an upbringing. It was a down-pulling. That goddamn woman lived in hell and pulled her boy right down through its hole."

"By 'that woman' I'm assuming you mean Jim Day's mother."

"All he ever knew as kin was his mama and his granmama. His daddy would have been some guy with twenty bucks and ten minutes to kill."

"Mrs Day was a prostitute?"

"That other lady said – and these are her exact words – 'Lorinn Day got up when the sun went down, opened her legs and mouth, and the parade started.'"

"Parade of customers?"

"Sometimes there was three–four men in that house at the same time. Women went in and out of there, too. Or both. Sometimes you couldn't tell which was which, the women looking more like men than the men. That lady didn't have no limits." Carla Joiner paused. "Or so I got told."

"Where was Jim Day during all of this?"

She frowned. "In the house, I guess. 'Cept when his mama got arrested a couple times, county jail. I heard little Jimmy was in custody of the child welfare people, sometimes. Or stayed with the grandmama."

"Day's mother, I take it."

"You could see where the bad seed had come from. She was a nasty woman, wicked. She dressed like a floozy and was always messed up on something. She didn't look scarcely older than her daughter, neither. I figgered she'd birthed Lorinn Day early, fourteen, fifteen years old. Lorinn Day weren't past being a girl herself, maybe twenny, when my ex and I bought this place way back when."

Making Lorinn Day eighteen or nineteen when she'd given birth to Jim Day, Nautilus thought. She'd likely found the kid a serious impediment, but he would have upped the money and services from governmental sources.

"You don't think Jim Day's granny was good for him?"

Carla Joiner looked over the rim of her glass. "Neither of them women had the right feelings toward the boy. There was sickness there."

Nautilus felt his stomach curdle. "How so?"

"I remember the first time Lorinn Day got

pulled off to jail. I mean, I remember when the other lady told me about it. The grandmama was in the house. Two men came to visit. One of the men had a fluffy toy dog on a string and was hopping it on the ground. Jimmy was mebbe six. He came running after that toy, trying to wrap it up in his arms, but every time he was about to pounce, the man yanked it away. He pulled that toy into the car and Jimmy climbed in after it."

"They gone long?" Nautilus asked.

Carla Joiner hid behind a cloud of smoke. "For a few days. Week maybe."

Nautilus kept his voice even. "That other woman who knew Lorinn Day better – she didn't tell anyone? Have the police check things out?"

Carla Joiner turned her face away and took a long pull from her drink. "That woman . . . she didn't know things was wrong. She thought them men was kin or the like. People around here keep to themselves."

Three excuses in one breath, Nautilus noted, resisting the inclination to grab the front of the woman's dress and ask if she'd slept through the rest of her life as well. Joiner burned off a quarter of her cigarette in two hard pulls, downed her drink in a single swig. She rattled the ice in the glass. "I need another roo' beer."

This time the drink she brought back was the color of weak tea, three-quarters blast juice, Nautilus figured. There wasn't much time to grab information before it started getting muddled.

"You gonna be here much longer?" she asked.

"Just a couple more questions, Miz Joiner. While the Days lived over there, nothing really changed?"

A shrug. "I guess every day was the same thing over again. I never knew . . . I mean that other lady never really knew when Jimmy was around and when he wasn't. Kid kept to himself like a quiet little ghost."

"And nothing was ever said to anyone?"

"An old man lived down the street went up to the Day lady once, asked what was going on. Three days later his house burnt down. He went away and never came back. An' that's all I know about anything to do with them people. It was almost forever ago."

Nautilus stood, feeling the onset of a headache from the smoke. Or the story of Jim Day's childhood.

"Thanks for your time and your recollections, Miz Joiner. If you think of anything else, please call me." He left the card on the table and let himself out. When he got to the sidewalk, the door of the house opened, a wavering Carla Joiner at the threshold. She pushed the two-tone hair from her face with fingers holding a cigarette, ash tumbling unnoticed down her cheek.

"Hey . . . I just thought of somethin' else. About the way the kid acted. Or maybe how he didn't act."

"What, Miz Joiner?"

"He never knew how to be like a kid. Once I was watching out my window about the time school let out. Jimmy was eight maybe. All the kids jumped off the bus and was laughing at him, shoving and pinching him. They ended up in my front yard and I went outside to run 'em off. I thought Jimmy'd be crying, but he wasn't. He was looking up at me with a face as blank as a pie tin and said the weirdest fuckin' thing."

"What was that, Miz Joiner?"

Carla Joiner tossed ice from the glass into the parched ground of her yard. She took a final pinching suck from the cigarette, tossed it into the dirt as well.

"He said, 'What do they want me to be, Miss Carla? I don't know what they want me to be.'"

"What do they want me to be?" Nautilus echoed, wishing he was anywhere but on this sad little street in the dead center of nowhere.

# THIRTY-FOUR

Nautilus checked a county map. He had another stop on his snapshot tour of Jim Day's life, a former foster home where a teenaged Day had lived for several months. Day had been at several foster homes, but Nautilus only found one former foster who hadn't died or moved.

Marlene Cullers lived just south of Carrollton. She looked younger than mid-sixties, a tall and heavy-boned woman with waist-length gray hair, half-round glasses, and a smile as wide and bright as a truck grille. She wore a Neil Young tee-shirt, patched blue jeans, and backless plastic shoes like helmets for your feet. If she'd been a lady wrestler, Nautilus figured, her name would have been Big Hippie Mama. She took him from front porch to coffee at the kitchen table in twenty seconds flat.

"Jimmy was a foster kid with us when his mama got arrested for dealing, went to prison. We were one of three families he stayed with. We talk, fosters, and all of us had the same experience."

"What kind of experience was that?"

She shook back the free-falling shock of gray hair. "Jimmy didn't do anything. He sat and looked at you, like trying to figure something out. Or making up a movie in his head where you had a part to play, but only he could see how it came out. He never seemed angry, never acted out. But that's because he never really seemed to be there."

"Was he dull? I mean . . ."

"Mentally? No, quite the opposite. He did very well in school. But when we'd talk to his teachers, they'd all ask the same questions: Is he always this quiet? Does he have these mannerisms at home?"

"Mannerisms, ma'am?"

Cullers frowned, trying to find words. "Sometimes he'd say things that didn't fit. You'd say, 'The Smith's new kittens got stole from their back porch last night,' and Jimmy'd laugh and say, 'At school today we ate hot dogs for lunch.' Stuff like that. No connection, not one anyone could figure, anyway. And he'd watch television all the time, war movies, police shows. And old cowboy movies. He dearly loved old John Wayne movies. Especially one about, about . . ." She spun her fingers, trying to gather the memory. "Rio something or other."

"*Rio Grande*?"

"That's it. He'd read the *TV Guide* cover to cover to see if it was on that week, get up at three a.m. to see it. We didn't stop him because television seemed to keep his attention, one of the few things that did."

"How long did he stay with you?"

"Eleven months. He wasn't a problem. He was barely here. But my husband tore up his back in a fall, couldn't work. I had to take a job clerking at the co-op until he got better."

Nautilus pushed the empty coffee cup to the center of the table and sat back in the chair, almost ready to leave. "So, outside of the occasional inappropriate mannerism, there were no behavioral hassles for Jim Day?"

"No, not really . . ." A hesitation.

"What, Miz Cullers?"

"Jimmy wet the bed a bit. Actually more than

351

a bit. It was almost a nightly occurrence. No big deal. I put a plastic pad beneath the sheet, kept fresh sheets in his room so he could fix things, and we all played like no one noticed."

Nautilus felt a stirring in his gut. *That's one. One of three.* He leaned forward and put his elbows on the table.

"Tell me, Miz Cullers, were there any suspicious fires around your house, or in the neighborhood during the time Jimmy was here?"

Puzzlement filled the woman's eyes. "How did you know about that? The fires?"

"Tell me about them."

"There were two that I remember. One was a grass fire out by the highway. Usually they're started by cigarettes tossed from cars, but this one started in the woods and burned out to the highway. Someone had built a fire in an old shed and it got out of control. It was no big deal. But there was another fire a couple months later."

"Bigger, I take it?"

"Burnt down an abandoned house a half-mile away. The fire department said it was set deliberate, gasoline. It was just part of the strangeness that day."

"Strangeness, Miz Cullers?"

The woman's voice dropped low. "The fire-fighters found the bodies of three dogs. The poor things had been tore up while alive and hid away in the house. One had gone missing from down the street, the Lovells' place."

"Do you remember where Jim was during those times?"

"I don't remember with the grass fire. I was calling for him when the house burnt, scared by all the smoke. He showed up mumbling that he'd been playing by the creek, the other direction. Oh Lord, I just remembered something else. Something I forgot completely about . . ."

"What?"

"He smelled like smoke. I thought it was from the air, the smoke in the air. There was a lot of smoke from the house fire. But it smelled so thick on him."

*Two and three,* Nautilus thought.

He thanked Marlene Cullers and left. Next, he had a phone call to make, area code 325, somewhere around Abilene, Texas. It could be a very interesting call and he pulled off by the Tombigbee River to let his eyes wander over water as he read his notes again. He slipped a photo from his pocket, the picture made from a courthouse microfiche of old copies of the local newspaper. He set the photo on his lap, took another look at the sweeping river, then dialed the number.

# THIRTY-FIVE

"You were married to Jim Day, Miz Pelgin? I've got the right person, I hope?"

"I was. But it was just a few months. Under a year."

"May I ask what cut the marriage short?"

"Where is he?" she asked.

"I don't know."

"I cain't tell you anything. I'm hanging up."

Nautilus felt a flash of irritation, jumped from friendly voice to hard-ass cop. "I'll be in Abilene by morning, Miz Pelgin. On your doorstep. You go to work, I'll be there. You run off and come back, I'm there. The best thing you can do is talk to me."

"H-He'll never hear what I say?" she stammered. "J-James."

Nautilus let warmth back into his voice. "Absolutely not, Miz Pelgin. There's no reason for it. I just need some background on his character. How'd you guys meet?"

*Come on, honey . . .* Nautilus thought, holding his breath. *One answer that I can turn into two and then . . .*

A long pause of decision. Pelgin said, "W-We met at a bowling alley. I was havin' trouble and he came over and showed me how to hold the ball and all that. He seemed super nice and I couldn't believe when he asked me out. We went together for two months and got married."

"You must have stolen his heart, Miz Pelgin."

Nautilus looked at the photo in his lap. It was the couple's wedding announcement photo archived in the weekly newspaper. Brenda Day, née Kugler, looked to be about two hundred pounds, her chin becoming her neck becoming her chest. Jim Day was beside her. He was good looking, boyish, like the actor Jon Voight at the same age. The new wife wore a billowing white dress, Day was in some kind of uniform. His eyes looked a thousand miles away.

"To tell the truth . . . I used to be kinda heavy and he was my first real boyfriend ever. I was seventeen, he was twenty-six, had a job as night security guard at the chicken-processing plant and talked about becoming a for-real cop. He seemed sweet and kinda lost and tongue-tied at times. He'd show off a lot, like how many push-ups he could do, how long he could hold his hand over a hot burner before yanking it back. He liked to tickle me until I had to push him off. We got married by a JP and on our honeymoon we, we –"

She stopped as if her voice had rammed a wall.

"Hello? Are you still there, Miz Pelgin?"

"I cain't tell it."

"Miss Pelgin, I'm part of a special unit that deals with highly disturbed individuals. I've heard everything. Please don't think you're embarrassing me."

Nautilus had discovered people were more likely to speak if he took the weight of embarrassment instead of them.

"W-We stayed in a motel in Branson for our honeymoon. On our wedding night he brought in this . . . a package. When he opened it up it was some kind of . . . thing, I don't know what you call it. It had straps. He wanted me to, to . . ."

"That's OK, Miss Pelgin. I'm reading you."

"He peed when he was trying to . . . do it. It was crazy."

"Did he ever get physically abusive?"

"Only after we was married. He started yelling at me and jabbing me when I didn't iron his shirts just so, fix his food this way or that. I told him he didn't want a wife, he wanted a dog."

"You asked for the divorce?"

"Two months and I was flat-out done with that shit. When I told him he went full loony. He said he'd hurt me so bad my mouth would scream a week after my body was dead."

Nautilus let his eyes drift to a towboat pushing a line of barges up the Tombigbee, the engines a steady rumble through his open window. The length of time a towboat wake continued to roil amazed Nautilus. The boat might be around a bend, but the river still shivered from its passage.

Pelgin said, "I didn't know what to do, I was so scared. I finally told my daddy. He come by one day and knocked on the door, said, 'Jim, Jimbo . . . how's about we go grab us a beer, son?'"

"Your father got along with Jim?"

"Jim always went all gooey around Daddy, like a little boy. He made sure we kept Daddy's favorite beer in the refrigerator, his favorite snacks around. But when Jim opened the door,

Daddy smashed his face with the butt of a shotgun and knocked him to the floor. Daddy pointed the gun at Jim's head and said I was leaving and never coming back, and if Jim wanted to argue the point, that was the time to do it."

"What'd Jim do?"

"He started singing like an Indian. Blood's pouring from his mouth and he's peed in his pants, but he's laying on the floor going Hi-yi-yi-yah, hi-yi-yi-yah and pumping his arm like he's chopping with a tomahawk. A month later I was living a thousand miles away and never saw him again."

"Why are you still so frightened, Miss Pelgin?"

"He's such a freak that time don't mean nothing. One day he'll see me in his head and remember some unfinished business. It's been over twenty years and I still look around for him before I step outside. You think I'm wrong to think like that?"

"No, ma'am," Harry Nautilus said. "I'm beginning to think that's a wise decision."

"*Rio Grande*?" I asked Harry to his face, a wonderful sight to behold at 10.43 in the evening.

"A John Wayne movie, bro. John Wayne was a –"

I leaned forward. "Jeez, Harry, I know who John Wayne was. A cowboy actor."

"Sit back, Carson. It's like you're bumping off my head."

"Oh, sorry."

I sat back in my chair. Computer cameras were new to me. When I'd told Harry the hotel had a business center with computer kiosks, he'd asked if the machines had cameras, like his new model. The desk sent a guy to press a couple buttons while Harry did the same. Presto, face-to-face conversation. It felt damn good to see his big square mug and bulldozer-blade mustache, even if he was jumping like a movie with half the frames missing. Harry looked amusingly eerie with a sepia tint and softened edges.

He said, "Wayne was more than a cowboy actor, but he was in a lot of Westerns. An icon, but more to folks a bit older than me. I guess the most common description of Wayne was a 'Man's Man'. He played macho roles before the term macho was popular."

"What's the tie?"

"I stopped by a video store, found a John Wayne compilation and watched *Rio Grande*

360

last night." Harry held a DVD box to the camera, a guy in a ten-gallon hat on the cover, bandana around his neck, smoking gun in hand. "The content shook me, Carson. A hard-bitten cavalry commander of a fort in Indian territory gets a new young recruit who is the son he hasn't seen in a dozen years."

"Let me guess, Harry. Sonny boy has to prove himself to Daddy."

Harry nodded. "Kind of the theme of Muhammad–Malvo, right? A subject very interesting to Doc Prowse."

I stared at Harry in his home office, a poster for the Newport Jazz Festival on the wall in the background. He had taken my request for Jim Day's telephone number and transformed it into a box in which long-separate pieces of the deadly puzzle were falling together.

Harry waggled a notepad at the camera. "I made some notes last night. You're leaning in again."

"Sorry."

"Day was a hideously abused child, probably rented out by his mother and grandmother, every day a fresh nightmare. Mama goes to prison when Day's thirteen and he starts the foster-home shuffle. By age fifteen, he's playing with fire and animal cruelty. Plus he's still wetting the bed."

"The big three," I said. Pyromania, animal cruelty and chronic bedwetting were three markers psychologists looked for in diagnosing sociopaths and psychopaths. One was not unusual, two were cause for concern, all three were a shrieking alarm.

"At the same time," Harry continued, "Day's watching emotion-heavy movies with John Wayne-types taking weak boys under their wing and – through carefully crafted doses of sternness and respect – making the boys into men. It becomes Day's pattern for maleness."

"A cartoon version, without emotional complexity."

Harry shot a jittery thumbs-up that filled my screen. "Day gets married but is incapable of relating to a woman in an intimate sense, like he has gender autism. Sex is a confusing and humiliating muddle and, in the end, Daddy rushes in and punishes him for being such a fuck-up."

"He really did that Indian thing: woo-woo-woo?" I chopped my hand at the camera.

"Vanquishing Indians was a recurring theme in old Westerns. My take is that Day was signaling surrender. It would have been a pivotal

362

moment in his psychic development. Know what I think Jimmy Day decided was the best thing to do?"

I thought for a few beats, adding it up.

"Become the daddy."

"As an abused boy lacking any father figure, he knew exactly what such kids were seeking. Day was screwed up bad, but learning to hide it better. He trades in the security guard uniform – he wore it to his wedding, how's that for sad? – for a cop uniform. He's suddenly become an authority figure, a man."

I felt the conclusion coming. It blew a cold wind across my spine.

Harry said, "Your father is killed. Day is consumed by the sense of revenge, of a trans-forming moment. A year passes and, unbeknownst to anyone, he figures the case out. And finds a troubled young man he can befriend, nurture, and guide."

"Day became Muhammad to Jeremy's Malvo," I whispered.

Harry nodded sadly. "Exactly, Carson. Your brother is Jim Day's son. Or was."

*The man opened the cabinet and set a bottle on the table. Once a day he had to see – needed* to see – his special bottle and its contents. So beautiful, so powerful. They were like tattered red flags that signaled conquest. He shook the bottle and watched the flags swirl and dance in the formalin, the preservative. History was racing toward him. He was racing toward history. These were his battle pennants.

"Charge," he whispered.

His work table was white. Everything in the echoing room was white. It had taken almost a year to apply seventeen coats of white sealer. The room had once been an office and women had worked here. Their smells had been trapped in the walls like stains. It took fourteen coats of paint to bury the smell of the women.

The other three coats were to make sure.

There was a tray on the table. It held a small bottle of model-maker's enamel, a brush, and a red doll small enough to clutch in his fist. He picked up the doll and smiled at the cartoon face, the bright lips.

At the corner of his eye . . . Movement! His face snapped to a shiver on one of the quartet of television monitors mounted on the wall; every side of the building was covered. He reached to the control, zoomed in on the motion.

It was just a stray dog sniffing at the trash behind the building. He released his held breath and turned back to the task at hand. Only one more time to do this. History was almost here.

He picked up the small red doll, grinned, and began to paint.

# THIRTY-SIX

My mind had reached its limit, and without sleep I'd be unable to function, so I fell away for several hours. It was lousy sleep, my dreams a moonscape populated with towering cowboys, broken Indians, dead women dragging themselves across the ground and leaving bloody trails from the ragged holes in their bellies. I could hear Alice's voice, but when I turned my head, she was gone. Jeremy's head popped from craters, laughing at me. When I'd run to his crater he'd pop from another one and I'd run in that direction.

From somewhere behind the sky, Vangie's somber voice would say, "Sorry, Carson."

I awakened for good at four and went to my butcher paper. I began a new section, the formerly perplexing stacks of words and questions making sense when I added the name Day. It was the bottom line to almost everything.

I was still puzzled by the message Jeremy had conveyed through the blind man, Parks. No matter how I tried to interpret it, the George Bernard Shaw quote seemed no more than a cutesy reflection on the country as an asylum. It seemed frivolous for Jeremy, who never did anything without a subtext.

I studied my ramble of words, irritated. I leaned close to see other words scribbled in that particular storyline. Parks, referring to my brother, had said, *"He called you something nice, said you was ever the hero on water or land.' Seems a nice thing to say, right?"*

I stepped back and frowned. *Ever the hero?* Hadn't Jeremy used the same phrase during his bedside visit?

Five minutes later I sat in the business center of the hotel, banging a computer keyboard, entering phrases into a search engine. *Ever, hero, water, land.* The engine returned tens of thousands of hits. I studied page after page, looking for anything to spark inspiration.

Thirty-seven screens in and about to bag the exercise, I noticed the name Walt Whitman. *Leaves of Grass* had been one of my brother's favorite works, a gift from his junior-year teacher at high school. Jeremy had loved Whitman, another searching spirit.

I added "Whitman" to my list of search terms and again scanned the results. On the second page of hits was a listing highlighting the terms "heroes of water and land". I followed the link to a poem, *Song For All Seas, All Ships*, twenty lines in length.

Several phrases stood out as if written in neon:

*To-day a rude brief recitative*
*Of ships sailing the Seas, each with its*
*special flag or ship-signal . . .*
*Ever the heroes on water or on land, by*
*ones or twos appearing,*
*. . . reserve especially for yourself . . . one*
*flag above all the rest . . .*
*Flaunt out, visible as ever, the various ship-*
*signals! . . .*

Flags. Signals. Heroes by ones or twos.

"You bastard," I whispered. "You tricky bastard."

I knew what Jeremy had given me: the key for making contact. But I had to figure it out on my own, another of his damned games.

As children, my brother and I built forts in the woods behind our house, haphazard derelicts constructed from junkyard leavings. We often imagined them as ships and ourselves as heroic sailors, signaling between our forts with flags of torn sheets my mother had discarded, yelling "ahoy!" and "avast!" and whatever else heroic sailors yelled while coursing the Spanish Main.

I hung a sheet in my window, thinking I'd wait hours, maybe days. I waited for twelve minutes. The phone rang.

"Took you long enough." Jeremy said. "Had a lobotomy recently?"

"You're hiding across the damned street?"

"Guess again, matey."

I went to the window and looked down into the crowd. Catty-corner was a pair of purse and luggage vendors, ink-black Somalians who hawked their wares in a succulent, musical language. They arrived at dawn and stayed past dark.

"One of the purse guys is doing recon on my window."

"I pay M'tiwmbe two hundred a week to check every now and then."

"How's Folger? Is she —"

"She's breathing and eating and, if I interpreted the sound correctly, she's urinating as well. All that commotion just to take a piss. It sounded like someone aiming a hose at a wall."

"How soon can we meet? We've got to meet. No tricks."

"About time you did something worthwhile. I'll send a cab. The driver has some odd notions. Play along with them."

I stood on the corner and watched as a yellow cab roared to the curb, the driver grinning and waving furiously.

"Get in. GET IN! We are going to be important major stars together."

The driver's eyes blazed in two directions with cockeyed bliss. His hair looked like a field of elephant grass plowed by tornadoes. He wore a silver lamé tux jacket over a black tee emblazoned with a Warhol Marilyn. He seemed to have consumed several hundred cups of coffee.

"Stars?" I said.

"I AM GOING TO BUILD A HOUSE IN MALIBU!"

After a disorienting two blocks I discerned that a powerful and elusive Hollywood casting director had convinced my loosely wrapped driver that he was bound for stardom as long as he stayed in the director's good graces. It appeared the director had cast me in the same movie.

I figured I knew who the director was.

When I exited at an address in Murray Hill, my driver wiggled his thumb and pinky at his mouth, screamed, "CALL WHEN YOU GET SETTLED," and vanished like he had a date at the edge of a galaxy far, far away.

I found myself on a sedate street of brownstones. I stepped to the door of a slender building of gray sandstone and rang the bell. Jeremy opened the door wearing a red jacket and blousy blue shirt. He was thick in the middle – a pillow or something. His hair was a layer of blond snips, his eyes brown with false contacts. He'd done something to emphasize the creases in his face. He had spent time at a tanning salon, or perhaps it was a chemical concoction.

"You look ridiculous," I said.

"I feel safe. Guess which is most important?"

We walked a long room with polished wood floors, tapestries, curio cabinets holding sculpture that looked pre-Columbian. The furniture was mismatched in a good way, selected for comfort instead of aesthetics. The fireplace was large and deep with a heavy oaken mantel.

The only out-of-synch note was the roll of duct tape on the mantel.

Jeremy said, "The owners are a brace of fag ophthalmologists fixing the eyeballs of peasant kiddies in Peru or some such dreadful, goody-goody thing. I'm renting for a month. I had another nest, but had to vacate when you dropped the bricks on my Portuguese cousin." He winked. "It was a splashy tip-off, *obrigado, irmão*."

"Where's Folger, Jeremy?"

"She's pissing like a trouper, brother. Keep me safe and you'll be swimming the ol' ween once again."

I hadn't expected to see Folger. I knew Jeremy too well.

He clapped his hands expectantly. "So, I guess it's down to bidness, Carson. Are you ready for me? For Sirius?" He lolled his tongue as if panting.

"You knew all along Sirius was a dog, didn't you?"

"Prowsie and me in flagrante delicto? It would have been the highlight of her life, but we have differing astrological signs. I don't wish to run afoul of my stars."

"What happened, Jeremy? To Vangie."

"She had an anxiety attack, nerves. Had to go for a run. He was waiting. Or he sent someone."

"Jim Day?"

"I TOLD HER TO STAY PUT. GODDAMN STUPID BITCH."

I backhanded him across the face. His head snapped sideways and he stumbled backward. His hand reached to his cheek.

"Never call Vangie anything like that again," I said. "Not in my presence."

His eyes narrowed and started to heat up. I said, "Don't even think of giving me that look. All it'll see is my back going out the door."

He raised his eyebrows, jammed his hands in his pockets, gave me a smile of plastic bonhomie.

"So you've heard of Jim Day, Carson?"

"Harry did my work well. But I've still got a lot of holes. Like how did it all come together. How did Day approach you?"

"Oh my," he said. "You want to start at the very beginning . . ."

# THIRTY-SEVEN

Folger listened closely to the voices. All she saw was black. Jeremy Ridgecliff had slipped through the trapdoor to the roof, set a wooden beam over the chimney, lashed a hardware-store block and tackle to the beam. He'd tied her into a rope harness and cranked her effortlessly up the chimney. Her toes swung just above the flue. A breeze sifted up the chimney. It smelled of incense and rustled her hair.

For a brief moment it occurred to her that she could die here. If something happened to Carson. If Ridgecliff took off. She'd spin in circles and die in a sooty chimney.

But Ridgecliff had, for the most part, seemed calm and in control of himself. Unnervingly so for someone pursued by an angry NYPD. As if he knew something no one else knew. Or perhaps that was a manifestation of the insanity. Another aspect of Ridgecliff struck her: He was like a very old man in a forty-year-old body. A strange notion, because he was like an adolescent child at the same time.

The voices started anew. Carson knew Ridgecliff, of course. They'd been familiar since Carson had interviewed Ridgecliff in the Institute. But it seemed he knew him better than she'd been led to believe . . .

"It was the summer after high school, Carson. A year after father died. I was walking to town and thinking about college in the fall, amazed some big university would give me a free education just for answering silly questions in a test. A guy in a truck pulled alongside. Jim Day, but I didn't know that yet. He said I'd brought honor to the whole county, him included. I was secretly pleased to have made a grown man so happy . . ."

We were in facing loveseats by the front bay window. Jeremy had insisted on killing the lights, arraying a dozen lit candles throughout the room. *"I haven't seen candlelight in years, Carson. We're not allowed fire, for obvious*

375

*reasons."* The air smelled of candle wax and the sticks of the lavender Japanese incense he had discovered in a drawer. Shadows jittered in the corners.

"Jimmy said he'd take me to the library, but took me to . . . the spot. When he showed a gun I remembered him as one of the cops from that day, the young one who never left the car.

"Jimmy started talking about rain and dams and rivers. How water builds up and threatens the dam. How it NEVER stopped raining. He was describing ME. He saw it in the clearing. He saw how my ANGER AND HATRED had been building under years of THOSE FUCKING BEATINGS RAINING DOWN AS I BURIED MY FACE IN THE PILLOW AND SCREAMED DOWN TOWARD HELL AND HOPED IT COULD SAVE ME BECAUSE GOD AND JESUS AND ANGELS IN HEAVEN AND ALL THAT SHIT MAMA YAPPED ABOUT WEREN'T DOING A DAMN THING!"

"Easy. It's all right. Relax."

My brother closed his eyes until his breath stilled. "Jim understood what had happened, Carson. He said our father must have been insane because any sane man would hold his head high if he had a son like me."

"Day was there from that moment on, right? When you went to college?"

*Like John Muhammad had moved into Lee Malvo's life until he owned his very breathing.*

"I told my counselor the dorm was so loud I couldn't concentrate. I was allowed to move off campus. Jim was with me. I finally had a father, Carson, a teacher. Not the usual things taught by ordinary fathers, but the special secrets of the world."

I could hear Day's voice applying the socio-pathic credo like a soothing balm: *We're not ordinary, Jeremy, we're special. Ordinary rules don't apply to us.*

"Day taught you secrets of women," I ventured. "That they were evil."

"Women had one ability: squirting other people out of them. It took FILTH AND DISGUST to put people in them, and then they squirted people out through the tube where FILTH and DISGUST took place. It's an UGLY and DEGRADING process, Carson. SICK!"

"And our mother?"

He snapped his head sideways and spat on the floor. He eyes turned to me to see if I'd challenge him on the act. I didn't. We'd regressed to a dangerous place. He was neither in the present nor the past, but an unstable junction of the two worlds.

"Day decided it was time to murder women?"

I saw his hands tighten toward fists. "Retribution is a holy act. We became warriors. Warriors can't commit murder." He spoke it like rote, and I figured he'd heard it a thousand times.

"Tell me how it started. The first one."

"We found a restaurant frequented by house-wifely types fighting middle age. I sat in a small nearby park and feigned emotional distress, my beloved cat hit by a car. A woman noticed my pain and comforted me. I asked if she'd accompany me to the restaurant. Jimmy was in his van at the edge of the park. He had a rag and chloroform. The right amount made them dopey but awake. Jimmy liked them to see what was coming."

"Coming where?"

"Jimmy had fixed the basement to be easy to clean. There was a bathroom with a sink, a hose connection. Four drains. Speaking of drains, I have to piss."

He unfolded his legs, bounded from the couch, and went to the bathroom.

When I heard the toilet flush I took a deep

breath. I had brought the story to the site of the killings. To the point where Jeremy's point of view changed in his interrogations. It was time to step through that final door.

To find out what happened in the kill zone.

Shelly Waltz walked into the Pelham campaign headquarters, feeling relief at being away from the station. The department was in uproar looking for Alice Folger. Knowing what he knew made him feel like a traitor. If it all fell apart, which was likely, that's how he would be remembered in the department: Shelly Waltz, traitor and scumbag.

The situation was all in Ryder's hands. What if Ryder was allied with his brother in some bizarre machination? What if they were sawing Alice Folger in pieces right now?

"Are you all right, Detective? You look a little pale."

Sarah Wensley, Pelham's majordomo, appeared at his side. The phone banks were still filled with happy faces. Did political activists ever sleep? The opposite contingent – across the street and behind the barricades – obviously didn't. The signs waved, chants echoed across the pavement.

"I'm fine, Ms Wensley. Indigestion or something. Anything in the mail today?"

"No dolls, mouths or otherwise, I'm happy to say. Another screaming letter from that Blankley guy."

"The candidate's still leaving tomorrow?"

"She heads to New England right after her address to the convention."

"Keep your eyes on that mail. Mr Borskov thinks there's one more doll in the series. If someone's been counting down to a message or whatever, it'll be in the final doll."

Waltz saw Secret Service agent Banks in the corner, coiled wire running to his earpiece as he kept a wary eye on the crowd across the way. Waltz pulled several sheets of newly manipulated photos from his briefcase, handed them to Banks.

"Our updates on Jeremy Ridgecliff, the guy suspected of killing the women. Pass 'em around your people."

Banks studied the faces: Ridgecliff as a blond, with dark hair, with a goatee, with mustache, and electronically shaved bald. Banks tapped the top sheet with his fingernail.

"Is this Ridgecliff really as smart as you say?"

"Rocket-scientist smart. Even worse, he likes being smart, know what I mean?"

Banks continued to absorb the photos. "Yeah. He wants to show it off. Make the perfect kill."

"Exactly. So far in his life, he's got eight kills attributed. Six for sure. Five were women."

Banks raised an eyebrow to Waltz. "He political?"

"He's a non-denominational, equal-opportunity psychopath."

Banks nodded toward Pelham. She was laughing and schmoozing a dozen head-bobbing reporters. "You think Ridgecliff is a direct threat to our lady?"

Waltz sighed, shook his head. He had to tell the truth.

"If you see Ridgecliff near Pelham, don't think twice. Blow Ridgecliff apart."

*We'll still find her, Waltz told himself. Even if Ridgecliff goes down, Ryder will find Alice.*

# THIRTY-EIGHT

Jeremy returned. He'd lost the wig, washed the makeup from his eyes and removed the concoction or mechanism altering their shape. Though his skin remained unnaturally dark, he again looked like my brother.

"Where were we? Oh yes, the –"

I interrupted. "Let's talk about the first woman you killed, Jeremy."

He spun away and began pacing, moving faster and faster, chased by a fire I couldn't see. The candle flames shivered as he swept past with his fists clenching and releasing. I jumped in front of him. Took his shoulders and pulled him tight.

He held on to me a full minute, as if finding his equilibrium. He reclined on the bright Oriental carpet and stared into the white ceiling, thinking a long time before he spoke.

"I was supposed to do it, the release. I entered the room, accepted the holy knife, and walked toward the woman, but my legs died."

"Died?"

"I fell to the floor. Nothing was holding my weight."

"You couldn't get to her?"

"I tried five times."

*Five?* "This happened on every attempt?"

"My legs worked backing up but died going forward."

I saw the women on the floor, naked and terrified, screaming into tape or a gag. My brother starting toward them with the weapon. Falling to the floor, wriggling and impotent.

"Day was there?" I asked. "In the room?"

"Of course, Carson. It was his party."

"What did he do?" I asked.

"The knife was dishonored by my cowardice. He took the knife to the bathroom to be reconsecrated beneath water. The knife returned, clean and bright and ready for its mission. The knife always returned."

*The knife entered the room . . .*

"What did you do, Jeremy? While Day butchered the women."

"I watched. And then I'd throw up and crawl away."

"You never once . . . ?"

He put his hands over his eyes and lay without motion. I walked to the window and stared out at a world where most people lived ordinary lives, no dark secrets, no hidden tragedies, no nights that followed you across the room with wadded sheets and covers.

I turned back to my brother. "You finally confessed to Vangie. The whole story. Everything."

"Every word, Carson. From my first memories."

"Because Vangie had become your psycho-analyst."

His hands slipped from his eyes. "At the Institute she was just a warden. Dealing with savages. Burnouts. People who thought devil dogs were eating their brains. 'You're different, Jeremy,' Prowse told me for years. 'I wish you'd let me behind that last door, Jeremy.'"

"So after all those years, you opened the door."

"I got tired of hiding." He rubbed his eyes

like he was getting weary. "I said we'd talk if I was a regular patient and not one of the savages. I told her get me a phone and we'll keep regular hours."

"You met – so to speak – on Saturdays."

"One to three o'clock. She sat at her desk in Gulf Shores, I laid on my bed with my phone and told her everything."

"Harry found a photo of you on her wall."

"She wanted a photo to look at when we spoke, something to personalize her experience and diminish the distance. I was baring my soul, Carson. I wanted my picture to reflect it, made her take it with my dingus and orbles hanging out. I made her promise to put the picture up just like I was in the room telling my story: JEREMY STRIPPED BARE."

Jeremy had always claimed to be viscerally disgusted by Vangie, and over the years had generated a litany of pejoratives: Slut Queen, Doctor Whore, the Cuntessa, Our Lady of Perpetual Misery. It would have been easy to shut Vangie out of his life: Simply stop talking, or request another psychiatrist be assigned to him. Had my brother actually respected Vangie Prowse? In his world, she'd have been his only equal in raw intelligence.

Were his relentless anti-Vangie rants and insults a mask?

I said, "When you told Vangie about Day, she tried to track him down, I take it?"

"She'd seen people like Jim Day before. She said he would be killing women. It was what he saw as his mission in life. She asked me everything I could remember about him, even the tiniest things, like the fact that his mama had once told him his daddy-o was from New Yawk City. She concluded Jimmy Day eventually HAD to be somewhere in the New York area, a spiritual destiny. He could come to New York when he was man enough. When he was ready."

"She was dead right," I said.

"One thing about old Prowsie, brother, she knew Mommy and Daddy issues."

I shook my head. "Unfortunately, she didn't know how to wipe away her prints as she investigated."

"The Prowster tracked down some of Jimmy's drooling relatives. Word got back to Jimmy that a doctor lady in the old home country of Alabama was asking after him. He wasn't a happy pup."

"Day went South, broke into Vangie's home."

Jeremy nodded. "And that's when he found old Prussy's precious little secret."

"The power he had over her," I said. "What was it?"

He rolled to his stomach and cradled his chin in his hands. A smile ghosted his thin lips. "The secret that made her spring *moi*? That brought her here? That made us stay in a hotel near Chelsea? The secret she traded her life for? You don't know what it is?"

"I have no idea."

He started laughing.

Shelly Waltz opened his desk drawer and removed a vial containing blood-pressure medicine. He was supposed to take one every morning with about a half-dozen other pills, but for the past two weeks he'd needed another in the evening. He could tell his BP was spiking by a tension in his neck, a low hiss in his ears.

He popped the pill, washed it down with coffee, and looked out over the detectives' room. It was quiet, most of the dicks out turning over rocks in the search for Folger.

He heard a rustle of paper from inside a gray cubicle. Cluff was still at work, hunched over the wide sheet of paper unfurled from the large roll on the floor beside the desk. Waltz had watched Cluff work out problems on the paper for so long it seemed normal.

Waltz walked over and leaned on the cubicle wall.

"What's up, Detective?"

"Ah, just scratching out some new shit," Cluff wheezed. Waltz saw him push the edge of the paper over a dog-eared pair of files. Hiding them.

"What's with the files?" Waltz asked.

Cluff's hairy ears reddened. "Nothing. Just a few loose ends."

Waltz's hand pushed the paper away. "Then you won't mind if I take a look, right?"

Cluff leaned back in his chair, made a sound like a steam train shutting down, his lung-scarred version of a sigh. "It's not anything. Just some old records from a couple different places."

Waltz studied the pages. "My, my . . . old admission records from Newark's Child Welfare office and Bridges Juvenile Center. I thought the Lieutenant shut down this area of inquiry so we could –"

Cluff swatted the air. "Yeah, I know. Look for a crazy in an Armani eating at the Four Seasons and living in a Park Avenue penthouse. I can't run all over like I once did, Waltz. I hate it, but that's the way it is. I got to spend half my time in my goddamn chair catching my breath, so I figured I'd do a little something while I sat. And Ryder never really convinced me there was no New York in Ridgecliff's background."

"Sounds like an admirable line of inquiry, Detective," Waltz said, rapping his knuckles on the top of the cubicle. "Have at it."

If Cluff was at his desk digging through moth-eaten records, Waltz thought, it was one less chance to find Jeremy Ridgecliff. And thereby doom Alice Folger.

# THIRTY-NINE

"Jesus, Jeremy, what is it? What was Day's hold over Vangie?"

My brother jumped to his feet and walked to the fireplace, sat on the elevated brick hearth, leaning back with legs crossed elegantly at the ankles. He'd set a candle beside the fireplace opening, its flame quivering in the draft.

"Jimmy believes in tit for tat, Carson. Prowsie killed Jim Day's boy, *moi*, by tracking me down for the FBI."

"Tit for . . . ?"

"TIT FOR GODDAMN TAT, CARSON! I'll say it slowly: Prowsie . . . killing . . . Jimmy's . . . boy. Now, what's the inversion? Tat for tit?"

"The inversion would be Day killing Prowse's girl."

Jeremy winked lasciviously. "There you go, brother. You finally got your tits in a row."

"What the hell are you talking about?"

"YOUR LOVE-MUFFIN, CARSON."

"My love muf— . . . you mean Alice Folger?"

"Jimmy found little Alice when he went through Prowsie's records. Jimmy must have felt like he'd hit the lottery. Prowsie's girl in his own backyard. WHAT INCREDIBLE LUCK! No, not luck . . . Jimmy probably took it as a sign from God."

I looked like a dolt when reality hit; mouth open, eyes staring numbly at my brother.

"You mean Alice is . . ."

"Proud Prowsie's legacy," Jeremy grinned. "Squirted from Mama Prowse thirty-two years ago. HI MAMA, I'M HERE! GET RID OF ME!"

"Rid of? You mean . . . " I was still tracking slow.

"Adoption brother. Prowsie was afeared a kiddy would slow her steps. She had something of the huh-huh-hots for the daddy, but if he knew, she'd get tied down. Prowsie had a big career looming, nuts to open. She had no time to stick a busy titty in a screaming mouth."

An early conversation with Waltz rang in my head . . .

*"I get your point, Shelly. Folger has cop in her DNA."*

*"Or overcompensating to create the genes . . . I always found families more custom and tradition than blood . . ."*

Waltz had meant Folger wasn't blood-related to the cop family, but worked hard to fit expectations. In the photo of Folger's parents I had been struck by their smiling-potato blandness in comparison to Folger's crisp, potent features. Now that I knew, Folger resembled Vangie more than Waltz, but with her own interpretation of both.

Jeremy said, "Prowse's dah-dah was a cop. Myrt and Johnny Folger were family friends of Daddy Prowse. The Folgers were good stock, but older and barren, a boo-hoo situation. When Prowsie's belly started puffing, she went off to 'research' in another city for a bit. She popped little Alice, made the hand-off to the Folgers. The deed was done."

"No. It stung for the rest of her life."

"Conscience is a hard piper to pay. Prowsie felt giving up Baby Alice displayed heartlessness, career over child, job over love, betrayal of the sperm donor . . . all those maudlin clichés. So Prowsie watched from a distance, making sure the little package she'd left in New York was doing all right. When Alice the New Detective Girl was living in a swamp, ol' Prowsie bought her a house. So very motherly, so very late."

A mystery solved. An angel revealed.

"Vangie made Alice safer. Don't make light of her efforts."

"I did my part, too." He winked. "Jimmy Boy was diddling at your chicklet's door a few nights back. I was doing my daily reconnaissance from Ludis's cab. When I saw the movement at her window, I yelled in the voice of Hulk Hogan: 'HEY YOU! WHAT THE HELL YOU DOING?' You should have seen jumpin' Jimmy run. I knew I'd better snatch up Miss Alice before Jimmy came calling again. As it turned out, he came calling a few hours later, right? But all he found was the curious lady upstairs. Jimmy was never very stealthy; that was my chore."

"Why did you do it, Jeremy? You helped Vangie. You saved her daughter even after Vangie was dead. It's . . . idealistic."

My brother let a sound on the street draw him away, finding interest outside the window. He was quiet for a long time. When he turned, it was to change the subject.

"Is Prowsie's lovechild a bimbo or a braino? She seems rather astute, actually."

"Alice Folger is fascinated by the weather, Jeremy. Climatology. She studies upper-level books on the subject, runs a sophisticated weather station and network from her home. She's been fascinated by meteorology from childhood. Sometimes the depth of the fascination freaks her out. She thinks it's an illness, an obsession."

He nodded, seemed pleased by the concept. "Science for Mommy, science for daughter. You can't outrun DNA, it has its own special needs." He clapped his hands and widened his eyes as if struck by a great idea. "Hey, speaking of special needs, brother, what say we go visit Jimmy Day?"

"What? You know where he is?"

"I sniffed out Prowsie's bomb my fifth day here. I've been waiting for you to catch up."

Jeremy sauntered outside with me in his footsteps. I started pulling the door shut, then stopped, canted my head. I swore I heard a distant sound, as soft and muffled as if carried on the last beat of a dying echo.

Crying?

Not hearing it again, I shrugged, closed the door. A cab appeared like magic as we stepped to the curb.

# FORTY

"You know De Niro? Bobby and me are LIKE THIS!"

Jeremy's delusional Latvian drove with his head canted over his shoulder, talking between Jeremy and me. Sometimes he yelled at things I couldn't see. Sometimes he sang. Jeremy pretty much ignored him.

"How did you find Day?" I asked. "He can't be using the name."

"No," my brother grinned. "He's using Knight."

My mouth fell open. Jeremy said, "Prowsie made the conjecture. We added it to my interpretation of his needs. We were actually quite the little team, Carson."

"Day needs control. I know that much."

"Ah, but to exercise that control, he needs boys. Very special boys. So he's where all the lost and troubled little fellows are, Carson. Where Jimmy can wait for the special lad that comes along maybe once a decade."

"Juvenile detention?"

"Juvie detention is too busy an environment, Carson. Guards, social workers, parents, cops, shrinks running in and out. Too many curious eyes. You need time alone with your boy if you want to make him a man. A very special man."

"Where are we going?"

"Long Island. It's a bit of a trip. Damn, I haven't eaten in seven hours, I need some repast. Is the Four Seasons near? They have a Chocolate Velvet that's simply –"

"We're in a hurry. There's your choice."

I pointed to a vendor on a corner. Jeremy got a skewer of beef, chicken for me. We ate as we crossed the East River and headed out to Long Island. The air began to smell of burned rubber and bitter chemicals as we wound past factories and warehouses. Ludis kept up a running dialogue with himself, seemingly oblivious to anything but the surrealist movie playing in his head.

After a half-hour, we passed a long stretch

of hurricane fencing. On the other side, on a scruffy field, a guy in crisp military fatigues was putting several dozen teenage boys through a regimen of calisthenics. They'd do a few jumping Jacks, then the instructor blew his whistle and everyone dropped for push-ups. Another blast from the whistle and they were up and flailing again. Half the kids looked as if they were ready to pass out.

I looked ahead and saw a big red sign: CAMP WILDERNESS.

"Boot camp," I said, putting it all together. "Juvie version."

A juvenile boot camp was where hardened, streetwise kids were sent for rehabilitation through hard work and regimentation. They spent most of their days with the supervisory personnel, often cast in a mentoring position.

"Tough love for wayward lads," Jeremy said. "But for Jimmy, it's a bad-boy buffet."

Ludis turned in his seat. "We been this camp place three times. You still gonna shoot a film here, Hollywood?"

"I think this location will play a big role, Ludis. It has an atmosphere of forebod—"

Ludis jammed on the brakes as a bright red Camaro fishtailed from the camp's staff parking lot. A guy in shades was at the wheel, teeth flashing as he blew by.

"That was him," Jeremy whispered. "Jim Day. James Knight, these days. He's leaving early. He's usually here until four."

My phone rang. Waltz. I looked at Jeremy and put my finger to my lips, *be quiet*.

"What's going on, Detective?" he asked, tension beneath his voice. Behind it, I heard a babble of voices.

"Things are unfolding, Shelly."

"That's all you can say?"

"Bear with me a few more hours. What's the commotion in the background?"

"It's the big event, remember? Pelham's addressing the conference. She's still an hour away, but the street's jammed with supporters and protestors. Never seen so many goddamn signs. I got pressed into service. No, the Chief pressed me into service, showing the NYPD flag for Pelham. We hauled two guys from the crowd for wearing NEUTER THE BITCH buttons."

"Does that go against free speech?"

"Underneath the words was an AK-47."

"Gotcha. Any more dolls show up?"

"No." His voice drew tight. "What have

you got on Folger? What are you planning to –"

"Can't hear, Shelly. You're breaking up."

I snapped the phone closed and we became a bolt of yellow lightning, picking up Day five blocks later at a red light. Ludis pulled three cars behind, yelling out the song "My Way". Day drove without fear, as if unfettered passage was his due. He cut, swerved, dove across lanes, drawing gestures and horn blasts.

We followed to an industrial area just south of the Harlem River, watching from a distance as Day's car roared toward a windowless brick building on a corner, a small two-story warehouse. Faded lettering on the building's side said CASSINI'S PRODUCE.

An electronically controlled door rolled open and Day's car disappeared inside.

Jeremy said, "We're jumping out here, Ludis."

"No," I said. "Let's take some time and figure out a –"

Jeremy was out and sprinting away. I cursed and jumped from the cab, following him around the corner of the building. I saw my brother pushing through a broken hurricane fence into an adjoining weed-strewn lot and studying the warehouse. I noticed something

399

else: a surveillance camera mounted on the side of the building, maybe a hundred feet away. I saw another at the corner.

"Jeremy," I hissed. "Cameras."

He nodded from two dozen feet away, waved, crept to a loading dock piled with broken pallets, his attention riveted on the building. I ran after him. Stealth be damned, all I wanted was out of there. My brother was peeking around a corner toward the rear of the structure.

"Jeremy, come on. We could be in Day's sight."

"Just a sec. I'm checking to see if there's another door."

"Get over here. We've got to step back and figure how to . . ."

He leaned around the corner, looking away. "How to what, Carson?"

I couldn't answer. I was looking into the eyes of Jim Day.

Detective Abel Alphonse Cluff sat in his office with his butcher paper pushed to the side, staring at two stacks of records on his desk. One was a computer printout of the clients Dora Anderson had served in her two years in Newark's Children's Services department, the other was admissions to the Bridges juvenile treatment facility during the same two-year period. Cluff shouldn't have had either set of lists, probably, from a legal point of view, but in twenty-five years with the NYPD he had developed a network that moved information a bit more efficiently than official channels.

He looked down at the records, sighed. Page after page of names.

"This crap don't ever go anywhere," he wheezed, wishing he was out on the street with a real hand in the game.

# FORTY-ONE

Day had snuck round the far side of the building, caught us from behind. Under .45-caliber gunpoint, my brother and I moved inside. We entered a concrete-floored area with targets on a far wall, a shooting range. I smelled powder and gun oil. At the other end of the room were exercise machines, free weights, kick bag and speed bag. Day's car was inside the steel door, engine ticking as it cooled. The walls were two feet thick, window openings bricked solid to keep thieves out. It was a fortress, which fit everything I'd recently learned about Jim Day.

He was utterly calm, said, "I want you to put your hands against the wall."

Day kicked my feet back further to keep me off balance. He reached into a metal box beside the door, pulled out a hand-held metal detector. It squealed at the Glock beneath my jacket and the .25 Colt holstered at my ankle. It found my two-inch pocket knife. And forty cents in change.

He studied my ID. "My, we are out of our district. I can't imagine the stories Jerry's told you. Not that it matters any more."

He swept the wand across my brother. It beeped at his belt buckle and pocket. "Empty," Day said.

Jeremy held out two quarters, one dime, and three Krugerrands. Day flicked the silver to the floor, put the gold in his own pocket. My brother started to back away.

"Uh-uh, Jerry. I need you to hokey-pokey."

"Pardon, Jim?"

"You know, the old dance. You put your right in, you put your left foot out. Step the feet out, slow and one at a time."

The wand beeped at Jeremy's left foot. "Pull your shoe and sock off," Day ordered.

Hidden in the curl of Jeremy's instep, in a thin plastic sheath, was a small knife. Basically a razor blade with a grip, the knife would be deadly in experienced hands.

"Wasn't I the one taught you to always keep

403

a blade close?" Day grinned. "Trouble is, I was also the one taught you that hiding place, remember? Let's go upstairs to more comfortable quarters."

The wooden steps creaked. Upstairs was like walking into a snow palace, everything painted white: walls, floor, ceiling. I saw a steel-framed bed beside two chests of drawers, three couches arranged like the letter C, a hard wooden chair at the C's mouth. A television was in the corner. The kitchen area was stripped to appliance essentials, restaurant-quality equipment. A beam-thick table and four chairs. Lighting was metal cones hanging from above. At the far corner an open door revealed a metal shower stall and toilet fixture gleaming like a new dime. The living area held one quarter of the space, the bulk of the area open floor.

Echoing Day, the living area was mostly empty, but the equipment in place was strong and efficient. Day stopped us in the center of the plank floor, outside the nest-like array of couches and chair. He would not be bringing us *inside*, so to speak.

Not good.

"I knew you'd stay ahead of the cops, Jeremy-boy. You have everything figured out.

You always kept us three jumps ahead of ol' John Law." Day looked at me. "Jeremy's wickedly smart. Give him enough time to plan and he could get into the main vault at Fort Knox."

"Not bright enough, obviously. He caught your attention."

"I been watching out for Jerry. Seems we been watching the same little lady." He looked to my brother. "Where is she?"

I answered instead. "Alice Folger doesn't know you. Why hurt her?"

Day whipped the gun across my face. The room exploded into crackling yellow stars. "Because her filthy mother stole him from me," he hissed. "She stole my boy and killed him."

"Your boy is back," I spat, pointing at Jeremy, holding my hand against my screaming cheek-bone, hoping something hadn't shattered. "He's right here, asshole."

Day snapped a side kick into my knee and dropped me to the floor beside the back of the couch. He had no real interest in me; I was a loud bug itching to be swatted. He turned to my brother.

"You squealed on me, son. Ratted me out."

My brother's chin started to quiver. He held

his hands up, palms out. A tear traced down his cheek.

"I-I'm sorry, Jimmy. I kept quiet for years."

*Don't fall apart, Jeremy,* I thought. *Keep it together, keep Day off balance. Resist. You can do it.*

"Time ain't nothing. A minute, a year, it's all the fucking same. You don't rat out your family."

"I'm sorry, Jimmy. I was wrong. It was Prowse's fault. She was evil. They're all evil. Just like you always –"

Day's hand slashed like a snake, slapping my brother's face.

"STOP WHIMPERING! WOMEN WHIMPER!"

Jeremy knuckled tears from his eyes. "I w-won't whimper, Jimmy." He sounded like he was five years old.

I scanned my area of the floor for anything usable as a weapon, a light cord, screwdriver dropped under a couch, nothing near. All I saw was an empty cardboard box with black type on a white label.

Russian Nesting Dolls
Matryoshka – Mother
1 set, 7 pieces

Day turned to Jeremy. "I keep a juice bottle

in the fridge, Jerry. Go fetch it. Use it on your cop buddy."

*Juice bottle?*

"He's not my buddy, Jimmy. I swear he's –"

"GET THE GODDAMN BOTTLE, BOY!"

"Yes, sir."

Wiping tears with the back of his hand, Jeremy went to the fridge and returned with a gleaming metal bottle. Day pulled a handkerchief from his back pocket, tossed it to my brother.

"Juice him, Jerry. I want him kept down so we can talk."

Jeremy put the rag over my face, looking away, like I wasn't there. He poured. The cloth turned icy. Fumes blazed in my throat and nostrils. When Jeremy stood back, he was in slow motion.

Day begin raging at my brother. Words were cutting in and out like a poorly tuned radio.

"We could have . . . history together, Jerry . . . your brains and my . . ."

"I got tired, Jimmy . . . I couldn't take any . . ."

"they hate us . . . teach them the knife . . . revenge for what they . . ."

Jeremy turned away and put one hand to his stomach, the other to his mouth. Started gagging.

"Talking about . . . killing . . . me sick . . . gonna puke." He bent over, hands clutching at his stomach.

Day punched Jeremy's head, sending him to his knees. ". . . woman turned you into . . . puking pussy-boy . . . ittle queer . . . kill you and maybe . . . can be a man about it."

Day pulled a curved gutting knife from his belt. He straddled my brother, grabbing Jeremy's chin and yanking his head back.

". . . take it . . . death like a man. Daddy needs you . . . die like a man. The knife needs you to . . ."

Jeremy put his hands together. I thought he was praying, his last living action. His hands jolted toward Day's face. The motion was hard and fast, like a punch. Day stumbled away, hands clawing at his right eye, grunting like a wounded animal. The knife tumbled to the floor. Day dropped to his knees.

I tried to speak but it came out as a moan. Jeremy crouched and picked me up like I was a child, carried me gently to the couch. I looked over his back, saw Day's hands pressed to his face, blood jetting from between fingers.

My vision sharpened as the toxins dissipated. I studied Day's face. Three inches of wood protruded from his left eye: Jeremy had concealed his beef skewer under his shirt, eluding Day's metal detector. Day's brain was emptying between his fingers. He lay on his side now, making noises more akin to a crying child than a wounded beast. We watched until Jim Day was still.

Then, something utterly strange: A burst of cricket sounds came from Day's corpse. I was still breathing out the poisonous vapors, unsteady in my head.

The crickets started again.

"It's his phone, Carson," Jeremy said, pulling the device free of Day's pocket and snapping it open. The screen showed a blurred movie of people in a tunnel. They had white circles on their heads. I heard laughter. The blur whirled to a group of people talking. Shelly Waltz centered the group. The camera moved on and the scenes became a muddy roar.

It wasn't a movie, it was cell-phone video from the convention. The tunnel was a wide hall. The white circles were campaign boaters emblazoned with VOTE FOR PELHAM.

Jeremy studied the phone over my shoulder. The screen went black.

"Daddy's new boy is sending postcards of his travels," my brother said. "He seems a busy lad."

# FORTY-TWO

"I've got to get from Spanish Harlem to the conference, Shelly," I said into my phone, heart pounding. "Something bad's going to happen to Pelham."

"She'll be here at the hotel in minutes. When she arrives, she'll be wrapped in a tight cocoon of security. We're got cops and tech staff crawling everywhere, checking everything from the underside of the tables to the podium. What could go wrong?"

"One minute ago you were talking to a group of people in a hallway. You looked worried. Everyone around you has white hats."

A stunned pause. "How'd you know that?"

I gave him the ten-second explanation. He said, "I'll send a car."

"Uh, Shelly? Jeremy's here. He's coming with me. It's essential."

"*What*?"

"Shelly, you've got to trust me."

"Where the hell is Folger?"

"Jeremy says she'll be returned today."

"He can't come here. You can't expect me to –"

"I expect you to go the distance," I said. "We're almost there, Shelly. If it falls apart now, it falls apart hard."

"I can't let a serial killer in the same hotel as the person who's probably our next President. No way."

"Pelham's in grave danger. Jeremy can help find that danger. Vangie gave her life for this moment, Shelly. Don't take it from her."

It was a lie and a below-the-belt punch, but it was all I had. Five minutes later the blue-and-white approached at what appeared to be mach one, siren, lights, horn honking. The cruiser banged up over the curb, Koslowski at the wheel. I pushed Jeremy into the back seat, jumped beside him. Koslowski shot a look in the rear-view, recognized my brother.

"Mary, Mother of God," Koslowski whispered. "Did Shelly tell you we'd be . . .'

Koslowski turned his eyes from the mirror, jammed the cruiser in gear and roared away. He kept his eyes straight, muttering, "I don't see him. I don't see a thing."

I hunkered down and watched the phone screen. Twice the device burred, followed by a brief stream of video, our quarry sending mission feedback to Daddy. The pics – crowd shots and hotel interiors – lasted five to ten seconds before the screen went blank.

Koslowski fishtailed to the hotel's rear delivery door. He shot a final glance at Jeremy. My brother pushed his hand through the open Plexiglas divider, thumb-flipped a bright gold coin on to the dashboard, spoke in a refined British accent.

"Spirited run, driver. Keep the change."

I yanked him out by the collar. The service door opened: Waltz. He shot fierce eyes at my brother.

Day's phone rasped. Waltz and Jeremy leaned close to see a grainy shot of a limo gliding to a curb, a door opening. Pelham exited, waving to the crowd.

"He's at the front of the hotel," I said.

We pushed through the crowded lobby, Waltz on my right, Jeremy on my left.

Waltz said, "Another doll arrived at Pelham's headquarters this morning. It was the final doll, the solid one."

"The mouth was painted over, right?"

"Judge for yourself."

We sidestepped a group of reporters as Waltz pulled a clear evidence bag from his pocket, the doll looking out. One glance and my stomach slipped sideways: The entire head had been painted away.

Bullard was across the room, near the front window, watching Pelham's progress. He held a phone or walkie-talkie in his hand, shiny black with a silver antenna. I figured he was sending progress reports to a command post in the hotel. I shot a look at Jeremy. Somehow in our brief walk he'd acquired a ball cap and reading glasses, an impromptu disguise.

The lobby was a flood of yelling, surging bodies, pandemonium. The smaller and security-cleared audience for Pelham's address was dining in the meeting arena on the second floor, awaiting The Candidate. Pelham was still outside, pressing the flesh. The three of us were looking for cellphones, not difficult, every other person had one lifted, ready to record Cynthia Pelham's entrance. Jeremy stiffened, stood stock-still. Focused his eyes on someone across the lobby.

"Jeremy?"

"Shhhh." He kept staring.

Pelham entered the hotel, her entourage whipping through the revolving doors. She was encircled by staffers, NYPD officers, and two men whose earpieces marked them as Secret Service. My brother tapped my arm, pointed across the lobby.

"That kid over there. He's afflicted. Look at his eyes."

I turned to see a blond male in his late teens, tall and well built, a first-string linebacker. He wore a suit and tie, held a clipboard in one hand. He had a cellphone in the other, the same style as Day's hi-tech model. His eyes looked absolutely normal to me.

"Daddy's boy," Jeremy sang.

I darted ahead of Pelham's group, noted that Bullard had joined her entourage, doing the *keep-back* motion with his hands to hold the fawning crowd at bay. The kid was standing in the wide hallway in front of a door that said KITCHEN TWO. He shot me a glance. Jeremy was right, the kid's eyes resembled frosted marbles. He saw no threat in me and aimed the marbles toward Pelham. He pointed the phone her way, thinking he was broadcasting to Daddy, not knowing the show was playing in the pocket of a guy two steps away.

"Excuse me, I've got to get into the kitchen," I said. "The hors d'oeuvres are ready."

"Sure," he grunted, stepping away from the door, keeping the camera angled at Pelham. I swung the door open, held it with my leg. Just as Pelham swept past, I shot my arm around the kid's neck and yanked him into the kitchen, yelling for Security.

Four guys were there in seconds, Waltz right behind. I had my knee in the kid's back and my arm around his neck. The security detail took control cautiously, the kid snapping like a shark, eyes wild, foam pouring down his chin. When the kid's strength poured out, the cops put him in restraints, one cop emptying the kid's pockets. He held up a plasticized card.

"An ID for a student newspaper. Never heard of the school."

"Fake," I said. "The kid attends or attended a place called Camp Wilderness."

"I got a knife. Small, three-inch blade."

"Plenty long enough to slice to the carotid," Waltz said.

The knife, the cellphone, a few bucks and a subway pass were all the kid was carrying. I watched as he was toted off to a different kind of camp.

Waltz put his hand on my shoulder. "Jesus, how close was he to Pelham? Ten feet? Less?"

Day's phone rasped in my pocket. Puzzled, I slipped it out. On the screen was a jittery shot of Pelham stepping into the second-floor meeting hall, walking toward the podium alone, people at tables standing and cheering. All guests and otherwise who had business on the secured second floor had been vetted and approved. Pelham's circle of protection had melted away.

"How nice," Jeremy said, looking over my shoulder. "There's another boy in the game and he's made it to level two."

# FORTY-THREE

Papers, photos, files, and reports surrounded Cluff as if scattered by an explosion, laying where they fell when he pushed everything from his desk but the files from the two juvenile facilities. He leaned close, giving them the third look in a minute, his anxious eyes moving from the Newark report on his left to the report from the Bridges juvenile facility on his right. He re-checked admission and release dates. Making sure the names were the same.

*It don't necessarily mean anything. People change . . . but why do I feel like there's a siren screaming in my head?*

He pulled his phone and started dialing.

*   *   *

I bolted toward the stairs, not caring who I pushed aside. I turned into the stairwell and felt a hard blow to my sternum. The rock-hard hand of a massive uniformed cop. Two other walls of beef stood beside him, giving me laser eyes.

"Show me ID," the guy with his hand in my belly said. "You need special ID for the second floor."

The cop beside him said, "I don't see any kind of ID."

Waltz ran up, breathing hard. "He's with me, Barney. He's OK. Let him go."

"My orders are no one without clearance or an NYPD identification can go past —"

"I'll take responsibility. Let him go!"

I continued up the steps, Waltz laboring behind. I saw my brother following and waved him back, hoping he saw my warning. I hit the second floor, the doors to the cavernous meeting room in front of me. I slipped into the room, saw a couple hundred women at round tables with carafes and glassware in front of them. Pelham was seated to the side of the podium, another woman droning at the mic, the introduction part of the proceedings.

"... *tireless advocate of the disenfranchised* ..."

I looked toward the side of the room and saw Bullard, his phone raised, his eyes dark and angry. *Bullard? Could it be?*

I sidled along the wall and snatched the phone from his face. It was a bargain brand with no video function. Bullard wasn't the one.

"What the fuck's with you, asshole?" he whispered, snatching it back. "I'm trying to talk to Cluff. His signal keeps breaking up in here." He put the phone back to his face. "You gotta talk louder, Cluff, I can't goddamn hear."

Day's phone sounded. I studied the screen. A tight tunnel, empty, probably one of the service corridors. Where could it be?

"*. . . great pleasure to introduce the next President of the United States, Congresswoman Cynthia Pelham . . .*"

I started to move away when Bullard grabbed my arm. I turned. He held up a finger, *just a second*, while frowning into the phone. I looked at Day's device. The sender was still moving through the corridor, the video murky, undefined. The screen turned black.

Bullard closed his phone. He looked confused. "Cluff did more checking of Newark and Bridges. There were a half-dozen crossover juvie admissions to both facilities when Bernal and

420

Anderson were working. One of them was named Jonathan Cargyle."

"Cargyle?"

"Like that newbie in Tech Services. He was here earlier, working. Making sure everything was safe."

I looked to the dais, saw a wide-smiled Pelham at ease in her element.

"... *gives me a feeling of satisfaction to look out over the faces of so many accomplished women. When I am President I vow that ...*"

"Cargyle?" I saw a mind picture of the innocuous kid who was never without tools or telephones. "What was he doing?"

"He was up on the stage. Checking the microphones or something."

"... *making sure all women can achieve full equality in all fields of endeavor ...*"

I turned and saw Cynthia Pelham, a black microphone directly in front of her face. To the side, I saw Cargyle peeking through the curtain. He had a phone in his hand, held high, ready to send Jim Day the record of his triumph.

I started running to the dais. When I yelled, "Everyone down," panic ensued. I was suddenly swimming against a tide of screaming bodies, women falling, folding chairs tumbling over,

421

glasses breaking on the floor. Pelham held her ground. There was nowhere for her to run but into the tumult.

I saw Pelham's Secret Service protectors fall beneath the crush of bodies. I was ten feet from the podium.

I pushed a woman aside, dove across another. Five feet.

I grabbed the microphone, cast-iron stand and all. Wires popped free as I sprinted to the window and launched it into the glass with every bit of strength in me, stand, microphone and wires tumbling. I saw it hit the storm-proof glass, bounce back like rubber, fall to the floor inside the room. I dove away, rolling desperately. A white flash enveloped everything. The floor shuddered beneath my body.

Only then did I hear the explosion.

# FORTY-FOUR

As explosions go, it wasn't very big, a few grams of plastique, a bomb tech would later estimate. Just enough to fit within the tight confines of the microphone. But enough to remove Cynthia Pelham's face and everything behind it. I sat in a second-floor room as a paramedic tweezed a small shard of microphone casing from my hand, the only wound sustained in the explosion.

Waltz walked into the room, leaned against the wall. The paramedic closed his bag and left. Waltz's face was expressionless.

"Where's Jeremy?" I asked.

"In security headquarters off the lobby, under arrest. He tried to follow us to the second floor. He got looked at real close and didn't pass inspection."

"Did Jeremy resist?"

"Your brother surrendered peacefully. He wanted to call his lawyer, to have the attorney waiting at the station. I traded him the lawyer call for Folger's whereabouts. She's getting picked up now."

"Lawyer?"

"Solomon Epperman, your brother said. Doesn't matter. Epperman can't do diddly for your brother. He's about to be transported to lock-up."

"How about Cargyle?"

"Whisked off to Bellevue. He was having some sort of episode, screaming about his father."

"If Cargyle doesn't go full tilt down the crazy pipe, I expect he'll tell amazing tales. Get a good shrink on his case. Male."

Waltz's phone rang. His face went dead serious. Relaxed as he talked. Was grinning when he hung up.

"We got Alice. She's fine. Covered with soot, but she's kicking and bitching and not a scratch on her." Waltz looked like he was about to swoon, this time in delight.

"I'm gonna check on Jeremy, Shelly. Tell Alice I'll see her shortly."

I got to the front door as my brother was put in the back of a cruiser. He seemed relaxed, resigned to his fate. Once everything got sorted out, my brother would return to the Institute.

Bullard appeared at my side. His hand was out and I took it. "Good job today, Ryder. Good job on the whole freaking everything. Between you and old Cluff, it's got a happy ending."

"If I wouldn't have insisted I knew everything and let Cluff dig," I admitted, "we'd have been onto Cargyle days ago."

Bullard could have agreed, but damn if he wasn't magnanimous. "Maybe. But it wasn't your call to make, Ryder, it was the Lieutenant's. I'm heading downtown. Want a ride?"

I accepted and we pulled away with my brother ahead of us by three car lengths, two bull-necked cops in the front of the cruiser, Jeremy in back. The car holding my brother stopped at a light. Jeremy craned his head around, studying the city, knowing he'd never return.

"Pull over by that drugstore a minute?" I asked Bullard.

"No problem. Whatcha need?"

"Gotta buy someone a toothbrush."

He angled to the curb. I started to hop out, but was distracted by horns behind us, a wall of sound growing louder, followed by a roaring engine, a diesel wound to max rpm's, red-lined.

"What's all the racket?" Bullard said. He glanced in his rear-view. Whispered, "Holy shit."

The roar became a scream of tearing metal and breaking glass. We turned in our seats to see a garbage truck fishtailing wildly, ripping the sides from parked cars like a can opener, pushing vehicles from its path like paper. A smashed motorcycle was snagged on the truck's bumper, throwing sparks. Black smoke boiled, locomotive style, from the truck's vertical exhaust.

The garbage hauler tagged our bumper and spun us as it howled past, trash pouring to the street from its open compacter. The hauler rammed the cruiser carrying Jeremy. Metal sheared away as the cruiser swirled, cops tumbling out. The truck stopped in the middle of the street and the door exploded open. A naked man leapt out, bandoliers draping his body, assault rifles in both hands.

He screamed, "Hail Asmodeus!"

And launched a fusillade of bullets in all directions.

Bullard howled, diving behind the cruiser, me scrambling after him. Two crashed vehicles exploded into flames. The dense smoke was acrid and blinding. I heard screams of bystanders as they stumbled over one another to escape. The air stank of garbage and gunpowder.

"Hail Asmodeus," the man howled again, punctuating his slogan with bursts of fire. Our cruiser's window dissolved into powdered glass. I stuck one eye above the hood and saw our assailant toss away one of the banana-clipped rifles, grab another. He jumped on the running board of the truck, stuck a foot and hand inside, flooring the accelerator and roaring in a circle as he fired, shoveling aside cars and tearing down light poles. Sparks dripped from broken wires. A store sign across the street crashed to the sidewalk.

The truck turned and started in our direction.

"Let's book," Bullard said. We sprinted a dozen feet to low concrete planters, dove for cover. Bullets skittered into the planters, ricochets whined.

Bullard seemed to be talking to himself and I realized he was praying. He sucked down a deep breath, stood, held his weapon in the classic double-hand stance. He narrowed an eye and emptied his clip. The truck veered left and smashed into the drugstore. The engine died. The first three feet of the vehicle's snout was buried in the store. The naked man was nowhere in sight. Heat ticked from the truck's engine. Bullard crept to the driver's side, me a few paces behind.

"The bastard's down," Bullard said. "He's staying down."

The assailant had tumbled to the street, the upper right quarter of his head still in the truck cab. We stared at the man's arms and torso, a webwork of bizarre tattoos, as if screaming his madness in ink. An automatic rifle was in his hands. Two more rifles and a shotgun were in the truck cab, plus eight sticks of dynamite.

"So what you think that was all about?" Bullard said.

I ran to the cruiser transporting Jeremy. Empty. His escorts crept from a storefront on the far side of the street, weapons drawn. Bullard waved the guns down. Smoke and sirens overwhelmed the street as emergency vehicles arrived. I ran the avenue, looking down cross streets, alleys. Every street for blocks was crawling with law enforcement.

"Any sign of Ridgecliff?" I asked every cop I saw.

There wasn't.

I don't think it was Epperman my brother called.

# EPILOGUE

The sky was clean blue, the sun tipped halfway to the water. Gulls wheeled and keened in the hot air. Harry set his cranberry hiking shorts against the railing of my deck, leaned against the planks with arms crossed over an aloha shirt with pink shrimp frolicking in an electric-green sea. I'd been giving him the play-by-play of New York.

"They found the two uteruses in Day's house?" he asked.

"In formalin in a jar in his apartment. Trophies. And there were seven of them, unfortunately."

"Uh-oh."

"When Jeremy went to the Institute, Day picked up and headed to Minneapolis. He also seems to have ramped up. There was a spate of women's disappearances during those years. There are already four police jurisdictions involved. Given the emerging patterns, few of the cops have doubts that they'll find Day in the thick of the horror."

"Day would have had a son or sons, right?"

"The bodies of two young males, twenty-three and twenty-one were found three years ago near the Canadian border. The bodies had taken a lot of punishment. No clues were ever found."

"Maybe a rebellion in his army?" Harry wondered. "The boys got tired of Daddy? Or vice versa?"

I shrugged, drank the last chug of beer in my bottle. "Who knows?"

I looked out over the Gulf of Mexico, a sheet of glittering cobalt. Who ever knows with a monster like Jim Day? The only certainty was that Day didn't set out to become a monster. He was created by his mother and grandmother. But who or what had turned them into monsters? How far back did the poison reach . . . generations? Centuries?

Harry said, "Cargyle and the young kid were Day's new army?"

"Plus three other boys Day was 'developing'. They expect to uncover a few more. The juvie boot camp was perfect for his kind of need. The kid Jeremy found in the hotel lobby, Billy Hoople, is nineteen, a trainee not as developed as Cargyle."

"Cargyle was the kid the Anderson vic saw? Her happy ending?"

"Seeing a former client working NYPD's tech services made Anderson's day. It also made her a target when Cargyle told Day about the meeting. Cargyle was a client of Child Welfare in Newark, an ugly childhood. The family moved to New York and Cargyle got in gang trouble in his mid teens, ended up at Bridges. His tested IQ of 135 bought him a rehab stay at Camp Wilderness four years back. Day was waiting."

"The other vic?"

"Angela Bernal befriended Cargyle while he was at Bridges juvie facility, tried to mother him. Compassion made her a target. Day also needed another mutilated female to ramp up the search for Jeremy. Like Anderson, Bernal served a double need."

The back door slid open and a barefoot Folger stepped out, wearing a white chef's apron over a pair of shorts and halter top, a beer in each hand. Alice had three weeks' leave from the NYPD. She was spending the first with me, getting a first-hand look at the weather systems along the Gulf Coast. She was liking how they moved.

She was also liking how her life was opening. She finally had a road map of her interior landscape, a map stretching from Evangeline Prowse's past to Alice Folger's future. She was still trying to fathom how a mother she'd never known had given her life to ensure that Alice kept hers. And that a father she'd never figured on knowing was as near as a desk down the hall, inspiring her, exasperating her, challenging her to new heights, and through it all remaining her staunchest supporter. In short, acting much like a father.

Sometimes life's circles leave me breathless.

Shelly? Suffice to say that his life, too, had opened. He would always grieve for the singular love of his life, but his joy at having a daughter was thrilling, and when he laughed – now a regular event – I swear it sounded like dimes raining into a punchbowl.

Alice and I had concluded that exposing my relationship with Jeremy at this point would change nothing. It saved a lot of needless explanations all around.

"Anyone want to explain the long faces?" Alice said, handing Harry and me fresh brews. "Or should I think it's me?"

Harry smiled. "We were talking about Jim Day, Miz Folger. And we just closed that chapter. Time to move to happier discussions, like what's for supper?"

"It's Alice, Harry, and as for chow, I'm having my maiden foray into making seafood gumbo. It's okay to make it with canned tuna, right?"

She winked at me, retreated to the kitchen to attend a bubbling pot of shrimp and crab.

Harry turned to watch a pair of dolphins just past the last sandbar. There was a squall on the horizon, a smudge of dark clouds joined to the sea by a curtain of rain. The storm would blow eastward and die when it rained itself out.

"Heard anything from Jeremy?" Harry said, still looking seaward.

"Not a word. He was in New York long enough to have enlisted a dozen afflicted citizens to jump at his call. He finds and controls those folks as easily as you and I put on shoes."

Harry turned from the water, pushed his blue-framed shades to his forehead, looked me in the eyes. "I know it all hasn't had time to settle. But have you noticed how Jeremy stayed one step ahead of everything?"

I sipped, nodded. "Self-preservation instincts. He's an incredible planner."

"Good word, planner. All starting when he finally decided to tell his story to Doc Prowse."

"He held his past inside a long time, Harry. It was ready to come out."

"Maybe it wasn't the only thing ready to come out."

"Pardon, bro?"

Harry ticked off points on his fingers. "Your brother's story got the Doc investigating Day, pulling him into the picture. Jeremy tutored the Doc in the slickest way out of the Institute, got her to make the tape that brought you to New York. He had Day scoped out at Camp Wilderness. How about Sirius? Didn't that fit just perfect?"

"You're losing me, Harry. What are you saying?"

"It's interesting that everything fell together the way it did. Who was Jeremy's biggest threat if he ever escaped? Jim Day, now deceased."

"You're suggesting – ?"

"I'm suggesting that your brother seems able

435

to control about anything, given the right opportunities and ample time to plan."

Harry's words triggered Day's description of my brother: *He's a wickedly bright boy. Give him enough time to plan and he could get into the main vault at Fort Knox.*

Into it? I wondered. Or out of it?

Harry gestured between the mainland and the sea, meaning the whole country, the world, everywhere.

"Jeremy's out there, Carson. He's brilliant, adaptive, and learning more ways to game the system every day. You ever think that might have been the big plan all along?"

I started to argue. Couldn't find the words. Alice slid open the door, smiled a smile so bright it shamed the sun.

Said, "Who's ready for a feast?"

# The Hundredth Man
## Jack Kerley

A body is found in the sweating heat of an Alabama night; headless, words inked on the skin. Detective Carson Ryder is good at this sort of thing – crazies and freaks. To his eyes it is no crime of passion, and when another mutilated victim turns up his suspicions are confirmed. This is not the work of a 'normal' murderer, but that of a serial killer, a psychopath.

Famous for solving a series of crimes the year before, Carson Ryder has experience with psychopaths. But he had help with that case – strange help, from a past Ryder is trying to forget.

Now he needs it again.

When the truth finally begins to dawn, it shines on an evil so twisted, so dangerous, it could destroy everything that he cares about...

"Superb debut novel. A headless torso, the heat-soaked Alabama nights, a detective with a secret. Fantastic"
*Sunday Express*

Also available as an Audio Book in CD or cassette format. See order form for details!

# Jack Kerley Audiobooks

# The Death Collectors

*read by Kerry Shale*

Thirty years after his death, Marsden Hexcamp's "Art of the Final Moment" remains as sought after as ever. But this is no ordinary collection. Hexcamp's portfolio was completed with the aid of a devoted band of acolytes – and half a dozen victims, each of whom was slowly tortured to death so that their final agonies could be distilled into art.

When tiny scraps of Hexcamp's "art" begin appearing at murder scenes alongside gruesomely displayed corpses, Detective Carson Ryder and his partner Harry Nautilus must go back three decades in search of answers.

Meanwhile an auction has been announced and the death collectors are gathering. These wealthy connoisseurs of serial-killer memorabilia will pay millions to acquire Hexcamp's art – unless Carson and Harry can beat them in their quest for the anti-grail.

Now available on Audio CD or Double Cassette

**Kerry Shale**'s voice work has already earned him the title of "the best-known American voice on Radio Four", according to the *Evening Standard*. An experienced narrator, he is also the winner of 3 Sony awards for radio acting and writing.

Cassette: 0-00-721172-4
CD: 0-00-721173-2

# The Broken Souls

## Jack Kerley

**"Blood was everywhere, like the interior had been hosed down with an artery ..."**

The gore-sodden horror that greets homicide detective Carson Ryder on a late-night call out is enough to make him want to quit the case. Too late...

Now he and his partner Harry are up to their necks in a Southern swamp of the bizarre and disturbing. An investigation full of twists and strange clues looks like it's leading to the city's least likely suspects - a powerful family whose philanthropy has made them famous. But behind their money and smiles is a dynasty divided by hate.

Their strange and horrific past is about to engulf everyone around them in a storm of violence and depravity. And Ryder's right in the middle of it ...

'As good as *The Hundredth Man*... superb stuff'
*Independent on Sunday*

ISBN-13 978 0 00 721434 1

Also available as an Audio Book, read by Kerry Shale
ISBN-13 978 0 00 722~~~6
(CD)